VICTIM OF CIRCUMSTANCE

FREYA BARKER

Victim of Circumstance

Copyright © 2020 Freya Barker

ISBN: 978 1 988733 470
Cover Design: Lauren Dawes
Editing: Karen Hrdlicka
Proofreading: Joanne Thompson

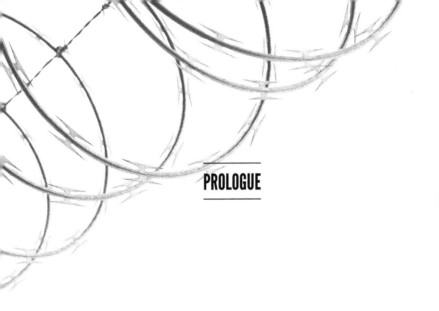

PROLOGUE

Fresh air.

I stop when I hear the harsh clank of the gate closing behind me and suck in a deep, desperate breath. It's like my lungs are able to expand fully for the first time in eighteen years. The full hit of oxygen makes me instantly lightheaded.

It's all between my ears, I realize that, but there's no denying the physical impact breathing actual free air after so many years has on me. I force myself not to bend over and gasp, like my body wants to. Instead I raise my eyes to a mostly cloudless sky, giving my senses a moment to adjust.

The shrill honk of a car horn interrupts my efforts to calibrate my senses and my eyes automatically dart to the end of the wide drive into Rockwood Penitentiary, where I've spent almost two decades in Cell Block C. My cab is waiting for me and I slowly start walking toward it, almost expecting a harsh voice to call me back.

All I have is a paper bag with the few meager, and by now meaningless, belongings I had on me when I was brought here. My clothes feel weird and unfamiliar, taken from a supply closet with stacks of unclaimed street clothes for people like me who have no one on the outside to send them some. I don't know where the clothes I was wearing back then disappeared to. Maybe some other guy wore those home.

Home. A weird concept, even before I ended up here it was an undefined place. At that time I had a tiny, rented studio apartment, but for two decades home had been a six-by-eight prison cell. Small, but it was mine. I didn't have much to fill it with except for the books given to me through Books to Prisoners, one of the many organizations trying to make life behind bars more livable.

I have eighteen books, one for each year I spent inside. Books I read over and over and over again. There'd been more, some borrowed from the prison library, but these eighteen came to mean something to me. They were representative of every year I spent inside. The ones that allowed me to disappear, even just for the time it took me to read them. They'd been my true sanctuary, my peaceful haven in an oppressive, sound-filled environment.

They're all in my paper bag, making it heavy as fuck to carry. Also in there are my toothbrush, my soap, and a leather wristband I forgot I had until it was handed to me earlier. My leather jacket, the only item of my own clothing remaining, is hot on my back in the midday sun. The wad of cash, both the hundred and fifteen dollars I had on me when I was arrested, and the gate money—a few weeks' worth of living expenses I'm supposed to pay back in a few months—are burning a hole in my pocket.

"Where are you heading?" the old man standing beside the taxi asks when I approach.

Isn't that the million-dollar question? One I don't have an answer for right away—it's been so long since I've had to make any decisions—so I buy myself some time by answering, "The closest bus station."

Clutching my paper bag, I climb in the back seat and immediately open the window, wanting to feel the air move on my face.

"Is that okay?" I ask politely.

"Sure," he says, climbing behind the wheel. "You're not the only one who does that."

I don't talk much. Never have, and certainly not while I was inside. I kept mostly to myself. I'm relieved when the driver doesn't make an effort to engage in small talk.

I look out the window, letting the landscape roll by as I consider where I might want to go. Big cities where I can disappear anonymously pass my mind's eye, but during the twenty-minute ride, the one place that keeps coming to the forefront is my hometown of Beaverton.

It seems crazy to go back to a small town where most people will remember what you did, but somehow I find myself compelled to ask for a ticket there when I walk up to the window at the bus station.

CHAPTER ONE

Gray

"This is too much."

I look at the stack of bills stuffed in the envelope Jimmy shoves in my hand, which was just supposed to hold my earnings for the past two weeks.

Jimmy Olson was still in Beaverton when I arrived last month. We'd been best friends since elementary school and he'd even visited me in jail twice, until I finally refused to see him. My head had been fucked up—hell, it likely still is—and watching Jimmy walk out of there twice had almost done me in. I was sad, I was scared, and I struggled finding my equilibrium inside. As much as seeing him gave me a brief moment of reprieve, seeing that door close behind him would leave me raw.

Hope becomes a hot searing pain that scars your soul when it has nowhere to go.

It was easier to live without, move through my days in a tedious repetition of the last. No highs, no particular lows, just a narrow existence within the walls of my prison.

But hope flared when he was the first person I saw, getting off the bus in Beaverton last month. Jimmy fucking Olson, coming out of a diner with a coffee in his hand and walking up to a red tow truck, *Olson's Automotive* printed on the side.

I might've avoided him, but he saw me. How he recognized me I don't know. I've gotten old. My former dark hair has gone completely gray inside. I used to be bigger than I am now, after discovering the prison gym is not a place you want to be without a posse at your back. I never had one. My body is much leaner now; the only exercise what I managed to do in my own cell.

Still he took one look at me and that boyish grin I remember so well spread wide over his face. He hadn't changed much at all and apparently had no hard feelings about me blowing him off, because he came tearing across the street, wrapping me in a bone-crushing hug.

I almost fucking cried right there in front of the bus station.

An hour later I was moved into the small apartment over his business. It used to be Old Man Stephenson's garage when both Jimmy and I worked there, but apparently he's dead and Jimmy bought the place. I was floored when Jimmy said he'd known I was released—had been keeping track—and was hoping I'd be smart enough to come home.

He gave me a week to settle in; a week I mostly spent in isolation in the small apartment he had stocked with food so I didn't have to go out. After that week, he barged in at seven in the morning, ordering me to get my ass downstairs, and give him a hand. I've been doing long days in the shop since.

"Fuck no, it's not. You had me sell off your shit, remember? I've had it sitting in a savings account all this time, gathering dust."

"You're shitting me? This is at least ten grand, my stuff wouldn't have made more than a couple of hundred."

"Seventeen thousand three hundred and twenty-five dollars to be exact," he says and my jaw hits the floor. "Most of it for your old Mustang."

"That was a pile of rust. I hadn't even started working on it," I point out, remembering the 1965 Mustang I hauled out of a field near Coleman for the measly two hundred bucks the farmer wanted for it. That was supposed to be my next project before everything went to shit.

"I know. It got done," Jimmy says with a shrug, and I feel my throat close. "Anyway, you may wanna open up a bank account, unless you're gonna walk around with that kinda cash."

Opening up an account would require going into the bank, a public building, something I'm not sure I'm ready to do. Even these past few weeks working in the shop, I would duck out of sight whenever a customer walked in. Jimmy seemed to understand, at least he hadn't commented on it. Not yet.

"I know. I will eventually. And Jimmy...thanks, man."

He shrugs again and dives under the pickup truck we have up on the car lift.

"Just don't go spending it all at once," he mumbles from under there.

"Only spending I'll be doing is buying a ticket to New York," I tell him offhand, as I shove the envelope in my pocket and duck under the hood of the Charger brought in this morning.

"You're going?" Jimmy asks.

"I need to. Never got to say goodbye to Reagan."

"Who's Reagan?" Kyle, the apprentice working with us this morning wants to know.

I can't even bring myself to explain, but Jimmy answers for me.

"His sister, dipstick. She died."

I glance over at the young kid, who looks miserable.

"Long time ago, kid," I assure him. He nods, looking only moderately better as he turns to focus on the tires he's checking for leaks. He doesn't need to know I haven't even begun to deal with that loss.

It's almost six thirty when Jimmy calls it a day.

"Wanna go grab a bite to eat?"

I know he's trying to get me outside of this place, but just like the bank, the diner seems like too public a place. Chances are big I'd bump into people who remember me, and I'm not ready to face them yet. Besides, I've gotten used to my own company and it's enough for now.

"I think I'll just stay here. Got a book to finish," I tell him.

It's a lame excuse and I know it, but the thought of walking into a crowded diner fills me with anxiety.

"How are you gonna go to New York if you can't even manage to cross the street?"

I guess it's a valid question, but there's a simple and clear answer.

"Nobody knows me there."

———

Robin

I like my nights to myself.

The first year after Paige left for college, I was desperate to fill any alone time with activity to cover the hole she left behind, but these days I'm perfectly content with just a book, or a good show on TV, and my own company.

We call a couple of times a week just to touch base, and see each other on half a dozen or so occasions throughout the year. Since my daughter left home, our relationship has gone through a transition and I have to say I really enjoy the connection we share now. We're equals. I don't carry the heavy, sole responsibility over someone else's life and welfare anymore; she does that herself, and does it well.

Paige is twenty-three and just graduated this May with a bachelor's degree in nursing from Rutgers University in New Jersey. Her late father's alma mater, except he studied accounting. It was also mine, but that was years later. I met him by chance when I volunteered at an alumni event and less than a year later dropped out when I got pregnant with her. New Jersey is where she was born and where we lived until I moved us back to Michigan when she was still young.

She'd had her sights set on Rutgers, and when my daughter wants something, she'll move heaven and earth to get it. Despite my mixed bag of emotions on it, I supported her decision. Ironically she loves it so much there, she decided to stick around and look for work this summer. Ended up with a fabulous job at a medical clinic. She loves it and though I don't love her living halfway across the country, I'm glad she's happy there.

I'm happy here, where I'm not too far from my mother, who needs me more now than my daughter does. Mom has struggled a bit since Dad died three years ago at only sixty-six, quite unexpectedly. They've always lived in Lansing where Dad worked for GM, at the assembly plant, for almost forty years before he retired at sixty-five. Less than two years later he passed in his sleep from a massive heart attack. They'd just finished planning what was supposed to have been their bucket list trip.

Life sucks sometimes.

Almost by rote I grab my phone and dial my mother.

"Hey, Mom."

"Sweetie, how are you?"

"Good. Just thinking about you."

"How come?"

"No particular reason. I talked to Paige earlier today and we made plans for me to head down there for a week next month, and I was just thinking, maybe you want to come?"

I've asked Mom to join me before when I go to visit my daughter but she always declined, which is why I'm surprised when she suddenly seems to consider it.

"I might. It depends."

"That would be amazing. Paige would be tickled. Let me know when you make up your mind, Mom. I can book you a flight."

The rest of the conversation we chat about her latest checkup, my aunt, Ditty, who apparently has a new beau—again—and the dirt on a cousin going through a nasty divorce. Half an hour later, I'm more up-to-date with family than I care to be.

I've always been the listener, never the talker, which is why my family knows little of my years in New Jersey. Something I'm grateful for since it wouldn't have served any purpose. Fortunately Paige remembers little of that time, so the only one with bad memories is me, and I've got ways to deal with those.

I feel better having talked to the two most important people in my life and settle into my evening with a book and a glass of wine. I've become good at counting my blessings and ignoring the small pangs of longing for things out of my reach.

———

"Shirley called in sick."

I'm donning my apron when Kim sticks her head into the small office where we leave our personal stuff when on shift.

I've been working at Over Easy for well over ten years now. When I started out I was just doing Kim's books part time, along with several other bookkeeping clients, but with Paige getting older and being home less, I craved some human interaction. One of Kim's waitresses left on maternity leave and she was in a bind, so I offered to help. That turned into a full-time job, while still doing the diner's books on the side. I've since dropped my other clients so I work at Over Easy exclusively.

My parents as well as Paige had a hard time understanding

why I would take on a menial job that didn't pay all that well. Despite what they think they know, the truth is I don't need much. I own my small home outright and the cost of living here is relatively low.

There was a time I had it all—the big house, fancy car, designer threads, platinum credit cards—but nothing about that made me happy. My life now does, and that includes working at the diner.

"What's wrong with her?"

"She says the flu." I see the skepticism on Kim's face.

"But..."

"But I'm not buying it. I could hear Mike yelling in the background."

Shirley's marriage is not a happy one. At least not anymore.

Two years ago, her husband Mike was laid off from the same GM plant where my father worked most of his life, and he hadn't been able to find anything new. At fifty-two, that's a hard pill to swallow—I get it—but Mike's idea of coping is hitting the bottle hard and taking his frustration out on Shirley, mostly.

Kim and I have talked about our concern for her, especially these past few months. She's called in sick a few times and looks like she's aged a decade. Drawn and pale, her normal exuberant smile now only a shadow. One of their boys is in college and the other works in the oilfields up in Canada, so it's just Shirley and Mike at home.

"I'll try and give her a call later," I volunteer.

Shirley and I aren't besties necessarily—I think we both have too much to hide for that—but I consider us friends and we've worked this shift together for years.

"Okay. I called Debra and she'll come in a few hours, and Jason has the kitchen so I can run the counter and cash register."

"Sounds good. We've got this."

This isn't the first time we've had just three of us here, but rarely on a Saturday morning.

From the moment I unlock the door at seven o'clock, the place is busy. I've had to warm up my own coffee twice already, and never manage more than a quick sip, hoping it'll tide me over until I can shove something in my face.

It was even a struggle to be patient with poor Mrs. Chapman who, as usual, took her sweet time with the menu, despite it showing the same things as last week. The widow comes in like clockwork on Saturday mornings. Her one weekly indulgence, she once told me. She turns it into this big production, pretends she's at a fancy restaurant, even dresses up for it, and we usually play along.

"Thank you, Robin," she says, smiling when I put the wine-glass with tap water and a slice of lime by her plate. It's little things like that—the linen placemat and napkin Kim keeps just for her, the cup and saucer for her coffee instead of our normal mugs, the fancy plating of her simple food—which make this weekly visit of hers special.

"My pleasure. Will there be anything else?"

"No, thank you. This is perfect."

With a nod I head for the counter, where I grab a coffeepot to offer refills to some of the tables. In the far corner, by the window, I spot one of our regular patrons with a few of his buddies. Tank occasionally comes in by himself during the week—he owns a business in town—but on weekends during the summer he often shows up with some of his biker friends to grab a bite before they ride. I glance out the window where their gleaming bikes are lined up in the parking lot.

It always gives me a secret little thrill to imagine being on the back of one of those. I've never actually been on a bike, but have fantasized plenty.

"Hey, Robin."

"Morning. What can I get you today?" After flipping over their mugs and filling them, I set down the coffeepot, and slip my pad and pen from my apron.

I take down their orders and am about to drop them off at the kitchen, when a hand grabs me by the wrist.

"Is today the day I can convince you to hop on for a ride?"

I grin down in the rugged but friendly face.

"Sorry, Tank. I value my life too much," I joke, and the other guys chuckle. "Besides, we're shorthanded today."

He slaps his hand to his chest dramatically.

"You wound me, Robin. I swear I'd keep you safe."

"I'm sure you'll live," I tease.

I dismiss the tingle of excitement I feel every time he asks me, wondering briefly if I'll ever work up the courage to say yes. Instead I wink, grab my coffeepot, and head to the kitchen.

I'm pretty sure a ride on the back of Tank's bike comes with some consequences and—nice enough guy as he is—I don't think that would be wise.

It's safer to stick with my fantasies.

CHAPTER TWO

Gray

"Are you okay?"

I glance up to find a friendly flight attendant leaning over the empty seat beside me.

"I'm fine," I lie.

My hands are gripping the armrests so tightly my knuckles are white. I force myself to relax them. To my relief she just smiles and nods before moving down the aisle.

It's not so much the flying as it is being cooped up in a relatively small cylinder with wings that has the spit drying up in my mouth. Aside from the wings part, it feels confining in here. No escape. I consciously steady my breathing before I pass out from hyperventilation.

The only good thing about traveling is no one knows me. They have no idea they're looking at an ex-convict, which is something I can't say for the few people I've been exposed to at home. I'm still keeping as low a profile as I can, even after two months back. At the shop I've become a little more relaxed, but I still do my groceries late at night to avoid more than the occa-sional late shopper.

I was lucky to be able to keep up my skills while incarcerated. Being a licensed mechanic gave me an advantage to get into the automotive program as a mentor, while staying up-to-date with changes in the industry. As a result, I feel I can carry my weight at the shop and am even working with the few apprentices Jimmy took on.

He claims business has been up since I started. I'm pretty sure he says it to make me feel better for accepting his help, but it doesn't make me any less grateful to him.

Jimmy is also the one who pushed for me to make this trip when anxiety had me threaten to back out. I might have cowered in the small apartment above the garage, but he told me—in no uncertain terms—I wouldn't be able to get on with my future if I didn't get real with my past.

That's why I willingly let myself be locked up with a large number of strangers in this flying tuna can—to get real with my past.

The sun is just coming up outside the small window as the engines suddenly roar, driving the plane down the runway. I can feel the exact moment we lose touch with the ground, our path suddenly smooth as I see the earth fall away below us. I realize I'm holding my breath.

I've only flown once before, when I was young and invincible. Jimmy and I took off to Mexico for one of those all-inclusive deals. I can't remember much, just that there was a lot of booze and pussy involved.

This time I know all too well how fragile life is, especially at the mercy of an airplane.

There also won't be any booze or pussy this trip. I'll only be away for one night, which already costs a sweet penny; I had no fucking clue how expensive things have gotten. Tomorrow I get to do this again to get back home.

"Would you like something to drink?"

I glance up to find the flight attendant back, this time with a cart.

"Water, please."

"Headphones?"

She motions to the monitor in the back of the seat in front of me.

"No thanks."

"You need anything else, you just let me know, okay?"

I'm not an idiot, even if I were blind and wasn't able to recognize the come-on in her eyes, I'd still be able to hear the invitation in her voice. But I'm not interested.

I fucked my way through my twenties pretty indiscriminately, but I have no interest in picking up where I left off. I have become quite familiar with my hand these past two decades. He and I get along fine. For now.

Instead of watching something stupid on that tiny little screen in front of me, I pull out the phone Jimmy made me buy. An iPhone X, whatever the hell that means. I had a flip phone when I went in, but those don't work anymore, apparently. So now I have this sleek looking thing that doesn't even have fucking buttons.

Kyle showed me how to work it. He even downloaded something so I could play Sudoku on it. I got pretty good at those inside. It's a great way to kill time, I've discovered. So great, I don't even notice an hour and a half has passed, when the pilot announces over the intercom we've started our descent and the seat belt light dings on again.

Instead of joining the slow-moving throng for the exit, I stay in my seat until the aisle is free before grabbing my overnight bag from the bin.

"Thank you," I mumble at the flight attendant, who tries to grab my hand, but I'm too adept at avoiding physical contact and am already out the door. A quick glance over my shoulder shows her crouching down to pick up a piece of paper I'm pretty sure holds her phone number.

Without any baggage to collect, I make my way to the exit, flinching at the smells, sounds, and crowds. I flag down a taxi, and give the driver the address to the hotel.

It's only seven fifteen in the morning and already I feel like I traveled to a completely different world.

The clerk at the hotel desk tells me it's too early to check in, but I can leave my bag with the concierge to pick up later, which I do. Then I walk out into the street, following the directions I printed out in Jimmy's office at the back of the shop.

There's already a substantial crowd gathering around the monument. For a moment I contemplate heading back to the hotel, but I came here with a purpose. I owe Reagan a proper goodbye.

I make my way through bodies to the edge of the first of the twin basins, cascading into the void left behind by the buildings that once stood here. I'd seen pictures of the memorial left in their place and know somewhere on the bronze parapet, lining the north pool, the name Reagan Bennet would be engraved.

Eighteen years too late, but I'm finally here to claim my sister.

———

Robin

"What are you doing up so early?"

Shit. I'd hoped to slip out and leave her a note.

Mom walks into the sitting room of the small two-bedroom suite I booked when she told me she was coming. Paige has a tiny spare bedroom that only fits a twin bed, so instead we're in a hotel only a block away from her place.

"I was just going to head out for a bit, Mom."

We arrived here the day before yesterday and had a chance to spend some quality time with Paige, who had to work today. My plan had been to grab a taxi downtown, just a twenty-minute ride from the hotel, and then come back here to take Mom out for lunch. Tonight Paige is supposed to join us for dinner and to see the Tribute in Light.

"You're going there, aren't you?" she asks, already knowing the answer.

"Do you mind?"

"No, sweetheart. I understand you need some time by your-self. I have no intention of interfering in that. I'm happy to putz around here, maybe read a bit, until you come back."

I walk up to her and wrap her in a hug.

"Thanks, Mom. We'll grab a late lunch when I come back, okay? Maybe try out that Caribbean place down the street? They have a nice outdoor patio and it's supposed to be a clear, sunny day."

"That sounds wonderful. Be careful out there."

I press a kiss to her cheek and throw her a smile before exiting the room.

Half an hour and forty bucks later, I'm let off at the curb and climb up the steps to the memorial. They've already started with the reading of the names and I find a spot sitting on the edge of a planter where I can listen. It's a long process—a lot of names—and as much as I ache for those grieving around me, I can't help closing my eyes and blowing out a deep breath when I hear the name I've been waiting for.

It's the same every year, the pain of loss so thick around me a good reminder how fragile we are. Yet with each return to this place, I feel more blessed.

"It never gets easier, does it?" A woman around my age takes a seat beside me on the ledge. I don't have the heart to disagree with her.

"It doesn't."

"Do you come every year?"

"Since they finished the memorial, yes," I inform her.

"Me too. Powerful, isn't it?"

"It is."

"Your husband?" she asks.

"Yes. And you?"

"Me too. Firefighter."

"My husband was here for a meeting."

We share the details quite matter-of-factly, nodding at each other in acknowledgment. Something brings each of us back year after year, but I doubt our motivations are the same.

"Do you have children?" I ask, curious.

The woman smiles.

"Two boys and a girl. It was the boys' father who died, I had my daughter with my current husband." She tilts her head slightly. "What about you?"

"We had a daughter together. No other kids."

"Did you remarry?"

Under any other circumstances these questions would be too personal for such a casual meeting, but somehow it doesn't feel that way here.

"I never did."

For some reason that makes me tear up, and the woman— whose name I don't even know—briefly squeezes my hand. Little does she know, my emotions have little to do with the loss of the man who was my husband. I grieve for the years I allowed him to take from me long after he was gone.

That's why I come here. To remind myself I'm still here, still breathing, still very much alive.

"Are you ready?" A handsome man I would guess to be quite a bit older ambles up, putting a hand on the woman's shoulder.

"I am," she responds, getting to her feet. Then she swivels back to face me. "Good luck," she says simply.

"Same to you."

With a smile and a nod, she links her arm with the man's and strides off.

I stay seated, waiting for the crowd to thin a little before I get up and amble to the edge of the north pool, where I know his name is engraved for eternity. I run my fingers along his name.

Then I lift my face into the sun and spread my arms, embracing the warmth it radiates.

The taste of freedom fills my senses and I feel a smile form on my lips.

When I take a last deep breath, before finally taking stock of my surroundings, I notice a handful of people trying not to stare. I turn a kind smile on them and navigate my way through the passage between the pools, to get to the other side, where I can grab a cab.

Someone in front of me suddenly steps aside and I almost run right into a man coming in the opposite direction. Strong hands grab me by the shoulders when I stumble and I lift my gaze up.

I notice his pale blue eyes first. They're focused on mine, studying me with a deep frown between them.

"Sorry," he mumbles, his voice rough.

"My fault, I wasn't paying attention," I quickly respond, taking a step back.

I can't help taking in all that is him. From the gray hair sticking up like he's just run his hand through it to the firm mouth framed by a short, somewhat unkempt gray beard. A black leather jacket covers a white T-shirt over a pair of worn jeans.

I realize I'm ogling him, but he appears to be doing the same to me. I don't look nearly as appealing as he does. Comfort was the name of my game this morning getting ready, so my hair is air-dried, I'm without makeup, and I'm wearing slouchy camo pants, white tennis shoes, and a white, long-sleeved shirt covered with my red, down vest.

I didn't expect to be scrutinized the way this man is doing in this awkward standoff.

"I'm—" I start, but before I can lift my hand to introduce myself, he suddenly darts around me.

I pivot just to see him stalking off, ducking between bodies before he disappears into the crowd.

Weird.

CHAPTER THREE

Gray

I'm not sure what first drew my eyes to her.

My fingers had just found the name I'd been looking for and traced them letter by letter, until I could feel my hardened heart crack and bleed all over what is left of my sister. The fist around my chest so tight I didn't think I could ever find my next breath. The somber atmosphere, the air heavy with grief, the drawn faces around me...and her.

With her head thrown back she appeared to be worshiping the sun, her pose almost sacrilegious. In contrast to those around her, this woman looked unburdened.

My feet started moving on their own accord, until I literally ran into her.

I shake my head, clearing the memories of earlier today. For those few moments I forgot who I was. Idiot. I force myself not to scan the crowd for a glimpse of red, or that untamed mane of hair, and instead look up where two columns of light pierce the dark sky.

The chili dog I bought from a street vendor earlier is starting to burn a hole in my gut as I make my way back to the hotel. I'm wiped. Up at the crack of dawn this morning to get here, and overwhelmed by the crowds and the surprisingly raw emotions, this has been a long fucking day.

I spent hours in the museum this afternoon, touching the twisted columns of steel, staring at the original retaining wall holding back the Hudson River; my sister's remains forever part of the landscape. I'm not a man of prayer, but I prayed for her there, sitting on a bench in the bowels of what once was the World Trade Center, feeling connected to her in a way that had the hair on my arms stand up.

Now I'm drained. I've done what I came here to do and still I know going home tomorrow those ghosts will be right there with me.

9/11 was a brutal catalyst for the dark path that followed.

"How may I help you?"

The young man behind the front desk smiles pleasantly when I walk up.

"The concierge has my bag. I arrived too early to check in."

"Of course, your name, please?"

I give him my name and wait as he goes in search of my stuff, while I scan the luxurious lobby. Marble floors and columns, gleaming copper and shiny oak, and so far removed from what I know it's not even funny. I can't imagine sleeping a wink in what I'm sure will be a soft bed surrounded by this level of luxury.

I don't belong here.

"Can you call me a taxi for Newark airport?" I ask the moment the hotel clerk appears with my bag.

He looks confused at my request.

"I'm afraid I don't understand. Weren't you checking in?"

"I changed my mind."

"Sir, your room is nonrefundable at this point."

Almost three hundred dollars for a room I never even set foot in and I don't give a shit.

"I'm aware of that. It doesn't matter, I have to go."

All pretense abandoned, the guy looks at me with mild disgust as he picks up a phone. I listen to him order me a cab and nod my gratitude before walking outside to wait for my ride.

The airport is much quieter than when I arrived this morning. The United employee I spot behind the desk informs me I'm too early to check-in, so I make my way over to a coffee shop in the terminal, buy a bottle of water and look for a place to spend the night. It doesn't take long to find an empty row of seats. All of them with armrests. Using my bag as a pillow, I lie down on the floor in front and close my eyes.

"Excuse me."

Startled I shoot up in a sitting position, almost knocking the guard leaning down on his ass.

It takes me a minute to get my bearings. My first thought is I'm back behind bars, the man's uniform reminiscent of the prison guards. They were never quite so polite waking us up, though. Usually that was accomplished by a sharp rattle on the steel door closing me in. Then my surroundings filter through and I realize I'm at the airport, waiting for my flight.

"Sorry to startle you," the older man says. "You were sleeping deeply and I was afraid you might be missing a flight. It's almost eight thirty."

"Shit!" I scramble to my feet. "My flight leaves in thirty minutes."

"Where to?"

"Detroit." My eyes dart around the terminal trying to figure out where to go.

"Come with me," he says, not waiting for an answer as he starts walking away at a fair clip. I hurry after him, hoping he can help me catch my flight.

With only a few minutes to spare, I run up to the gate where an attendant scans my boarding pass and waves me through. Out of breath, I drop in my seat by the window, willing my heart to slow down. Moments later the airplane backs away from the gate and I'm once again hanging on to the armrests for dear life when we take off.

I can't wait to get home.

———

Robin

I'm frozen in my seat, a few rows behind him.

He never looked at me, and even if he did he may not have recognized me. There's no reason to believe our very brief encounter yesterday made as much of an impression on him as it did on me.

What are the odds, though? I wasn't even supposed to be on this flight, but Kim called last night, telling me Shirley had ended up in MidMichigan Medical Center in Clare. A neighbor called 911 after finding Shirley bleeding on her porch.

I immediately called the airline and was able to change my flight to the first one back to Detroit this morning. Mom decided to stay and Paige was going to help her move her stuff from the hotel to her apartment today, since I had to leave early.

The blue-eyed man had been on my mind until Kim's phone call cleared my head, and all I've been able to think about since is poor Shirley. Apparently Kim's been camped out at the hospital and the text I received this morning detailed the extent of Shirley's injuries. The list is nothing to sneeze at: a swollen jaw, three-inch gash to the head, two cracked teeth, a broken forearm, and several bruised ribs. He did a number on her this time.

"Please fasten your seat belt."

The friendly flight attendant indicates the belt I was in the middle of buckling when he rushed through the door.

"Yes, of course," I mutter with an apologetic smile, quickly finishing the task.

My eyes drift over the seats in front of me, focusing on the gray mop sticking up three rows down. I wonder if he lost someone when the towers came down. Over the years, I've run into a surprising number of people who knew someone who died that day. Of course, when they found out my husband had been one of them, I always drew sympathetic looks. Those would've been best saved for someone who deserved them.

I try to distract myself with some cooking show I found on the small monitor in front of me, since I forgot my book back at the hotel when I rushed out this morning. I have a Kindle app on my phone, but I don't want to waste my battery reading. Besides, I don't think reading would be enough to keep my mind off things right now.

About halfway through the Pavlova the three contestants are supposed to create, my neighbor—an older lady with painfully bad breath—engages me in conversation. I politely look at pictures of the new grandbaby she just went to visit, and to my surprise, time passes quickly.

I've almost forgotten about Blue Eyes when I shuffle off the plane with the other passengers and spot him still in his seat. He's looking out the window, his broad back—still wearing the black leather jacket—turned to the aisle. I almost reach out to tap him on the shoulder so he can get out in front of me, but at the last second the line starts moving again, taking me along.

My car is in long-term parking and I shoot off a silent thank you when it starts up without a problem. It's getting up there both in years and mileage. I bought it new when I moved back to Michigan and it's due for a replacement. Unfortunately, what I'm able to afford now versus then has changed a lot.

I would've put all of the money from the insurance policy in trust for Paige, but we needed a roof over our head and a means of transportation. I bought the small two-bedroom ranch just outside of town and a standard Mazda Tribute. No bells and whistles on either. The rest of the money I put away for Paige. It was used for her tuition and the remainder went into her bank account when she turned twenty-one.

I try not to break any speed limits on the two-and-a-half-hour drive to Clare, but I'm anxious to get to the hospital. Kim mentioned she'd stay with Shirley, but she also has a diner to run so I don't want to waste time stopping off at home. I didn't think to ask if her sons had been notified and were perhaps on their way, but I guess I'll find out when I get there.

It's just after one when I pull into the hospital parking lot, and my stomach is growling from lack of food. Breakfast was a granola bar I picked up in a small store at the airport, and that was at six this morning. The smell of fresh coffee and pastries assaults me when I walk into the lobby. I eye the coffee shop counter, but decide to wait until after I find Shirley.

"Mrs. Hancock is in room 317," the volunteer at the front desk informs me. "Up to the third floor and to your right."

"Thank you." I throw her a smile over my shoulder as I head to bank of elevators she indicates.

Upstairs I easily find the room. Shirley is no more than a hump in the bed but before I can step inside, Kim gets up from the chair in the corner and presses a finger to her lips as she walks toward me.

"She just fell asleep," she whispers, as she turns me back into the hallway.

We stop by the nurses' station where she tells the young woman working on a computer that Mrs. Hancock is sleeping, and we'll be down in the lobby, before dragging me back to the elevators.

"What's going on?"

"She's been up all damn night," Kim groans, running a hand

through her haphazard hair. "First arguing with me about whether or not to call the boys. I wanted to but she was adamantly against it. Says she doesn't want to alarm them unnecessarily. Can you believe it? Alarm them?" She agitatedly blows a breath through pursed lips before continuing. "Then when the cops came in to take her statement this morning, she claimed she fell down the stairs. Not that they believed her. They don't need her to file charges against Mike, and I'm waiting to hear if they've picked him up yet."

"Jesus. So other than stubborn; how is she?" I ask, gratefully following Kim to the coffee shop.

"Eating through a straw for the foreseeable future, until her teeth can get fixed and her jaw heals. They had to surgically set her forearm, she's still groggy from the anesthetic."

"That bastard," I growl.

"No shit. She's going to need looking after for a while."

I don't even think; I react.

"She can stay with me."

I'd like to think, if I'd had a friend I could trust back then, I might've gotten away sooner, but any friends were his, not mine.

"I can take her," Kim counters, turning to the kid behind the counter to put in an order and I quickly add my own.

"You have a wife and young kids at home, as well as a diner to run. You have your hands full. I've got the space and the time," I push while we wait for our orders.

It's true. Just sixteen months after Kim and her longtime lover, Janice, got married, she gave birth to their first child, Chester. Less than two years ago Janice had Amber, a little girl to complete their family. With two kids under five, a busy household, and a full-time business to keep track of, I'm sure they have better things to do than look after Shirley.

"Fair enough," Kim says, her mouth full with her cheese croissant. "She can stay with you, but you promise to let me know if you need help."

"First thing we need to do is convince her to let us call her kids," I suggest, sinking my teeth into my own lunch and I groan at the buttery taste.

"Have some mercy." Kim finally glares at me as I enjoy every bite audibly. "I haven't seen my wife in over twenty-four hours."

I roll my eyes. "TMI, Kim. Nobody wants to know that shit."

Of course she finds that funny. She opens her mouth to say something else, I'm sure I don't need to hear, so I quickly shove the last of my Danish in my mouth and get up to toss my napkin and coffee cup in the trash.

"Let's go." I nudge her shoulder as she tosses back the dregs of her coffee.

We walk into the room as a nurse is taking Shirley's blood pressure. Her eyes are open and briefly on me before she turns her head away.

We're in for a battle.

CHAPTER FOUR

Robin

"I have an appointment tomorrow."

Shirley looks at me from her perch on my couch as I walk in the door.

It's been almost two weeks since I brought her home from the hospital, and I'm about ready to pull my hair out. She's been impassive all this time. Stuck in denial. Unwilling to let us call her boys, talk about packing some of her things, or discuss anything to do with her future.

Not that I blame her. I guess everyone needs time to process their life won't be the same as it was before. For some it's difficult to see anything beyond the situation they're in.

The one thing Kim and I got her to agree to, with the aid of the kind police officer who came to the hospital, was a restraining order against Mike. He'd been charged with domestic assault and battery, but was out on bail walking the streets already.

This morning she promised to contact her dentist for an

appointment to fix her teeth after pushing her on the subject for the past week.

Small steps.

"That's great news." I smile at her and move to the kitchen island, dumping the groceries I picked up after my shift. "When can he see you?"

"Thursday at two."

"Either Kim or I can take you, we'll work something out."

"Actually..." I look up from emptying the bags on the counter. "There's something else." She lowers her eyes to where her fingers are plucking at the throw on her lap. "I have an aunt in Grand Rapids I talked to this morning. She wants me to come stay with her. Only problem is she doesn't drive. I know I'm asking a lot, but do you think it's possible to drive me to her place Thursday after my appointment?"

I set down the box of crackers I've been holding and go sit beside her on the couch, grabbing her good hand in mine.

"Sounds like you did a bit more than just make a dental appointment."

"Are you upset?"

"What, me? Why would I be upset?"

"I'm really grateful to you for letting me stay here—looking after me—but I just feel I need to get out of here. Beaverton, I mean," she quickly adds. "Make a clean break, you know?"

I understand better than she knows. Besides, some distance between her and that douchebag would be safer for her. Not that we've heard or seen anything from him yet, but it would be naïve to think after so many years of abuse he'd simply let her walk away. Statistics show that protective orders in domestic violence cases only go so far.

"It was my pleasure and for what it's worth, I think you're doing the right thing. A fresh start is probably just what you need, and I'll be happy to drive you to Grand Rapids."

———

"I'll call them."

I shoot a quick glance at Shirley before focusing back on the road.

"My boys," she clarifies. "When I get to my aunt's place, I'll call them."

I reach over and squeeze her hand.

"I'm glad. Who knows, they may have been trying to reach you all this time and are worried."

"They don't call often," she admits softly. "They've been upset with me for years for staying."

"Your kids know?"

"He was never an easy man to live with. They know that much. The physical stuff started after the youngest went off to college a few years ago, but I think maybe they can guess. Mike was a big believer in corporal punishment when the boys were growing up." She blows out a deep sigh. "I'm afraid they'll be mad I waited so long."

"Or maybe just happy you finally found the courage to walk away," I suggest.

"Maybe," she repeats wistfully.

Her aunt, Meg, is a rotund woman with a radiant smile and she permanently corners herself a place in my heart when she greets Shirley with, "Never liked the asshole. Is it bad I hope he tries to show his face so I can use my brand-new shotgun to blow him off my steps?"

I chuckle through Shirley's protests and Aunt Meg tosses me a wink over her niece's shoulder. It's clear she's in good hands.

I accept the dinner invitation, and even stay for the offered tea, and a slice of homemade apple pie, before saying my goodbyes.

"I'm sorry I'm leaving you guys minus a waitress," Shirley sniffles on my shoulder, as I carefully hug her.

"Don't you worry about that. Kim already has a few interviews lined up. We'll have the schedule filled in no time," I assure her.

"Thank you. For everything."

"Anything and anytime. I mean it. It may take a while for you to get your feet back under you, but you will. I promise."

As I drive away from her aunt's house, I remember telling myself the same thing years ago. *Many* years ago. It isn't until now, seeing Shirley take those first few steps to freedom, I realize how far I've come, and yet I'm still holding back.

I'm forty-five-years old—almost forty-six—and I've spent the last eighteen of those cautiously tiptoeing through life. I've found stability; have a roof over my head, a job that pays the bills, and a daughter who is all grown and on a path of her own. It's high time I throw caution to the wind and actively start living again.

The man with the intriguing, pale blue eyes immediately comes to mind, along with the regret I didn't grab the opportunity to talk to him.

I'm about fifteen minutes away from home when my Tribute dies.

———

Gray

"You should come with us tonight. Get out for a bit."

I watch the last customer of the day drive off the lot in the truck I just replaced the brake lines on before I turn to Jimmy.

"I'm good."

"Come on," he pushes. "It's been over two months and other than your twenty-four-hour turnaround to New York, you've barely been outside this building. At least come grab a bite, meet the guys. A few of them have been in your shoes."

He's asked me at least half a dozen times over the past weeks, and although I no longer duck out of sight when someone comes into the shop, it's different going out there. He's also mentioned a few of his biker buddies did time before.

Maybe it's time. Either I move away somewhere people don't know me, or I stay here and face whatever's coming my way. All I'm doing right now is dragging out the sentence I already served in full.

"Okay, fine. Do I have time for a shower?"

Smiling broadly, Jimmy claps a hand on my shoulder.

"Absolutely. I'm gonna grab a quick one myself. I'll swing by in twenty and pick you up."

I nod, grateful he seems to understand walking into a restaurant by myself would be much harder. I just hope I don't disappoint him. I'm not exactly the most social guy to be around. Inside I stuck to my books, avoiding most interaction, and leading a pretty solitary existence. Sitting around, shooting the shit, with a bunch of his friends may well be more than I can deliver on.

But I can try.

Twenty minutes later and freshly showered, I wait outside the shop when Jimmy rides up on his bike.

"I'm not gonna ride bitch," I announce when he stops in front of me.

"Don't worry. You're not pretty enough anyway," he deadpans. "We're walking. It's just two blocks down. I'll swing by to pick up the bike after."

Last I remember, Beaverton only had about a handful of restaurants, two of those fast food, one barbecue joint, a tavern, and the diner two blocks away. I'm guessing that's where we're going.

"Hudson's Diner?"

"It's called Over Easy now. The Hudsons retired...shit, it's been a long time. Their daughter took over. Remember Kim?"

Yeah, I remember Kim. She worked at her parents' place from

the time she was fourteen, two years behind me in school. I noticed because she was one of the prettiest girls in town at the time. I can't recall how many times she shut me down asking her out. Fuck, I used to be a cocky bastard, and she seriously messed with my confidence.

I remember my relief when she came out of the closet and I realized it wasn't me; it was my gender that was lacking. That can't have been an easy time for her. A small town this size, anyone different than what people consider the norm stands out like a sore thumb.

"I remember her. Used to crush on her," I admit with a grin.

"Hell, yeah. Me too and I'm guessing we weren't the only ones. She's still pretty but so is her wife."

I turn to him with raised eyebrows.

"Wife?"

"Gay marriage was legalized in 2015, brother. She didn't waste any time. They've got a couple of kids too."

I try not to think too hard about the logistics. It's not my business.

"Good for her," I mumble.

"Was married myself for a spin."

I throw him a side-glance and catch him with a lopsided grin on his face.

"Who was the unlucky lady?"

"Fuck you. You wouldn't know her. I met her at a bike rally in 2005. She got on the back of my bike and came back to Beaverton. Got hitched three months after."

"What happened?"

He shrugs. "She was wild. Couldn't keep up with all the shit she was into. Called it after barely a year."

"No offspring?"

"Fuck no. She was so far from mother material, it's not even funny, and honestly, I wasn't ready to be any kind of parent myself."

"And now?" I ask, glancing over again.

I'm curious. It's an issue I struggled with, especially at first; the knowledge I'd never have kids. There'd been a time I wanted that—kids, a family—but I would never put the burden of having a murderer for a father on a child. Fuck, I lived it.

Jimmy shrugs. "Whatever happens...happens. But I have it on good authority, I should probably meet a good woman first."

I chuckle as he pulls open the door to the diner. It looks pretty much the same, although I can tell there've been some upgrades.

"Fucking Gray Bennet!"

Well, shit.

I notice the heads swiveling in my direction before I see an older, but still beautiful, version of Kim heading my way. The smile on her face is not exactly the welcome I expected, nor is the bone-crushing hug she folds me in.

Jesus. I have to firmly remind my body this woman is as out of reach as the stunning New York stranger who's been plaguing my dreams.

"Kim," I grunt, peeling myself from her hold.

"God, it's good to see you. How long have you been back? I've heard rumors you were in town."

"You too. Been back since July."

She opens her mouth to say something else when she suddenly seems to realize we've become the center of attention.

"Shit," she hisses, leaning into me. "We're gonna have to catch up later. I'm short a waitress today."

Relieved, I nod before following Jimmy to the round table in the corner where four tough-looking guys sit, watching us approach.

"Tank," the one with the bald head and goatee says to Jimmy.

"Rooster," he answers.

"Tank?" I repeat before I can check it.

My friend grins sheepishly. "My road name." Then he turns to the men. "Guys, meet Gray. Gray, from right to left; Bear, Tattoo Bob, Shortie, and that's Rooster."

The guys grunt a greeting and I return the favor before taking a free seat. Kim shows up shortly after to take orders.

I eat and mostly listen to the conversation centering around an upcoming event in Kalamazoo these guys are heading to next weekend.

"You coming?" Shortie asks me. A tongue-in-cheek name, since he's at least six four, if not taller.

"We need someone to haul the trailer," Bear adds.

"You should." Jimmy nudges me. "It's like a giant swap meet. You can find every fucking motorcycle part you can imagine. I bet you they even have those parts you were missing on that old Knucklehead of yours."

"Would be a moot point since that bike is long gone," I point out.

I found that old bike at the dump out in Clare, when I was digging around for parts for my Mustang. It was missing a back wheel and most of the engine block was stripped for parts, but the seat, the frame, and the tank still looked to be in good condition, so I loaded it up on my old pickup.

It was supposed to be my project after I got done the Mustang, but that never happened.

"It's in my parents' garage," Jimmy explains. "When the bank foreclosed on the farm, I managed to haul it out of the barn."

I'm not sure what to say. I didn't think there'd be anything left after my lawyer notified me the farm was gone. I know it's probably a pile of unsalvageable rust by now, but it means something he cared enough to hang on to it for me.

"I..." I have to clear my throat before I can continue. "I'll come. Next weekend; I'll come."

"Sorry to interrupt." Kim walks up to the table and turns to Jimmy. "One of my girls is stuck on Dale Road, about fifteen minutes out of town with a dead engine."

"Fuck. Sorry, guys. Rain check for me." He starts getting up when I grab his arm and pull him back down.

"I'll go. What does she drive?" I ask Kim.

"Black Mazda Tribute."

I get out of my seat and grab my wallet from my back pocket, but Kim stops me.

"On the house if you get my girl off the side of the road before all light is gone. Nothing but trees out there."

"Keys for the tow truck are on the tackboard in the office," Jimmy says. "I owe you one."

"Fuck no, I'm not even close to paying you back."

Before he has a chance to respond, I make my way through the diner, ignoring a few curious stares. The crisp night air feels good as I jog the two blocks back to the shop. It's still twilight, but it can get dark real fast up here. A girl alone, on the side of the road, in the middle of nowhere is not a good thing.

I have to be careful with my speed. I don't want to draw the attention of law enforcement—they generally don't feel that forgiving when dealing with an ex-con.

She must've seen my headlights coming toward her because I see hers flashing a few times. I use a widening of the shoulder to turn the truck around and carefully back up to the black SUV.

I drop down from the cab and have to raise a hand to my eyes to block the glare of her headlights as I walk up. She seems to catch on when they suddenly turn off. By the time I get to the driver's side door, my eyes have adjusted to the dark and I catch sight of her.

A woman—not a girl—and one I would've recognized anywhere, even though I only saw her for a brief moment once before.

In New York.

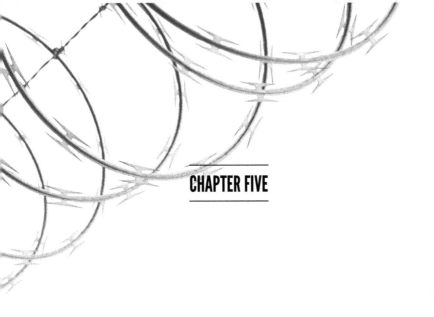

CHAPTER FIVE

Robin

I sit frozen as the man approaches.

Those blue eyes. The same white shirt and leather jacket.

I turn the headlights off and blink furiously, positive my mind is playing tricks. When I open them he's right beside my window, staring in slack-jawed, but then his features even out. Should I open my door? This is too much of a coincidence.

I grab my phone from the passenger seat and dial the diner back.

"Over Easy."

"Kim? It's Robin. The guy you said was going to pick me up, what does he look like?"

"Gray? Tall, lean build, silver-haired, blue eyes. I think he was wearing a black leather jacket. Why?"

That's him to a T.

"Never mind. He's here, I've gotta go."

I quickly end the call and unlock my door, opening it carefully.

"Are you Gray?"

"Gray Bennet. You work for Kim?"

"I do. I'm Robin."

I'm about to offer my hand but he moves around me, sticking his upper body into the car.

"Keys?"

"Oh. I have them here."

He holds up his hand and I pass them over. Then he climbs behind the wheel and tries to start the engine. It sputters a few times but doesn't engage. He gets out again, and I have to take a step back to give him room.

"Need anything from the car?" he asks, and I take a minute to clue in.

"Just my purse. Do you know what's wrong?"

He leans in and grabs my bag off the passenger seat, handing it to me.

"I'm guessing fuel pump," he mumbles, walking to the back of his truck where he starts to roll out chains.

He's not very talkative. In fact, he's borderline rude, not even looking me in the eye when I know damn well he recognized me too.

"You were at the 9/11 Memorial, weren't you?" I probe when he drags the chains to the front of my SUV.

"It's safer for you in my truck. Door's open."

He totally ignores my question and it's clear he wants me out of the way. Fine. Glad to know he's really an asshole so I can stop fantasizing about him.

It still freaks me out to bump into the same man I ran into in New York, a few weeks ago, at the side of a dark road in nowhere Michigan.

I resist the urge to call him out on it, step over the chains he's attaching somewhere under the bumper of my vehicle, and because it's getting chilly out, climb inside the warm cab of his truck.

Minutes later, his door opens and he gets in behind the wheel. I try hard not to glance at him, keeping my eyes firmly on the road ahead as I wait for him to start driving. When significant time passes and we're still in the same spot, I glance over to find him watching me.

"That was me. In New York," he says, his rough voice so low it's almost a whisper.

"I know," I answer, matching his volume. "This is weird."

"Sure as fuck is." His raw chuckle is a surprise, as are the dimples popping up by the corners of his mouth, but the next moment his face irons out again. "Where to?"

"The garage?" Seems like a no-brainer to me.

"Car won't get fixed tonight. Where's home? I'll drop you off."

I can't count the times I cautioned my daughter about sharing information like her phone number or our address with strangers, and here I am, contemplating doing just that.

"How do you know Kim?" I ask, trying for a little more assurance that he's on the up and up.

"We were in high school together. She was a couple of years behind me."

"You grew up here? I've never seen you around and I've been here now for almost seventeen years."

A muscle ticks in his jaw as his eyes stare out the front window.

"I just recently moved back to town," he says brusquely.

"And you work at Tank's shop?"

"Olson's. Yes."

He turns his head and I meet his eyes, amazed again at how light they are.

"Okay," I concede, giving him my address.

I watch his hands on the steering wheel as he pulls onto the road. You can tell a lot from a person's hands. Gray's are large, with a wide palm and long fingers. The remains of a hard day of manual labor not quite gone from around the blunt nail beds.

Callused hands I imagine would feel rough to the touch. Slightly abrasive on skin.

My face flushes at the direction my thoughts travel and I abruptly turn my focus on the road ahead, just in time to see a couple of deer dart out in front of us. He slams on the brakes at the same time his arm shoots out, bracing me in my seat. Much like I used to do with Paige, instinctively protecting what was precious to me.

We sit like that for what feels like much longer than it is. I'm acutely aware of the pressure of his forearm against my chest and forget to breathe.

"You okay? Robin?" He pulls back his arm and I can feel him looking at me.

"I'm good," I manage to rasp, despite feeling breathless and a little shaky. Although, I'm not sure whether from the near collision or his unexpected touch.

I need to get a grip. It's clearly been too long since I've been in close proximity to a man if I get flustered by this. Even as I'm silently berating myself, I know it's more than that.

I'm around men plenty at the diner, even handsome ones, but they don't make me feel unbalanced the way Gray does. He's quiet, seems self-contained and even distant, but I swear every time his gaze is on me, I can feel it. Probing and curious, yet shuttered. Like one-way mirrors, keenly observing while hiding behind them.

"I saw you, you know. On the plane. I almost stopped to talk to you." I'm not sure why I'm volunteering the information, other than to fill the silence. He looks startled. "You were looking out the window. I wasn't sure...I didn't want to interrupt."

"I don't like flying," he says, surprising me. Not so much he doesn't like it, but that he would admit it. "Looking out the window helps me forget I'm stuck in a small tin can."

I smile at that.

"I gather you don't fly often?"

He glances over at my question and I can almost see shutters coming down.

"Nope."

Silence stretches until he pulls into the long tree-lined driveway to my house. It's dark except for the porch light I left on when Shirley and I left. Being alone again will be a bit of an adjustment. Despite the not so happy reasons for Shirley's two-week stay, I enjoyed having company.

"You need more lights."

"Excuse me?"

"Your drive is too dark. You're out here alone, you need to be more careful."

I'm annoyed at his gruff, patronizing tone, while at the same time wondering if perhaps I should be worried instead.

"I'm five minutes out of town," I protest.

"By car. Which at this moment is hanging off the back of my truck." He stops in front of my house, peering out the front window. "A lot longer if you have to walk it."

Shit. I'm gonna need a car.

"About that, you guys wouldn't happen to have a loaner car, would you? I'm kinda stuck out here."

———

Gray

What the fuck was I thinking?

Not my smartest move, but the woman is out there alone without wheels so I volunteered driving her to the closest car rental place in the morning. Never mind that it's in Midland, half an hour drive away.

An even longer time in her presence than last night.

"This thing is a piece of shit," Jimmy says, poking his head from under the hood of the Mazda. "Robin should be looking for another ride instead of investing any more money in this one. You should tell her putting in a new fuel pump would be a waste. Unless you want me to?" he asks with a shit-eating grin on his face.

We've been over this since I told him this morning who the customer was. Apparently he's familiar with her, information which burned in my gut. Especially when he offered to take on the task of driving her to Midland. As much as I want to distance myself from the intense feeling of need she seems to stir in me, I still don't want Jimmy anywhere near her.

"Fuck off." I scowl at him before marching to the tackboard with keys, grabbing the ones to the pickup truck I've been using.

"Hey, hold up," he calls after me. "On your way back, can you pick up some parts at Advance? It'll save me shipping costs. I'll call in the order now."

Instead of answering, I flip up a couple of fingers in acknowledgment before walking out the bay doors.

I notice, getting in behind the wheel, I'm wearing my coveralls instead of my usual uniform of jeans and a white T-shirt, but I would never live it down if I were caught running upstairs to change. Who the hell cares anyway? It's not like this is a fucking date.

It only feels like one.

I run an agitated hand through my hair before I turn the key in the ignition. I'm out of sorts and short on sleep. I'm still trying to find my equilibrium in a world that is much more overwhelming than I remember, and this woman only adds to the confusion. What are the odds?

At the memorial she stood out like a bright beacon in a vast ocean of grief: a promise of hope I have no right to. Then she turns up here, in the town filled with dark memories, making me believe in a higher power when I know damn well there is none.

She's waiting when I pull up to her place, sitting on the steps of her porch. Already wearing her work clothes: jeans and a T-shirt with the name of the diner across her chest. As she walks up to the truck, I have a hard time looking away from those letters stretched over her ample tits. My dick, dormant far too long, picks now to rise to the occasion. Thank fuck I'm wearing my coveralls; they hide more than my jeans would.

"Morning," she chirps, as she gets into the passenger seat. Too sunny and trusting, and way the hell too appealing.

"The car's a write-off."

I'm being an asshole on purpose. I don't want to be like a fucking moth helplessly drawn to her flame, but when I see the light dim in her eyes, I regret it intensely. I'll just add it to the truckload of regret I'm already lugging around.

"Really?" She doesn't seem to expect an answer so I stay quiet, turning the truck down her driveway. From the corner of my eye, I see her working her bottom lip between her teeth as she stares out the window. "Guess I'll be shopping for a new car then," she finally says. "I figured that day was coming." I can sense her eyes on me. "Maybe I'll check out a few secondhand car dealers in Midland when you drop me off."

I will myself not to respond but it's useless, I have little control around her.

"They'll charge too much. Let me talk to Jimmy, he may be able to get you something reliable for a decent price."

"Thanks, that'd be awesome."

I make the mistake of looking at her, the smile on her face so genuine it hits me square in the chest. Pity to have her waste something that beautiful on me.

Still I engage when she asks my opinion about what she should be looking for. My responses are the bare minimum, but she doesn't seem to mind. Before I realize it, we're driving into the outskirts of Midland, a city much larger than the one thousand plus population of Beaverton.

I fight the urge to turn the truck around, not quite ready to end what had been a far too meaningful half hour with Robin. She seems surprised when I get out with her and follow her into the rental office, but Jimmy had asked me to make sure they gave her our preferred rate.

It takes about two seconds for me to want to put my fist in the face of the guy behind the counter, whose eyes never quite make it up to Robin's face. Fucking sleezeball is so focused on her tits; he doesn't notice me glaring until one of his colleagues elbows him in the ribs. The moment his eyes meet the murder in mine he blanches. He barely even looks at her after that, rushing her through the paperwork, and even throwing in an upgrade.

Within minutes, we're back outside, walking around the SUV they're giving her. I point out a few dings on the fender Robin missed, making sure they're all noted on her contract. Leaving her with the keys, he disappears inside and I stand awkwardly beside her, my hands buried deep in my pockets.

"I appreciate you driving me all the way out here," she says, turning her face up to me. All I can see is the warm light in her much darker blue eyes and the soft swell of her perfect lips.

"Not a problem," I mumble, backing away before I do something I'll regret.

"Wait," she calls out when I turn my back. "Can I buy you a coffee or something? It's the least I can do," she adds quickly, as I look over my shoulder. A deep blush darkens her cheekbones as her question hangs in the air.

So fucking tempting.

"I've got shit to do," I blurt out rudely, and watch that deep color bleach from her skin.

"Of course. Well, thanks again." This time her words are delivered with a tight smile, and I feel the loss of her warmth as she gets behind the wheel.

I'm still standing in the same spot when she drives by me and pulls out of the parking lot.

Never even sparing me a glance.

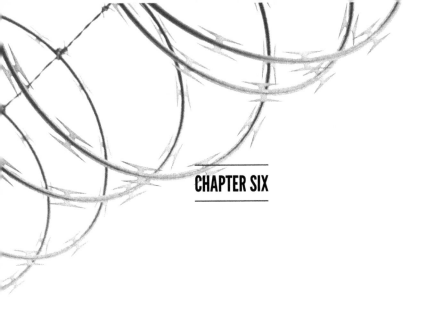

CHAPTER SIX

Robin

"And how did they react?"

I lean back on the couch and put my feet up on the coffee table, the phone beside me on speaker as I sip my morning coffee.

Shirley just told me she finally worked up the courage to contact her sons. We've been in touch a couple of times since I drove her to Grand Rapids a week and a half ago. I know Kim's been checking in on her as well. No one has heard from Mike, who'd been released on bail and has apparently been keeping a low profile. Who knows, he may not even be in town anymore. Good riddance if you ask me, but I'm not so sure it's the last we'll see of him.

"Angry. Mostly at their father, but some at me."

"At you? Why?"

"For not leaving him sooner." She's quiet for a moment before she adds, "For not talking to the cops. They want me to tell them everything from the start."

My fist pump is silent but I'm so relieved to hear that. I've been worried she might end up going back to him, like so many women do. I don't want her to become a statistic.

"What are you gonna do?" I ask her carefully.

"Tell it all."

I hang up twenty minutes later, feeling better about Shirley than I did before. Her kids sound like decent young men whole-heartedly supporting their mother; notwithstanding the shitty example their asshole dad had shown.

I'm just cutting vegetables for the stir-fry I had planned for dinner tonight when my phone on the counter starts ringing. I suck in a sharp breath when *Olson's Automotive* appears on my screen.

"Hello?"

"Hey, it's Tank. We may have found you something."

I pretend I'm not disappointed it's him instead of Gray call-ing. For some reason that man has made a lasting impression on me. One I can't seem to shake, no matter how hard I try.

Tank had come into the diner the day after I picked up my rental in Midland. Despite Gray blowing me off, he'd apparently still talked to his boss about finding me new wheels. He asked me what I was willing to spend and said he'd keep an eye out.

"Really?"

"Three-year-old Honda CRV with just thirty-five-thousand miles. Decked out, comes with winter tires, and all within your budget."

Since my budget is fifteen grand and I've done a little research myself, this sounds too good to be true.

"What's the catch? Those things go for at least twenty-two K if not more."

Tanks starts laughing.

"I told him you wouldn't fall for it."

"Told who?" I ask, but I'm not surprised when he mentions Gray's name.

"Look, it was a leased car he picked up at the auction for a steal. The engine needed some work and there was a small ding on a rear fender. He was able to push out the dent and fixed the engine. In fact, he spent the past week taking it apart and rebuilding it."

I'm struck silent, unsure what to think of that. The more I learn about this man, the more confused I get, and the more I want to know.

"How much for parts and labor?"

"He did it on his off time, Robin. You're gonna have to take it up with him."

"Wait a minute, if he's the one who found me the car, why isn't he the one on the phone?"

"Fuck if I know, pardon my French."

"Not to worry, I speak it fluently myself."

He chuckles. "I knew I liked you for a reason. Anyway, do you have time to come in tomorrow and take it for a ride? See if you like it?"

"I don't start until noon, if the morning is okay?"

"Any time is good. See you then."

I'm still puzzled when I put my phone down and turn back to my veggies. I would've sworn a week and a half ago Gray wanted nothing to do with me—it couldn't have been clearer—but now I find out he's been working on a car for me on his own time. It doesn't make sense.

A few weeks ago, I'd come to the conclusion I was ready to start living again but the first time I stuck my head out in an attempt to do that, I got slapped back. By Gray. I'd half convinced myself my radar was off because I had a feeling maybe there was interest on his part, until he made it abundantly clear I'd imagined it. Now he goes and does something like this. I don't understand what he's getting out of it.

I try to watch some TV after I eat, but not even the new series I've been devouring on Netflix can hold my attention.

Annoyed with myself, I end up going to bed early at ten, unfortunately my mind still won't settle.

Gray Bennet is not only an enigma; he's fast becoming an obsession.

———

"Can I help you?"

A young kid I've seen at the diner a couple of times before approaches me when I walk up to the bay, wiping his hands on a rag.

"Hi. Yes, Tank told me to come by for a test drive?"

"Oh, you're the lady for the CRV? My name is Kyle. The boss is out on a tow, but let me get Gray."

I knew the chances were good I'd run into him, but I still feel a niggle of excitement when the kid disappears into the shadows. It's quickly followed by disappointment when Kyle comes walking out, dangling a set of keys in his hand.

"He's in the middle of something, but he says to give it a good run. It's right over here."

He leads the way to a shiny black SUV, looking brand-new, opening the driver's door for me before handing me the keys.

"Thank you."

"The boss should be back in twenty minutes or so, to handle any paperwork. It's a great car. Gray fixed it up nice for ya."

Another reminder of his unexpected kindness, yet he didn't come out to show me the vehicle himself. I shrug it off and get behind the wheel. Kyle shows me how to adjust my seat and I take a moment to familiarize myself with the interior, which looks and smells like a new car.

I start the engine and can hear right away how much quieter it is than my Tribute. Pulling out of the parking spot, I catch a glimpse of a coverall-clad figure standing inside the shop, his face hidden in shadows. The gleam of silver hair is a dead giveaway, though.

Half an hour later I pull back into the lot, completely sold on the SUV.

"I love it," I announce when I walk in to find Tank talking to Kyle. "It's perfect."

"That's great. Come into the back and we'll get the paperwork sorted." I follow him into the small office where I hold out the keys. "Might as well keep those," he suggests.

"But I first have to get the rental back to Midland."

He indicates for me to sit down and slides a bill of sale toward me, detailing the vehicle and the price tag.

"We can take care of that for you. We make that trek regularly to pick up parts. Gray is making a run tomorrow and Kyle can drive the rental down."

"You guys have done enough. Which reminds me, how much for parts and labor? I don't see it included here."

Even before he says anything, I can feel his presence behind me.

"It's taken care of."

I twist in my seat and look up at him.

"You can't do that," I protest, despite those distracting eyes boring into mine.

"It's done," he states firmly. "Parts were nothing and the rest was just time. Got too much of that anyway."

There's a lot in that statement, but I'm not sure what any of it means. I'm determined to find out, though. Call me a sucker for punishment, but there has to be a reason a virtual stranger sacrifices hours on your behalf.

He may act like it's all the same to him, but I don't think I'm mistaking the keen interest in his eyes.

"Then, thank you." I turn back to face Tank, who seems to be amused by the interaction. "No need to bug Kyle. I'll be driving the rental back tomorrow myself, but I'd appreciate a ride back."

"Done," he says, a big grin on his face. "Gray would be happy to give you a ride."

There's definitely no mistaking the growl I hear behind me.

———

Gray

Fucker.

I don't know why he felt he needed to throw me under the bus, but he did. With a motherfuckin' grin on his face. I was also pissed to find out he'd told her about me working on the CRV. There was no reason for her to know that. So much for staying out of her way.

Who am I kidding? It's my own fault for getting involved in her quest for a new vehicle, but fuck, I didn't feel right about her driving something that wasn't completely reliable. I don't want her stuck on the side of the road in the dark again.

I'm not even sure there wasn't some intent on my part.

Christ, if I'm this confused about my own motivations, I can't even imagine how fucked up I must look to her.

I glance over to the passenger seat where she's buckling in. Robin; the woman whose face I haven't been able to get out of my mind since seeing it tilted back to the bright New York sun. I stopped believing in fate the day I lost my entire family, but I wonder what else to call bumping into this woman at every turn.

"It won't take long," I inform her, as I set out for the warehouse to pick up the parts for the garage.

"Good. That'll leave us time to grab a bite before heading back home. It's the least I can do."

I open my mouth for the automatic rejection, but shut it again when I realize she isn't exactly asking this time. She's stating. Not that I've been particularly friendly before, but I'd have to be a real asshole to blow her off now. The kicker is; I don't really have it in me.

After loading up the truck with boxes at the warehouse, I climb back behind the wheel, turn to her, and ask, "Where to?"

"Hamburgers good? I haven't had one in forever."

"Fine by me."

She directs me to a family restaurant close by she's pulled up on her phone.

"So..." she starts after we've been seated in a booth by the waiter. I brace. "Here's what I don't get. You give every indication you don't particularly like me, yet you go out of your way to get me a good vehicle."

"Who says I don't like you?" The truth is out before I let my brain process what I'm admitting to. The humor shimmering in her eyes tells me she planned it this way.

"Good to know I'm not crazy," she mutters under her breath before giving the waiter her drink order. I ask for water and find her eyes on me when the kid walks off. "Well, it may have been the fact you weren't exactly friendly in our previous encounters." She tilts her head and scrutinizes me so thoroughly that I'm starting to feel like a bug under a microscope.

"I don't talk much," I try to deflect, but that only makes her chuckle.

"That might be an understatement." Her delivery is dry but her smile is wide. "Here's what I think; your New York visit, like mine, is something you keep to yourself. The reasons, the motivations, they're private and kept away from day-to-day life. Am I right?" I grudgingly nod because she is. "So we already know more about each other than most people at home do, and you don't like that. Heck, I don't like it either, but it is what it is. Now, as I see it we can try to pretend we never saw each other, but frankly, I'm not very good at lying, especially to myself."

The return of the waiter gives me a chance to process her blunt, straightforward, and eerily accurate assessment. She scans the menu, but I don't need to, I know what I want, a cheese-burger with fries and coleslaw. She orders one with Swiss and the sweet potato fries she says she loves. When the kid walks away, she leans her elbows on the table.

"Or..." she continues as if she never stopped, "...we could be friends."

"Friends," I echo, and she nods to confirm.

"Yes. You said yourself you're back in town after a very long time, and I've recently decided I need to expand my horizons. We could both use a friend."

Her expression is dead serious and yet I want to laugh. She thinks we can be friends. If only she knew she's sitting across from a convicted felon—a killer. She'll undoubtedly find out soon enough, but I don't have the heart to laugh in her face when what she offers so generously has me swallow hard.

"Okay, friends," I agree.

Her responding bright smile warms me from the inside out with the kind of light I'd hate to see snuffed out.

As I'm sure it will be when she discovers the truth about me.

CHAPTER SEVEN

Gray

I watch her generous hips sway as she moves between the tables.

I've been here a few times this past week for lunch. Once with Jimmy and the other two times by myself. I'm putting myself out there and it wasn't nearly as bad as I thought it might be.

Oh, I got the looks I expected from some, but a couple of people I remember from before actually stopped by my table to welcome me back. I hadn't expected that. Truth is, even if the cold shoulder was all I got, it would've been worth it just to get warmed by Robin's smile for me when I walked in.

Our run to Midland last week was eye-opening for me. Sharing a meal as the friends she suggested we could be had me lower my walls a bit. I was surprised how good it felt just to talk to another person. A regular conversation—mostly. She told me about her daughter, and the fact her mother lives in Lansing. She asked about my family and I told her I didn't have any left. She didn't push though; instinctively knowing it wasn't a subject I was comfortable with. When we landed on the topic of books, though, we'd found safe ground.

I held off until day three after that before I ventured into Over Easy on my lunch hour. It had been a struggle between the need to stay out of the public eye, and the craving to see her again. Robin won.

"More coffee?"

She walks up with a carafe.

"Thanks, but I should get back to the shop. Just the bill, please."

"Sure." She starts turning away before swinging around. "You know, I'm off tomorrow, but I was planning to make a pot of goulash. Would you like to come for dinner? I mean, I usually make much more than I can eat and end up freezing—"

"That'd be great," I find myself saying.

She smiles wide, "Great. I'll just go get your bill then," and walks off.

"Be gentle with that one."

I turn around at the sound of a deep, familiar voice. Sitting behind me is Frank Hanson, owner of the town's favorite watering hole, The Dirty Dog. He has to be at least seventy-five or something. Last time I saw him he was pinning me against the side of the bar, his arm pressed up to my throat. I remember almost blacking out, wishing he'd finish the job.

"Mr. Hanson." I nod at him, hoping Robin will be back soon with the bill. I'm not in the mood for a confrontation.

"Gray. Good to see you, son."

I'm sure shock is visible on my face. This wasn't the welcome I anticipated from him. Frank had been a good friend to my father and the one to pull me off his body.

"Frank, I—"

"Was hoping I'd run into you," he continues, as if I never spoke. "I've got a few things I'd like to talk to you about."

"You do?"

"Come by The Dirty Dog? Maybe Sunday?"

I notice Robin approaching my table, the bill in her hand.

"Sure, okay," I tell Frank quickly before turning to her.

I pull my wallet from the pocket of my coveralls and leave a few bills on the table, enough to include a decent tip for Robin. I lift my chin at Frank, who does the same, and lightly touch Robin's arm when I pass her.

"Later," I mumble, a little startled by the charge that small touch caused as I walk out of the diner.

———

Robin

I'm not sure what moved me to ask him for dinner, but I've probably reconsidered half a dozen times since I blurted it out at the diner yesterday.

There is something about the man making me want to look after him. An awkward vulnerability simmering right under the gruff surface. He doesn't appear particularly skilled socially and seems to keep himself carefully shielded. Yet I've seen a few tiny cracks in that carefully impassive veneer, and I feel compelled to find out more about him. About why he affects me the way he does.

Then these past few days, since he started coming into the diner, I've heard some whispers. Things I find hard to reconcile to the quiet man with the intriguing pale blue eyes. I know about rumors and misperceptions, so I'm determined not to judge on what I hear, but on what I know. So far, all I know is Gray has been kind—although not always friendly—helpful, and quite generous with his time. I was also pleased to discover his love for reading, something we share.

It's not the only thing we have in common. We both lead a

quiet existence, don't socialize a whole lot, and we both carry secrets. Even without the rumors stirring, it wasn't hard to see that. Although the resulting impact on our existence may not have been the same, it's a safe guess both of us lost someone important in our lives on September 11th, 2001.

I'm nervous, almost slicing my finger as I cut vegetables for the goulash. I never mentioned a time, but I assume he won't be here until after five when Olson's closes, which is two hours from now.

My phone rings on the counter and for a moment I wonder if he's calling to cancel, but then I see my mother's name on the display.

"Hey, Mom."

"Hi, sweetheart, how are you?"

"I'm good, Mom. Cooking your goulash as we speak. I had the day off. How are you? Feeling any better?"

Mom had come back from New Jersey almost a month ago with a persistent cold she can't seem to get rid of.

"Goulash? Gosh, I could go for a bowl of that right now. I'm doing a little better. I ended up going to my book club with Betty last night. It was nice to get out for a bit."

Betty is Mom's longtime friend, as well as a neighbor in their apartment building. She lost her husband young and when my dad died, she moved into a condo just three doors down from Mom to be closer to her. The two are thick as thieves, and it's peace of mind for me to know Mom always has someone nearby in an emergency.

"I'm glad you went. As for the goulash, I'm cooking a massive amount; I can easily freeze some for you. I'll bring it down next week when we see Dr. Tracey."

"About that; Betty offered to take me if you're busy."

My mother doesn't drive. Never has. Betty does, so the two get their groceries together, but I've always driven down for any appointments Mom has.

"Not at all. Unless you prefer I don't come see you?" I tease her, eliciting the immediate protest I expected.

"Oh, that's not what I mean. I just hate to have you come down just for a regular physical."

"Not coming down just for that, Mom. I missed out on spending time with you at Paige's because of that thing with Shirley. We'll do something fun after the appointment. Maybe grab lunch and a movie?"

I wedge the phone between my ear and my shoulder as I dump the mushrooms, onions, and peppers in my Dutch oven. I already fried up the cubed beef and scooped it out on a plate. I'll combine it all, once the veggies are sautéed, and add some stock before it can simmer for a couple of hours.

"That sounds like a plan. So..." She drags the single syllable and I just know she's about to pry. "Cooking a massive amount, huh? Expecting guests?"

I swear the woman has a sixth sense. Ever since Rick died, she's been hopeful I'd get married again. I almost did, eight years ago, when Paige was still in high school. A local farmer, Andrew VanGuard, who'd also been relatively 'new' to Beaverton, had asked me after we'd casually dated for maybe a year. We clearly had different expectations. Casual was all I was in the market to offer, and I hated having to disappoint him.

Mom had been heartbroken to see her dream for me thwarted, but Dad had still been alive and he'd jumped to my defense. Dad just wanted me happy and I think he suspected my marriage to Rick had not been as perfect as my mother always viewed it.

That's why I'm hesitant telling her about Gray, because I'm afraid she'll build it up into something it isn't. At least not at this point in time. Still, I find myself wanting to share.

"I have a friend coming over for dinner."

"Oh?" She doesn't even hide her excitement.

"Mom—a *friend*," I emphasize. "Actually, it's a funny story..."

I proceed to tell her how we bumped into each other at the memorial and I spotted him on the same flight out the next day. Then I told her about my Mazda breaking down, and of course she immediately offered money so I could buy a new one before I had a chance to mention I already had one.

Thanks to the years Dad put in with General Motors, Mom is left with a decent pension and a good return on some of their investments. It doesn't mean she has to spend it on me.

It takes me ten minutes to convince her I'm fine, I purchased a good car with money I'd set aside for it. Then I mention how Gray had been instrumental in that, and how I'm thanking him with dinner.

Sadly it does little to curb my mother's romantic fantasies for me. In fact, I think it only encourages her.

"Mom, I should get going," I finally say. "I'll pick you up next Wednesday at ten, okay?"

"Yes, of course. You probably need to change. Put a nice dress on or something." I roll my eyes and try to hold back the exasperated sigh, but it's like she can hear me anyway. "There's nothing wrong with trying to look pretty, Robin."

"I know, Mom. I promise I'll brush my hair."

"Oh, I was going to mention that and I almost forgot; you may want to dye your hair, you're getting quite gray I noticed."

My mother has a standing appointment at the hairdresser, every four weeks, when she gets her hair meticulously dyed the same chestnut color she's had as long as I can remember. Not a single silver hair visible. She's been on my case ever since my first gray, not understanding why I don't want to hide them.

"Mom, I don't want to dye my hair. It is what it is and I actually quite like it."

"But you're still so young."

"I know, Mom," I give in. There's no way in hell she'll ever give up on this, and it's useless arguing the same subject expecting a different outcome. "We'll have to agree to disagree on this topic, okay? I really have to go."

"Of course. I love you."

"Love you too, Mom. See you Wednesday."

After adding the beef back in the pot, topping it off with broth, and covering it with a lid, I slide it into the oven where it'll simmer until soft. A quick peek at the clock shows it's already after five when I'm done peeling the potatoes and I put them on the burner, before rushing to my bedroom to get cleaned up.

I'm just running a brush through my hair when I hear the knock.

He looks freshly showered and a little lost when I open my door and when he catches sight of me, his eyes widen in appreciation.

I'm wearing the only dress I own.

Mom would be happy.

———

Gray

I thought I may have gone overboard bringing a box of chocolates and a bottle of wine—and I sure felt scrutinized carrying both to the cashier on my way here.

Looking at Robin wearing a dress, I don't feel as foolish anymore. Clearly I'm not the only one trying to make a good first impression. She looks gorgeous, her full curves on display in the retro dress. I try hard not to linger on her cleavage, where I'd love to bury my face.

"Hey," she says softly. "Come in."

"Hi." I step inside and shove bottle and box unceremoniously in her hands.

"You didn't have to do that," she protests.

"Yeah, I did. Haven't had a proper home-cooked meal in almost two decades," I find myself admitting to.

Where the fuck did that come from? What is it about this woman that has me spilling my guts every chance I get? I almost turn on my heel and beeline it back out the door, but she firmly closes it, grabs my arm, and steers me into a small, but warm and cozy living room.

"I'm glad you let me cook for you then," she says simply. "Have a seat. I'll check on dinner and grab us something to drink, what would you like?"

"Water is fine."

"No wine?"

"Better stick to water."

I barely keep myself from telling her I haven't had a drink in as many years either. I sit down at the end of a dark gray sectional couch, and take in as much as I can of my surroundings without appearing like I'm scanning the place. A modest TV is hanging over the mantel, and a collection of framed pictures sits underneath. I'm curious and want to take a closer look but stay seated.

The living room flows into the dining room toward the back of the house, and the kitchen opens up to that, forming an L-shaped living space. When I walked into the small entrance, I noted a hallway leading toward the back with what I assume are bedrooms and bathroom off to the other side.

I see her walk into the dining room with two glasses and a pitcher of water, which she sets in the middle of the table.

"It'll just be a few minutes," she says, smiling in my direction.

I shoot to my feet as if only now remembering my manners.

"Anything I can do?" I call out, having lost sight of her in the kitchen.

"No, I'm just—Fuck! Ouch!" I hear her swear and I rush around the corner, seeing her bent over the sink.

"What happened?"

I'm already crowding behind her, looking over her shoulder.

"It's nothing. I'm just clumsy."

I notice she's holding one hand with the other and a pot of half-drained potatoes sitting in the sink. Reaching around her, I fish the pot from the sink, set it on the cutting board on the counter. Then I turn on the cold tap, take a firm hold of her hand, and guide it under the stream of water.

She hisses sharply and I try not to notice how her back seems to fit effortlessly against my front. Too late I realize my dick—hard as a rock since she opened her door—is notably pressed against her soft ass. In addition my nose is almost touching her hair, I can smell what I assume is her shampoo, which isn't helping my condition.

"I think I'm okay now," she finally says in a raspy voice, as she pulls her hand back. I immediately step out of the way.

"Here, let me do this." I take the pan she reaches for and finish draining it.

"Thanks. I just need to get the goulash from the oven and then we can eat."

"Why don't you sit down, I'll get the food on the table," I offer, easing her aside. "Smells amazing."

"Thanks. It's my mom's recipe."

She's pouring water in our glasses as I set the pots on the table.

"Is this okay?" I ask her.

"It's fine. As long as you don't mind eating from the pot."

I chuckle at that. If only she knew.

"It's the only way I know."

The food is amazing and I'm tempted to undo the button on my new jeans after I've cleaned my third helping. The conversation has safely circled around books again, and we've discovered neither of us are fans of movies based on books. We agree too much is lost in the transition from paper to screen, but then she asks a question that makes it personal.

"Have you seen any of the movies based on the events of

9/11?" She notes my sudden silence and quickly adds. "I'm sorry, I didn't mean to be insensitive."

"You're not, and I haven't. I avoid those."

"I understand. I shouldn't have brought it up."

She immediately gets up and starts clearing the dishes.

The mood seems to have shifted and it doesn't sit well with me. What I like best about Robin is the fact she is what she is, no more and no less. It's my fault she tenses up and tiptoes around me.

"Robin..." I cover her hand with mine when she reaches to take my plate. When I look up at her I notice how close her face is to mine. "I lost my little sister that day."

Immediately her eyes well and her free hand lifts to my face in a gesture of comfort I haven't felt in so long. I can't help but lean into her touch and watch as her lips form words.

"Oh, Gray, I'm so sorry."

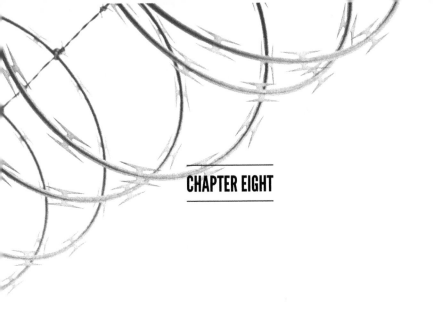

CHAPTER EIGHT

Robin

"She worked as a waitress at Windows on the World."

I sit down on the chair beside him, putting a hand on his leg and he covers it with his. His eyes are fixed on them.

"What was her name?" I ask gently.

"Reagan." He opens his mouth, as if to say more, but then closes it again, studying our hands as he slides his fingers around my wrist.

"You don't have to talk about it," I offer gently, turning my palm against his and twining our fingers.

"And you?" he asks.

I know what he means, but I'm hesitant to give him the answer. I'm afraid the moment I tell him, he'll shut down and I'll have lost the tenuous bond we seem to be forging. I suddenly feel guilty for all the years I've gone to the memorial. While I spent time with others grieving over the collective loss, I silently celebrated my freedom. All those lives changed in devastating ways, while for me it meant a new beginning.

It's the reason I go back alone every year—keep distant from the crowds as much as I can. I come to remind myself to be grateful for the life I've made; yet the last thing I want is to offend those who continue to suffer with their loss.

"You don't need to—"

"My husband. Paige's father."

"I'm sorry," he says, his voice deep and soothing as his thumb strokes the back of my hand.

It's a comfort I don't deserve.

Maybe that's what has me blurt out the truth.

"Don't be. I'm not."

I see I've shocked him with my declaration. I automatically withdraw my hand from his, but he grabs on at the last second.

"He beat you?" The words come out as a growl.

I'm surprised he immediately goes there, it seems like quite a jump to make.

"God no," I clarify quickly. "That might've left marks."

I notice his flinch and I immediately press my lips shut. I can't believe I've shared as much as I have. Most people know I lost Rick in the attacks on 9/11, but not even my mother knows what my life had been like leading up to that day.

Shame burns itself on my cheeks and I abruptly stand up from the table, grabbing his plate and walking into the kitchen. I hear his footsteps behind me, but don't stop rinsing the dishes in the sink. When I turn he's only a step away, looking down on me.

"I watched you," he says, his eyes on my mouth, "from across the pond. You looked like light and hope, with your face lifted up to the sun. Something drew me to you and my feet were moving before I realized it." He reaches his hand to my face, brushing his thumb over my cheek. "You have a very expressive face. It doesn't lie."

"Gray..."

His name slides out on a breath. I barely recognize my own voice, my own feelings. This man has me open up doors I've had locked tight for so many years. The light brush of his thumb on my skin does more for me than sex with any other man I've ever been intimate with. The need to open myself up, share my deepest, darkest secrets is as terrifying as it is liberating, but for now fear holds out.

So I lift up on my toes and press my lips to his.

This isn't me—so forward and claiming—and yet it is.

I feel him freeze under hands I slide up his chest and loop around his neck, pulling him farther down. I tilt my head slightly for a better fit and lick my tongue along the seam of his still lips. It's as if his body jolts against mine and suddenly comes alive. An arm slips around my waist, his hand spreading over the small of my back, fingers pressing into the slope of my ass, as he pushes me into his hips. There is no mistaking the hard evidence of my effect on him pressing into my belly. His other hand slides up my spine and tangles almost painfully in my hair, grabbing a fistful as he slants his open mouth over mine.

The kiss is that of a starving man; hungry and voracious as he feasts, stealing my will and my breath. I go limp in his arms at the overwhelming onslaught of emotion and sensation, but his bruising grip on me holds me in place.

The next moment I'm suddenly released, panting as I reach for the counter behind me for stability when Gray takes a sudden step back, his hand running through his hair.

"I'm...did I hurt you?"

He sounds tortured and I instinctively reach for him, grabbing onto his arm.

"No. No, not at all. You just...that was intense," I ramble, much like my thoughts.

"It's just..." He seems to be no better off forming coherent sentences, which makes me feel a little better. Until I almost see a firm resolve slide into place as his features smooth into an impassive mask. "I should go. Dinner was wonderful. Thank you."

His back ramrod straight, he stalks in the direction of the front door and I scramble to keep up with him.

"Gray..." I start when he's already pulling the front door open.

"Thanks again," he says, before he slips outside and pulls the door firmly closed behind him.

I'm not sure how long I'm standing there with my mouth open, wondering what the fuck just happened. Then I move, locking the door and turning off lights. I head straight for bed where I lie awake for hours, more than a little confused and—frankly—hurt.

———

Gray

"Late night?" Jimmy asks when he catches me yawning again.

More like an early morning for the third time in a row, but who's counting?

Fuck, with every night since I almost mauled Robin in her kitchen my anxiety has gone up. I lost control, something I cannot afford to do. God, the feel of her soft body pressed up against me, willing and pliant. If I hadn't pulled away when I did, she would've ended up on the floor with me ripping at her clothes.

There's a reason I haven't looked for easy pussy since I got out a little over three months ago. A reason after eighteen years, with just my hand for company, that's still the only way to relief I allow myself. The reason I landed in there was my out of control rage. It cost a life. Hell, it cost me most of *my* life.

I'm afraid of the damage I could do if I'm unable to rein in my emotions. Afraid to hurt, and maybe be hurt.

Something happens when you spend most of your days with pain, fears, needs, and regrets as your only company. You push them down and a thin layer of veneer forms, like a film of dust, growing as time passes. You welcome each layer of reinforcement until it becomes an impenetrable shield, protecting not just you, but everyone around you.

Until I met Robin.

From the first time I laid eyes on her, she managed to rub my resistance thin without even trying. Then when she kissed me, stroked her fingers through my hair as her tongue demanded entry, she broke right through.

I can't let that happen again.

"Yeah," I finally answer Jimmy. "Just restless."

"Mmm," he hums, eyeing me carefully. "Maybe you need a little distraction? Snow is expected for next week so the guys and I are going for a ride up to Lake Huron Beach this weekend. Staying over for a night and then back home the next day."

I hung out with him and his biker buddies in Kalamazoo a couple of weeks ago. I like them. Pretty much straightforward guys I didn't mind spending time with. There's only one problem.

"Bike's not done."

"I know," Jimmy acknowledges. "But Rooster has a second bike I'm sure he'd lend you."

Rooster was the big, bald-headed guy, and pretty much the leader of their small motorcycle club. He'd mentioned doing some time decades ago for armed robbery, but had avoided getting into trouble since. That's how he got the name for the MC, the Converts. He said he stopped being an ex-convict years ago and considered himself a convert instead. Interesting viewpoint, I guess, but one I'm not quite ready to adopt.

Maybe getting away for a couple of days will help me stop thinking about Robin.

"Sure. Yeah, if he's okay me riding his bike. It's been a while."

"He ain't gonna mind. I'll call him." He gives my shoulder a shove when I yawn again. "Go upstairs, get some fucking sleep.

I'll finish up." He indicates the Nissan I'm just finishing an oil change on. "Fucking go," he repeats when I hesitate.

I pull the rag from my back pocket and wipe my hands, mumbling, "Thanks," as I walk away.

Upstairs I hit the shower, scrubbing at the grease and oil on my hands. It's a never-ending battle, the dirt always clinging in the creases and crevices. Symbolic, somehow.

With only a towel around my waist, I pad out of the bathroom and flop back on the bed, my arm covering my eyes. I'm exhausted, but still sleep won't come. My thoughts immediately go to Robin and the confused, almost hurt look on her face when I hightailed it out of her house the other day.

Guilt. It's a feeling I recognize. I wonder if that is what's been keeping me restless and awake; guilt.

I reach blindly for the cell phone I dropped on my nightstand when I walked in. I had copied her number from the blotter on Jimmy's desk, in the office downstairs, the day after we picked up her rental in Midland. I'm not sure why, other than it gave me a sense of calm, knowing I could reach her. I haven't used it yet.

Jimmy showed me how to text on this iPhone, but I'm having a hard time hitting the right buttons.

> Me: im sorty

Shit.

> Me: sorry
> Me: Fot leaving like that

Fuck.

> Me: For

Jesus. It's quicker and easier just to call, which I would've done if she'd had an early shift. She doesn't. I may have driven by the diner earlier, when I took one of the cars we were working on today out for a test drive. That was around three and I caught sight of her new SUV in the parking lot. It hadn't been there ten minutes prior, the first time I drove past.

What does that say about me? That I almost run out of her house in an attempt to get away only to stalk her work, eager for a glimpse. Fucking pathetic, that's what it is.

> Me: Dinner was food
> Me: good

Disgusted, both with this stupid texting and my sorry self, I shove the phone under my pillow and swing my legs out of bed.

I pull open the fridge and pull out a carton of eggs, some bacon, cheese, and mushrooms to make an omelet. My almost daily fare. Hard to cook much more on a small two-burner hotplate, but I don't mind. I'll never get enough of fresh-cooked food. Not like the partially congealed stuff we were fed inside.

I've just cracked the third egg in the small bowl when I hear a muffled ping from the bed. I drop the shell in the tiny sink and grab a towel to wipe my hands, as I dive for my phone. All I see on the screen is Robin's name and only a few words.

> Robin: Glad you...

I stab at the message to make it bigger but instead it's asking for my passcode. I've punched it in without thinking enough times by now, but for the life of me, I can't get it right now. I'm growling in frustration when at my third try, the phone finally unlocks and I see her full message.

> **Robin: Glad you liked it. Nothing to be sorry**
> **for. It's fine.**

It's fine.

I don't know a whole lot about women, but I know 'it's fine' is a euphemism for 'you fucked up good.'

Sinking down on the bed, I start typing out a message, this time reading it back before sending. I hesitate, a heavy feeling settling on my shoulders, and I use the back button to delete every last word, dropping the phone facedown on the mattress and heading back to my eggs.

Perhaps it's best this way.

CHAPTER NINE

Robin

"I'm sorry, Dr. Tracey is running behind a few minutes," his assistant apologizes when we walk into the clinic. "He'll be with you as soon as he can."

"No problem," Mom returns, and walks ahead to the waiting area.

The clinic houses three doctors, so I'm surprised to see the only other person in there is a young guy with earbuds in, probably listening to music on the phone his eyes are glued to.

"Good," Mom says, as soon as my ass hits the seat beside her. "That gives me a chance to ask you about your dinner last week. How was it?"

I'm not surprised. I may have distracted her with a funny work story Paige told me over the weekend, but Mom is as tenacious as a terrier and nosy to boot. Still, I don't want to talk about Gray, have done my best this past week not to think of him either, although I haven't been very successful. It hasn't helped that the rumor mill has been alive and well at Over Easy.

I was working a shift with Donna earlier this week. The woman is older than my mother, but still works harder than some of the part-timers we have. She mentioned 'that Bennet boy' and that neither time nor prison had made him any less handsome than he used to be.

Finding that out hadn't surprised me as much as one might think. Gray struck me as someone a little out of touch, maybe even unsure of his footing, and definitely socially awkward. Someone who seems to be tentatively testing out the world around him, but when he relaxed—as he had over dinner—he really came into his own.

That is until I kissed him. That is not something I'm about to share with my mother.

"It was nice. I still can't make my goulash taste the way yours does." I try for distraction wrapped in flattery. "Why is that?"

"Always tastes better when someone else cooks it. So, tell me more about this friend of yours."

I should've known she wouldn't let go.

"I already told you last week."

"You're being purposely evasive," she accuses.

"And doesn't that tell you something?" I snap, surreptitiously glancing at the woman by the front desk and the young man sitting three seats down from Mom. Both seem engrossed in whatever it is they're doing.

"I just want to see you happy, sweetheart." She puts a hand on my arm, and I immediately feel guilty for being short with her.

I soften my earlier sharp retort with a smile. "I know you do, Mom, but I don't think Gray is the answer."

"Why do you say that?" she asks, just as someone comes out of Dr. Tracey's office on the other side of reception.

"Mrs. Bishop?" The woman behind the desk stands up and grabs a file. "If you would come with me?"

I hold no illusions my mother will let the subject drop, but for now I have a reprieve.

I force my thoughts to the diner, where Kim apparently finally hired a new full-time waitress, who is scheduled to start on the weekend. It isn't easy in a town this size to find someone, so she ended up putting out some feelers in neighboring communities. Donna and I have been taking on extra shifts to cover for Shirley missing, but Kim's had to fill in the rest of the schedule with part-timers. It'll be nice to get back to our regular shifts, although the extra work has been good for my bank account.

I spoke to Shirley this past weekend and she seemed to be doing okay. Her sons, with the help of a police officer, had managed to pack up her personal possessions from the house here in Beaverton last week, and there'd been no sign of Mike. All stayed quiet on that front. She also found a job as a cashier at the local grocery store and sounded like she was slowly getting back on her feet. I'm sure it'll take some time—especially with the court case against her husband looming the week of Thanksgiving —but Shirley sounds determined to forge ahead.

Good for her.

When Mom surfaces twenty minutes later, I've successfully avoided spending all that time thinking about Gray. It only lasts as long as the drive to Mom's favorite restaurant.

The moment we're seated in the small booth by the window heralds the end of my reprieve.

"You didn't have a chance to answer my question earlier."

Rather than trying to give her the runaround, I decide to tell her the truth. Maybe then she'll give up on her romantic notions.

"Okay, look, I like Gray. He seems like a decent man, and I thought maybe there was something there to explore, but I get the sense he's not in the same place."

Perhaps it was a little more than a 'sense' when he took off like the devil was on his heels after I kissed him. Although seconds before, I sharply recall the way he kissed me back like his very life depended on it. I guess that's why I can't shrug it off as mixed signals so easily. It would've been easier if I hadn't heard from him at all after he marched out, but there'd been that endearing message I received a few days later. Proof he was thinking about me too.

Mom puts her hand on mine across the table.

"Maybe he'll come around or else, his loss, sweetheart." She sits back in the booth and resolutely changes the subject. "So, what are we doing for Thanksgiving this year?"

I love my Mom.

"Paige told me this weekend she's flying into Lansing on the twenty-sixth. So I thought maybe I'd pick you both up and bring you back to my place. Paige can bunk with me and you can have the spare. We'll cook together. What do you think?"

I know the holidays especially are still tough for her. Heck, they are for me too; Dad's loss seems to loom larger on those special days. It had been Paige's suggestion to celebrate here instead of at Mom's for a change. New traditions and all that.

"That sounds perfect," Mom agrees. "Let's just hope the snow holds off until after."

We don't tend to get piles of snow here—not like some places to the north of us—but things can get slick on the roads quickly.

"Perfect, so let's figure out what we want to make," I offer, glad we've moved on to a safer topic.

But as we're discussing our meal options, I can't help wonder what Gray will doing for Thanksgiving.

———

Gray

"How are you feeling?"

Frank looks a little the worse for wear when I walk into the bar at lunchtime.

We were supposed to meet last Sunday, but he got word to me

he wouldn't be able to make it. Yesterday he called the shop and asked if I could come today during my lunch break.

I'm still not clear why he wants to talk to me, but I guess I'm about to find out.

"I'll live, for now," he mumbles, leading the way into the bar after locking the front door. "Beer? I can do coffee as well."

"Not for me, thanks. I'll take a glass of water though."

I watch Frank's slow, measured movements and wonder what's going on with him. I don't have to wonder long.

"Two things," he starts, after setting a glass in front of me and taking a sip from his can of Vernors. "First—and I don't have time to pussyfoot around things—I owe you an apology." I startle at that. "I should'a known. We'd been friends for more years than I could count, even then, but I knew he was a drunk. I knew he could be a mean bastard when he'd had a few. I just never thought he'd..." He visibly swallows, taking another sip before he continues, "He was drunk when he came in that night. Sat at this bar, crying about how she was dead. I felt for him, we all did, thinking he was talking about your sister. All those years, and I had no idea—"

"Frank." I stop him with a hand on his arm and a lump in my throat. "Not your burden to carry."

"Seeing you out there." He shakes his head and his eyes drift out the window, as if he was reliving it all. "You deserved better, boy. Years I struggled when you refused to see anyone. Then when I heard you passed up on a parole opportunity, I was fucking ready to break you out of that godforsaken place. Can't tell you how happy I was to see you back in town. Didn't wanna spook you off right away, so I gave you some time to adjust, but I was watching."

"Water under the bridge, old man."

I try to stop the flow of words that hit me like paper cuts to my soul, but he ignores me.

"I've gotta do right by you, Gray. I let you down. Fuck, this whole town let you down. None'a that should've happened if we'd been payin' attention. Which brings me to my second point."

He takes a deep tug from his can and closes his eyes as he swallows it down. I worry when I see his hand start shaking as he pulls an envelope from under the bar.

"Are you okay, Frank?"

He doesn't sugarcoat it.

"Dying, son. Be a small miracle if I make Thanksgiving. I would'a let you be a little longer, but I plumb ain't got the time. The cancer got me good."

"Jesus," I hiss.

He shoves the envelope at me.

"It don't make up for the time you lost, son, but I hope it'll give you the future you deserve. I ain't got kids of my own, but if you were my boy, I couldn't be more proud of ya."

Those paper cuts from earlier are now deep slices, and emotions I've worked hard to keep in check flow freely. It hurts: feeling.

I don't deserve his words, and yet they penetrate deep.

"Open it."

He indicates the envelope in front of me and I pick it up, sliding my finger under the flap.

"What is this?" I manage, my voice a croak.

"Copy of my last will and testament. You lost everything that night, boy, and I wish I could give you your family back, but I can't. Least I can do is make sure you're taken care of."

As he speaks, my eyes scan the document full of legal jargon until they catch on a highlighted name:

I LEAVE TO **GRAY EDWARD BENNET**, SOLE BENEFICIARY, ALL MY PERSONAL BELONGINGS, INCLUDING (BUT NOT LIMITED TO) THE PROPERTY, BUILDING, AND CONTENTS AT 357 PARKER STREET, BEAVERTON, MI; THE DIRTY DOG BAR; MY

APARTMENT; AND THE 1965 FORD MUSTANG IN THE GARAGE ON
THE BACK OF THE PROPERTY.

"You can't do this," I mutter, trying to wrap my head around what
I'm reading.

"Already done," he says firmly.

"But—"

"The bar runs itself," he continues undeterred. "Bunker
manages the day-to-day, so you don't even have to be here unless
it's payday. Then all you need to do is sign the checks. Bunker
prepares all of it. He's been with me for fifteen years and can run
this place in his sleep. My place upstairs you can take or rent out
as you see fit. You can toss or keep the contents, I don't really
care.

"There's not a single person left who'd lay claim to any of it.
All I ask is that you take what I'm givin' ya not as some consola-
tion prize, but as the fulfillment of the wish of an old man waiting
for his last breath."

His gnarled, shaking hand lands on mine as my mind tries to
keep up with what he's saying.

"Do me this honor, son. Let me leave this life, knowing I've at
least tried to right some of the wrongs done to you."

Half an hour later, I walk out of the bar, dazed and overwhelmed with the magnitude of what just occurred. I signed
about a dozen forms and papers Frank had prepared for me, to
ensure the bar can be kept running since he'll be moving into a
palliative care facility over the weekend.

I'm not sure what to do with all this. I'm sad, the responsibility is heavy, and my mind is chaotic. I feel compelled to talk to
someone—to share and help me process what is happening—but
the first person who comes to mind is Robin, and that's clearly
not an option. I made sure of that.

"How's Frank?" Jimmy asks, when I walk into the bay doors of the garage. I'd told him where I was going earlier.

"He's...not good," I spill, unable to keep it all to myself.

Jimmy seems to see something in my expression because he calls out to Kyle, telling him to take over from him as he steers me to his office in the back.

"You're shitting me?" he says, when I've given him a rundown of the last hour.

"I know. I don't know what he's thinking just handing it all over."

"I'm talking about him having cancer. That damn old coot never said a word. I bet you he's told no one else," he clarifies. "Although, I'm not nearly as surprised about the will. He and I spent a lot of nights talking about you over a couple of beers at the bar, brother. Both of us worried but determined not to give up on you, even if it's what you seemed to prefer. We shared a common guilt, wondering if there was something we could've done."

I'm unable to speak; stunned to hear I'm not the only one carrying the burden of that day on my shoulders.

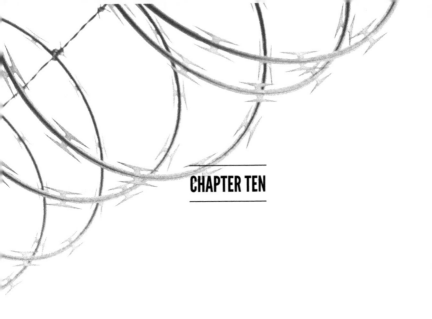

CHAPTER TEN

Robin

"Does Gray Bennet come in a lot?"

My head shoots up at those words, and I drop the cutlery I'm rolling into napkins for the dinner shift back on the tray.

The new waitress, Becca, isn't talking to me but to Kim, and I return to my task, listening in to their conversation.

She's nice enough: Becca. She started last weekend and seems to know what she's doing. She's been friendly to me, good with the customers, and it's been a relief to be back on our regular schedule.

"He's been in a couple of times, but I haven't seen him recently," I hear Kim say. "How do you know Gray?"

I glance over and catch the wink Becca directs at Kim as she leans in conspiratorially.

"He and I go back a ways," she explains. "Wouldn't mind catching up with him. For old time's sake."

Yikes.

I peek at her with a little more interest. She's very pretty;

dresses a little young perhaps, with skintight jeans and plunging necklines, but I figure if you have it there's nothing wrong with flaunting it. And Becca has it: the long legs, big rack, and long dyed-blonde locks framing a carefully made-up face. I could see her with Gray.

In my peripheral vision I see Mrs. Chapman trying to get our attention, and I stop what I'm doing and head over to her table.

"Have you decided?" I ask her. The poor woman seemed a little more confused than usual today and has been staring at the menu for the past thirty minutes. I tried to help her come to a decision earlier, but that only seemed to fluster her more.

"I think I'd like eggs Benedict. Is it too late?"

Normally we stop serving breakfast after the lunch rush, but I'm sure Jason is willing to make her some eggs Bennie. I put a hand on her arm.

"I'm sure we can whip those up for you, Mrs. Chapman. In the meantime, can I top you up with some fresh coffee?"

"Please."

The woman's thankful smile causes a twinge in my chest. I've long suspected the reason she takes forever to make menu choices and again to finish her meals, is because she craves the company. Her weekly visits to the diner may well be the only social interaction she has since her husband passed away about ten years ago.

Becca and Kim still appear to be in conversation by the cash register when I walk up to the window and put in Mrs. Chapman's order with Jason.

"What's with her?" Becca asks, when I grab the pot from the coffee station behind the counter. I instantly bristle at the somewhat judgmental tone.

"She's just lonely," I answer sharply, jumping to the old woman's defense. "She comes here to see a friendly face."

Becca seems to read me right, because she immediately smiles apologetically.

"Of course. I didn't mean to—"

"No worries," I interrupt her, feeling a tad guilty about my own knee-jerk reaction to Becca. Hearing her talk about Gray may have had something to do with that.

This is stupid. It's not her fault, or his for that matter; I've been unable to stop thinking about him. You'd think someone my age and life experience would be smarter than to spend time thinking about a guy who couldn't be more clear on where he stands. Instead my head jerks up every time the door to the diner opens; secretly hoping it's him. I've even held off bringing my SUV in to the shop to have them put on my winter tires because I'm too concerned how Gray will react when he sees me.

Ridiculous. After my shift, I'm driving straight to the shop.

"There you go, Mrs. Chapman." I smile at her, topping up her cup. "Jason is getting your eggs ready. Won't be long."

"Thank you, dear."

When Donna comes in at four, I take off my apron, grab my purse and coat, and say my goodbyes. Outside I can tell the temperature is dropping and a mean wind has picked up. The weather forecast included a chance for flurries this afternoon, but so far they've held out. Looking at the dark skies to the north, it won't be long.

I drive the two blocks to Olson's and pull into the wide driveway, my eyes automatically scanning for Gray, but I don't see him. Tank spots me, though, and comes walking up as I'm getting out from behind the wheel.

"Hey, Robin. Everything okay?"

"Yeah, I'm good. Just wondering when you might have a chance to put my winter tires on?"

He looks toward the shop before turning back to me.

"Not today. I'm in the middle of a job I have to finish before the end of day and Gray is out on a call with the tow truck. We can do it tomorrow, though. Drop it off in the morning and I'll give you a ride to the diner. I'll have Kyle drop it off there when we're done."

I admit I'm a little disappointed Gray isn't here, but I plaster on a smile for Tank.

"That's great, but I start at six tomorrow morning. Can I drop by a little later? I can probably sneak out for a few minutes after the breakfast rush."

He waves it off. "One of us'll drop by and pick it up. Don't worry about it."

One of us. That could mean Gray.

Tank's already heading back to the shop when I call out my thanks.

The next morning is busy, but every time I hear the door chime, my head bobs up. Finally, when I'm cleaning off a couple of tables in my section, Becca's squeal has me turn around to see Gray walking in. My heart skips, but instantly drops like a rock as I watch Becca throw herself in his arms. I turn away when they seem to close tightly around her.

———

Gray

Last person I expect to see when I walk into Over Easy is fucking Becca Simms.

Fuck, it takes me a second to recognize her, even as she's throwing herself against me. No sooner do her arms slip around my neck, I reach up to remove them. Prison made me uneasy with uninvited invasions of my space.

Oddly that didn't seem to bother me with Robin.

My eyes immediately seek her out and I find her bent over a table on the other side of the diner, her back to the door, thank God.

"I heard you got out a few months ago."

My head swings back to Becca, and I try to control the anger flooding me. I haven't seen the woman since September 10, 2001. Not one single time.

I take an immediate step back when she lifts a hand to my chest and it hangs suspended for a moment before she drops it to her side.

"What the fuck do you think you're doing?" I grind out in a low voice.

"I thought about you. Thought maybe..."

I shake my head sharply.

"Not happening. Not ever," I bite off before turning my back on her, eyes searching for Robin, who seems to have disappeared.

I barely notice Becca slipping past me to tend to a table, but I can't miss Kim who steps into my view.

"Go easy," she says. "Not sure what's going on, but you walk in, and I have one waitress almost in tears and another hiding in the washroom within minutes."

Fuck.

"Sorry."

Kim's expression softens.

"I know y'are. Did you need a table?"

I shake my head, suddenly in a hurry to get out of here.

"Jimmy sent me to pick up Robin's car."

"Let me see where she is."

I sit down on a stool at the counter while Kim goes in search of her. Becca returns, an uneasy smile on her face as her eyes meet mine.

"Can I get you anything?"

"I'm good. Look—" I start apologizing when a wave of her hand cuts me off.

"My bad. Don't mention it," she mutters, quickly turning her back to put an order in with the kitchen.

Robin appears from the narrow hallway leading to the bathrooms, Kim right behind her, immediately drawing my attention.

"Hi," she says, a tentative look matching the one Becca shot me just moments ago on her face.

Spreading fucking joy wherever I go, it seems.

"Hey, Robin. Jimmy asked me to swing by and pick up the CRV from you."

"Sure. Let me just fetch my keys."

She ducks behind the counter to grab them from her purse, handing them to me. I not so accidentally brush her palm with my fingers and it stings when she pulls back her hand as if burned.

As determined as I was to keep my distance, I can't let her think whatever it is putting those shadows in her eyes. We'll need to talk.

"What time does your shift end?" I ask, standing up.

"Around four, but I'll just walk over."

I glance out the window where the snow is still coming down.

"I'll pick you up."

"Really, there's no need."

It's clear she intends to avoid me, but I'm determined not to let that happen.

"Four. I'll be here," I insist, and almost smile at the irritated roll of her eyes.

Back at Olson's I make quick work of switching out her tires and parking her SUV behind the building.

"Aren't you taking it back?" Jimmy asks when I walk back into the shop.

"Figure I'd do it after her shift ends."

"I'll just have Kyle drive it over."

I know he's trying to get a rise out of me and I give him what he wants.

"Fuck off, Jimmy. I said I'm doing it."

He raises an eyebrow and one side of his mouth pulls up. Fucking smug bastard.

"Does that mean you smartened up?"

"The hell are you talking about?"

"Oh, I don't know. The fact you didn't fucking leave this building for weeks and one day suddenly start heading to the diner for lunch? Then not one week later, you're moping around here all day again? I'm not an idiot, brother. You forget, I spent more time than you at that goddamn diner, but never, not once, has that woman looked at me the way she does at you."

I'm shocked at his words. It's not only more insightful than I would've given him credit for, but it also makes me realize I'm not the only one who has more than a passing interest in Robin. Makes me feel like an even bigger idiot than I already did.

"I plan to talk to her," I share.

"You should."

"It could backfire on me, though."

"If you think that, you're an idiot. Don't you think she already knows you're an ex-con? Over Easy is a fucking hotbed for gossip. I'd be surprised if she doesn't already know your entire story by now."

I think about his words as I drive over to the diner some time later. I took the time to quickly wash up in my apartment and put on clean jeans and a fresh shirt.

Robin is already waiting outside, which ticks me off, because it's still snowing. No reason she couldn't have waited inside. I pull up at the curb and start getting out to open her door for her, but she's already taking care of that herself.

"You looking to catch a cold?" I snap, when she pulls the door shut.

Her eyes jerk up to meet my angry ones and she presses her lips together as she wipes her wet hair out of her face.

"That why you're picking me up? So you can bark at me? Because—"

She's working up a steam and I do the only thing I can think of to do. I hook a hand behind her head and meet her mouth halfway over the console, drowning the rest of her words in a hard, almost desperate kiss.

By the time I pull away her lips are swollen and slightly abraded, but her eyes are dazed.

"Fuck," I mumble under my breath, but she catches it and instantly her face hardens as she sits back in her seat.

"Are you gonna run again?"

"No," I respond instantly, straightening behind the wheel and snapping my belt in place, but I never let go of her eyes.

She stares at me for a beat before sharply nodding and buckling herself in. The moment I hear the snap, I yank the gear in drive and with spinning wheels on the slush, peel away from the curb.

As I drive off, I notice Becca watching us through the diner window.

"Where are we going?" Robin asks when I blow past Olson's, probably driving much too fast for the weather.

"Your place," I bite off, concentrating on staying on the road when all I want to do is pull off to the side, haul her over the console on my lap, and bury my hungry cock inside her.

We get out to her house in record time, despite the poor road conditions. The entire trip I avoid looking at her but I can feel every breath she takes. The moment I come to a stop in her driveway, I launch myself out of the SUV and round the hood, my eyes on hers through the window.

I open the door and she moves to get out, but I catch her before her feet touch the ground. With my arms banding around her I cover her mouth with mine, half-lifting her out of the vehicle. I'm not quite sure how we get to her front door with our mouths still fused. There she breaks the kiss and mumbles, "Keys," against my lips. Reluctantly I let her go so she can open the door, but I crowd her back, and the moment I hear the door release, I push her inside ahead of me.

My fingers find the tie around her messy knot and pull it out as I kick the door closed with my foot. I keep moving her toward the wall until she has to brace herself against it. I wrap the tumble of waves in my fist to expose her neck and open my mouth on the tendon stretching to her shoulder.

Thoughts swirl unchecked through my mind, but the only thing I can focus on is her taste, her scent, and my uncontrollable need. With shaking hands, I strip her out of her jacket and manage to get the zipper of her jeans down, shoving a hand inside. My fingers encounter her slick heat and I groan in the crook of her neck.

"Gray..." she mumbles, her cheek pressed against the wall.

"Tell me to stop," I plead, even as I'm pushing her jeans down over her hips, taking her underwear along.

"Please..."

As the single word leaves her lips, her feet step out of the jeans puddled at her ankles, and she presses her naked ass back, tilting her hips in invitation.

"Baby, I can't—"

Already I'm freeing my cock, sinking through my knees so I line the blunt tip up at her entrance.

"Please, Gray..."

What little restraint I had left vanishes when she whispers my name and I surge inside her tight heat.

CHAPTER ELEVEN

Robin

"Shit, Sunshine."

He leans heavily against me and I can feel aftershocks coursing through his body.

That was unexpected. And fast.

"I'm so sorry."

I feel him pull away and there's an instant chill at my back.

"You disappear on me again and I'll throat punch you," I mumble, my face still pressed to the wall. My legs are trembling too hard for me to stand on my own.

"Not gonna disappear."

I hear the sound of a zipper and feel his hand on my hip.

I swallow my 'Thank God' at the last second. I was hoping he wasn't done yet, because I'm sure not. The next second I feel a trickle down my leg.

Well, shit.

"I'm leaking."

I try to push off the wall but when that doesn't work, I roll until my back is against the wall and I'm facing him. I see the guilt written all over his face.

"I swear I'm clean. Been no one since I went in. Jesus, Robin, I'm clean."

The meaning of what he's telling me is slow to register but when it does, it makes me curious.

"How long were you in prison?"

It's clear he'd prefer not to answer by the way his eyes flit away.

"Can I grab a towel or something?"

Right. The slow drip down my leg.

I can't bring myself to move yet, though. I'm part in shock and part mortified at my lack of control. I'm standing here with my panties and jeans on the floor at my feet, my business on full display. I should be mortified but the kicker is, there's still part of me painfully aroused.

"Please," I answer him. "Second door on the right is the bathroom. Grab my robe while you're there," I add last minute.

He doesn't actually touch me, but I can feel his eyes on me, when he passes and heads down the hall.

I vaguely register sounds of running water as I test my legs and find them a bit sturdier. Before I have a chance to start moving, Gray appears with a washcloth and my ratty old robe. I hold out my hand but he ignores it, shocking me by dropping down on his knees in front of me.

"You don't—"

"Eighteen years," he interrupts me, as he carefully wipes the inside of my leg. I'm so shocked by his words; I forget what it is he's doing. "Lost control. Did I hurt you?"

I hiss when the rough terrycloth brushes my sensitive clit and his eyes shoot up to mine. Those pale blue eyes full of concern. I quickly shake my head.

"No. You didn't."

"I gotta ask; are you protected? On the pill?"

"No." Poor guy, I catch him flinching. "Had a hysterectomy after Paige was born," I quickly explain, as he gets to his feet.

He pulls me away from the wall and wraps my robe around me, tossing the washcloth down the hall in the direction of the bathroom. Then he grabs my hand and leads me inside where he pulls me down on the couch, tucking me to his side.

I don't fight him, I'm still trying to process what just happened, but at least I'm doing it with him right here.

"Eighteen years?" I tilt my head back and watch as an array of emotions plays out on his face. But I swear, the one left in his eyes when he turns them on me is guilt.

"Pled guilty to second-degree murder."

I'm unable to stop my sharp inhale, and I instantly feel his body stiffen as he removes his arm from around my shoulders.

"Were you?" I ask when I find my words.

I have to know. Just because I can't imagine him doing something like that doesn't mean he didn't. Still, I can tell my question makes him uncomfortable.

He stands up and walks over to the fireplace, where he studies my family pictures, while I wrap my robe around me a little tighter. Most of those photos are of Paige, but some include my parents and me. He trails a finger over a snapshot my father took of me when I was big as a house with my daughter, and still believed myself happy.

"Yes."

I can barely hear his whispered response. His back is turned to me and with his shoulders hunched, it's as if he's bracing for impact.

It's hard to reconcile the vulnerable man in front of me with someone who'd willingly take another's life. In fact, what little I've seen from Gray Bennet, he's a kind man and liked by people who know him better than I do.

"What happened?" I finally ask in a gentle tone.

He keeps his back turned, but I notice him gripping the edge of the mantle hard enough his knuckles turn white.

"My sister called me—crying. All I could hear was screaming in the background," he starts, and already my heart is bleeding for him. He grunts. "Hadn't even turned on the news yet, but then I did. Saw the smoke coming from those buildings, knowing Reagan was in there." He takes a step back and bends over with his hands braced on the mantle, his head hanging down. "Asked me to help her, but all I could do was watch helplessly. Told me she loved me, and to tell Mom as well. When the south tower came down the line went dead. I kept trying to call her back until I saw the north tower collapse and I knew..."

I get up from my seat and walk up behind him, putting a hand on his back, but he shrugs it off and starts pacing the room.

"I tried to get us tickets—Mom and me—but air traffic was shut down, so I told her to pack some things, that I was gonna pick her up and we'd drive to New York. Even then she was worried about leaving my father. Bastard was drunk already. All those years and I never could get her to leave his ass. She loved the farm but Reagan was her baby."

I'm already crying, watching him pace; four steps one way, then four the other. Never an extra step, as if there was an invisible barrier stopping him. I sit back down on the couch, something he doesn't even notice he's so far inside his memories.

"I was just about to walk out the door with my stuff when she called. Dad yelling and hollering in the background. Told her to take her bags and lock herself in the bathroom until I got there, but then that line went dead as well."

I wrap my arms around my midsection in an attempt to hold myself together. The raw agony in his voice is unlike anything I've ever heard. Every next word a painful step to what I already know in my bones will be a horrific conclusion.

"His truck was already gone when I got to the farm," he resumes, his eyes on something invisible in front of him as he continues to put one foot in front of the other. One, two, three, four steps, then turns a hundred and eighty degrees and does the same in the other direction. I just sit here and watch helplessly. "She was on the bedroom floor, her open suitcase upside down beside the bed, its contents spilled everywhere. I knew she was gone. Found my baseball bat in the closet of my old bedroom and drove straight to where I knew I'd find him."

"Gray..." I whisper, and he stops in his tracks, his eyes shooting to me, looking almost confused.

"I killed him."

———

Gray

I wait for judgment to cloud her face, but it doesn't come.

Tear tracks run down her cheeks but there is no disgust, or fear, or accusation in those warm, gray eyes turned on me.

"I know," she whispers, before getting to her feet and walking toward me.

I take in her appearance, the long light brown hair peppered with unapologetic gray framing her beautiful face, the ratty blue robe tied loosely around her waist, and the swell of generous hips I wish I'd spent more time appreciating.

"I killed him," I repeat, wanting to make sure she understands.

I feel the heat of her body as she rises up on tiptoes and takes my face in her hands, brushing her lips over mine.

"Yes," she confirms, her eyes open and seeing. "And I understand."

I find myself at a loss for words. I've spoken more to this woman than I have to anyone in a very long time. I feel empty and spent. So when her hand grabs mine and she leads me silently to her bedroom, I follow.

"Sit," she orders, indicating the bed.

When I comply, she kneels in front of me and starts pulling off my boots. Then she removes my socks and pushes my knees open, using them to push herself to her feet. Grabbing the hem of my shirt, she starts lifting it over my head, my arms rising willingly.

However, when she leans forward and presses a kiss to my chest, I have to close my eyes, overwhelmed by her gesture. I feel her move away and hear the rustling of clothes, then a drawer opening and closing, before I can sense her proximity again. When I look, she's wearing a pair of panties and my shirt.

I let go of the breath I've been holding. As willing as my dick seems to be, I'm not sure I would've been able to take her up on the invitation I thought she was extending.

"Come lie down with me," she asks, climbing into bed and opening her arms to me.

Even if I wanted to, I wouldn't have been able to get a word through the huge lump in my throat as I lower myself into her embrace. It's not even dinnertime and I'm suddenly bone weary.

Her body, her comfort, and her acceptance are like a balm to my soul, and in her arms I allow myself the first real tears of grief.

When I wake up the room is dark and I'm alone.

I hear a muted voice through the door and swing my legs over the side of the bed as I run a hand through my hair. I get up, aim for the open door to the en suite bathroom, and I relieve myself before washing my hands and splashing some water on my face.

I can't find my shirt—I assume Robin's still wearing it—and forfeit socks and boots when I go in search of her.

"Yes, sweetie; pumpkin cheesecake sounds amazing. Can't wait to try it."

She's sitting at the kitchen table but turns her head when I walk in, a soft smile on her lips. I find myself smiling back, the pull of underused muscles strange. I point at the fridge and raise my eyebrows in question. She nods and waves a hand.

"I thought the rice and mushroom stuffing?" I hear her say, as I pull a pitcher of what I hope is orange juice from the fridge.

My guess it's her mom or her daughter and they're discussing Thanksgiving dinner based on what I can hear.

"Oh, that sounds good too."

I sit down across from her and notice her eyes are almost sparkling.

"Okay, let's do that then. Yes, I'm still picking you up."

She grins at me as I sip my juice and listen in boldly. She doesn't seem to care.

"I'll be fine. I just had my winter tires put on. Sweetie, I gotta go."

Robin reaches her hand across the table, and I cover it with mine as the faint sound of a woman speaking filters from the phone.

"I will. I promise. Love you too. Night."

"Daughter?" I ask, when she puts her phone facedown on the table.

"Yeah, Paige. She's flying in for Thanksgiving."

"I gathered as much."

I'm still smiling like I never told this woman my deepest darkest secrets just a few hours ago. I don't even recognize myself as I rub my thumb over the back of her hand.

"Are you hungry?"

The question is innocuous enough, but my body's response is immediate. Her eyes darken when she catches the flare of my nostrils.

"Starving," I growl, already getting to my feet. I keep a firm hold of her hand and pull her up with me.

My turn to lead the way to the bedroom, where I rip my shirt off her body, her lush tits bouncing as she pulls her arms through. My breath sticks in my throat as I take in her soft curves.

"Jesus, Sunshine."

I reach out and run the tips of my fingers down the slope of her breast before weighing it in my hand, rubbing my thumb over its hard tip. A slight hiss comes from Robin's lips. I lift my eyes to hers and see the same heat I feel reflected there.

The same intense need I felt earlier surges to the surface, and I suck in a deep breath fighting to stay in control. This time I'm going to make absolutely fucking sure her needs come first.

With a light shove she falls back on the bed, her legs draped off the end of the mattress. I hook my fingers in the elastic of her panties, pulling them off. Then I drop to my knees, lift her legs over my shoulders, and drag her closer to the edge.

I inhale the scent of her arousal deeply before covering her with my mouth. Her taste, new and yet familiar, floods me. My mechanics may be rusty, but my hungry determination more than makes up for it. It doesn't take long before I feel her thighs trembling as she presses herself to my mouth.

I'm up and out of my jeans in a flash, poised at her entrance. I seek her eyes before I slide into her body; a light brush of my thumb over her clit has her scream out my name. With her tight channel pulsating around me, I let go of my control.

Embarrassingly few moments later, I buck and groan as my tight balls empty inside her.

CHAPTER TWELVE

Robin

"What happened to that smile?"

I shove my purse in the drawer behind the counter and stand up to face Kim.

"Didn't sleep too well."

Kim knows me pretty well, and although I'm not lying, I'm not exactly forthcoming either.

"I figure you haven't slept well since that hot as fuck kiss in the parking lot when we had our first snow."

I'll never live that down. I came in the next day and discovered that kiss had done the rounds through the small community. Of course it didn't help I dropped Gray off in front of Olson's the next morning, and did the same a few more times the week following. The resulting friendly ribbing didn't bother me then, but it bothers me now.

Because I haven't seen him for the past four days.

At first I figured it was the weather. We've been hit with a few early winter storms and that usually results in cars going off in the ditch. Every year it's like people forget how to drive in the snow and have to learn all over again. But when my message was ignored again last night, I clued in there was something else.

I spent most of the time I should've been sleeping mulling over events of the weeks prior instead, trying to figure out what I may have missed. Except for that first night, I'm ashamed to admit there wasn't a lot of talking involved. Too much time to make up for.

Then the weather turned and he got busy. Apparently, too busy to answer my messages. It doesn't sit right. The last answer I got was on Wednesday, when I'd messaged and asked what he was up to for Thanksgiving next week. I'd just talked to Mom, confirming I'd be picking her up, when it occurred to me it might be nice to ask him to come. I figured he might appreciate a decent home-cooked holiday meal.

His response was that he'd get back to me on that.

Four fucking days ago.

My last three messages have gone unanswered. At about three this morning, I decided the ball was firmly in his court and I wasn't about to chase him down.

I force a smile for Kim and breathe a sigh of relief when the door opens and the first table of the day walks in.

"Morning!" I call out to the trio shuffling in, and I'm greeted with subdued hellos.

I grab a carafe and cream and make my way over to where the three seniors sit down in their preferred booth. There used to be four of them, but I heard through the grapevine that Frank Hanson, owner of the Dirty Dog, was gravely ill. Apparently he had moved to a palliative care facility in Clare.

"Coffee, fellas?"

"Sure, sweetheart, hit me up," John McClusky, a retired school principal, is the first to answer.

"Yup," is the curt response from former postal worker, Eddie Banks.

The third in the trio, Enzo Trotti, whose family owns the local pizzeria, simply turns over his cup and holds it out.

I fill their cups and it's on my lips to inquire about their friend, but I don't want to pry. Kim has no such hang-ups and sidles up to me at the table.

"How's Frank doing, boys?" she asks, never mind that those 'boys' are almost twice her age.

It's Enzo who answers.

"Not long now."

"Said he didn't think he'd make Thanksgiving," John adds. "Looks like he may have been right."

"Well, shit. I'm sorry to hear it."

"We all gotta go sometime," Enzo declares. Despite the flippant tone of his statement, the expression on his face shows he's feeling this deeply.

"Doesn't make it any easier," I tell him gently, placing my hand on his arm.

His watery, red-rimmed eyes turn up to me.

"No. No it don't."

"What's gonna happen to the Dirty Dog?" Kim asks, and this time Eddie speaks up.

"Crazy bastard left it to that Bennet boy."

For the rest of my shift, I'm preoccupied with what Eddie said. Wondering if that's perhaps what has kept Gray busy these past days.

Becca, who has been scheduled on the afternoon shift, comes in at a little before four. She smiles at me as she has for a while now, reluctantly.

"Everything okay, Becca?" I ask when she slips around me behind the counter to tuck her purse away.

"I'm fine."

The response is instant and as fake as her smile has been, ever since the day I saw her greeting Gray when he came to pick up the keys to my SUV. The same day he picked me up after work and kissed the stuffing out of me, right outside the diner windows.

I had dismissed the earlier incident as maybe old acquaintances and what happened after between Gray and I solidified that conclusion. I'd never even bothered to ask him about it, but now I'm wondering if perhaps I should've.

I'm not a fan of confrontation, but I'm even less of a fan of stress in the workplace, so I turn to Becca.

"Are you sure? You seem a little tense."

Something flares in her eyes. Anger? Hurt? I can't quite place it when she turns her face away.

"Just some personal stuff. Sorry if I've been off."

"Don't apologize. I was worried perhaps it was something I'd done?"

She hesitates, just a fraction too long, before she answers with a forced smile on her face as she looks at me.

"Not at all."

Now I recognize the anger simmering behind her eyes.

"Good," I mumble, more than a bit taken aback as I grab my things and with a wave goodbye, head for the parking lot.

Maybe it's time to get some answers.

The snow is starting to come down again when I pull into Olson's, but I'm disappointed when I find only Tank inside.

———

Gray

"Asshole."

My head snaps up as I trudge into the shop, after pulling yet another fucking idiot out of the ditch. Eight of them today alone.

My mood is already in the sewer and having Jimmy greet me like that doesn't improve it one bit.

"What the fuck?" I snap.

"She was here. Looking for you."

"Who?"

I know damn well who he's talking about. The same 'she' I've been avoiding since she asked about Thanksgiving. For some reason that innocent message chilled the blood in my veins. I haven't talked to her since. An asshole move—Jimmy's right about that—but the prospect of Thanksgiving at her place, meeting her mother and daughter, made this whole thing a little too real. I'm not sure I'm ready for that.

Jimmy doesn't buy my feigned ignorance either.

"She's worried about you, since apparently you've been ghosting her for days. You can be a selfish bastard; you know that? First person she lets close in years. And you? You fucking dine and dash. Nice."

My temper flares and I shove my clenched fists in my pockets for fear of letting them fly.

"You don't know a fucking thing about it," I bite off.

"No. I don't," he spits, stepping dangerously close to my space and I take an inadvertent step back. "Because you don't talk." I flinch at the unexpected accusation. "I don't know what goes on in your head, but I know it can't be fucking easy. Because you... don't...talk." Every word is emphasized with a finger poking my chest and I have a hard time keeping from breaking his hand, so I take another step back.

"Nothing to talk about."

Exasperated, Jimmy throws his hands up in the air and lets loose a colorful string of curses. Then he closes his eyes and sucks air in through his nose before looking at me, and he continues in a carefully restrained voice.

"Then why is it, you suddenly blow off a woman most men would give their left nut to have in their bed? Last week you started to remind me of the man I knew, but over the past few days, I watched you crawl right back into your shell."

"Thanksgiving," I blurt out. I can tell from the confused look on his face he's not getting me, so I clarify. "I think she wants to invite me for dinner."

"So?"

"Her mother and daughter will be there."

"And?"

Apparently my explanations aren't helping him understand.

"Family holiday, Jimmy. I'm sure her family won't be happy she's slumming with an ex-con." He opens his mouth to protest, but I don't give him a chance. "Last Thanksgiving I celebrated, my baby sister was sitting across the table from me. Haven't had much to be thankful for since then."

Understanding dawns on his face and his eyes close again.

"Jesus," he mutters, shaking his head. "I hadn't even considered that."

"I hadn't either, until she brought up the subject," I admit. "Hit me like a ton of bricks."

"Why not just explain?"

I shrug.

"Does it matter? Not like this could've gone anywhere."

"Are you for fucking real? Are you so self-absorbed you can't see how unfair that is to her? Right now Robin worries it's because of something she's done. You at least owe her the truth on that, even if things don't work out, you can't let her believe it was in any way her fault."

Shit. I fucking hate it when I'm wrong.

"I'll tell her."

"When?" he pushes, like he did the first time he called me out on my self-defeatist bullshit.

"After work."

"Get the fuck out of here. You're done for the day."

I stare at him for a moment, catching the sincerity in his eyes. Then I turn on my heel, but before I even get back to the truck, my phone rings in my pocket. I don't recognize the number when I pull it out and am tempted to let it go, but end up answering.

"Hello?"

"Gray Bennet?"

"Speaking."

"It's Bunker. I manage the Dirty Dog?"

"Right." I remember the name Frank mentioned and right away a sense of doom comes over me. Last time I spoke with Frank was last week, but he told me again he didn't want me driving out. "Is there a problem?"

"Have you seen Frank recently?"

"I've talked to him. Apparently he prefers no visitors."

"Yeah, that's what he told me too," the man says, sounding annoyed. "Come to find out, just now from one of his buddies, Enzo Totti, Frank is at his end stage."

"How the hell does he know?"

"Apparently one of Frank's nurses is his niece."

That feeling of doom only gets heavier. I'll admit, I hadn't thought much about the man while I was inside, but that's changed since he sat me down for a talk a month ago.

"I'm driving out there," I announce, my plans changing on a dime.

"Was hoping you'd say that. Otherwise I'd have gone and you would've been stuck with the bar."

That would've been a disaster, since I don't have the first clue how to run a bar. Besides, I owe the old man.

"I'll keep you up-to-date."

"That'd be good. Give the old coot my love."

Before I can say I will, the line goes dead and I head back to the shop.

"I thought you were leaving?" Jimmy says, poking his head up from the engine he's working on.

"I am, but I'm going to Clare. Just got word Frank Hanson's dying. Don't know if I'll be on time, but I won't be leaving until he breathes his last."

I know don't have to explain to Jimmy why that is important, he seems to understand and nods right away.

"Of course. Go. Stay in touch. Do you need money?"

"I'm good. Thanks, Jimmy."

With that, I head up the steps to my apartment where I throw an overnight bag together, remember a book and the charger for my phone, and return downstairs.

Jimmy's waiting by my truck.

"Here. Just in case." He slaps some money in my hand. "Makes me feel better."

I pin him with a long hard look, before giving in with a nod. I shove the bills in my pocket, climb behind the wheel, and peel out of there.

Half an hour later, I walk into the main entrance of the one-story building and aim for the desk in the lobby. A gray-haired woman, probably in her sixties, smiles up at me when I approach.

"Can I help you?"

"I'm here to see Frank Hanson."

She dials her smile down to a sympathetic one immediately.

"Are you family?"

Without blinking I respond, "The only one he has."

It's not exactly lying.

"Room seventeen, in the south wing." She points at the hallway to the left. "Check in at the nurses' station first."

I can't find a nurse, but I find Frank.

Christ.

He looks much smaller lying down. His eyes are closed and his whole face has sunken in on itself. I stand there for a moment, watching to make sure his chest is still rising.

"Sir?"

I turn to find a nurse with a stern expression on her face.

"I'm here to sit with Frank," I announce, and stare her down.

She glances past me into the room at Frank's prone body, and then looks at me again.

"He didn't want anyone here."

"I know. I'm still here to sit with him."

A faint smile breaks through as she nods.

"Don't let him chase you off."

"Don't plan to."

She gives me a little shove into the room and I take the chair beside his bed.

I'm not sure how much time has passed when his eyes blink open and stare straight at me.

"Always were a stubborn little shit," he rasps, barely moving any air.

His fingers twitch on the bedspread, and without thinking I reach for his hand.

"Damn straight," I tell him, folding my hand around his.

I couldn't be there for my mother or my sister, and I sure as fuck am not going to let another person I care about die alone.

Whether he wants to or not.

CHAPTER THIRTEEN

Robin

"I can't believe I'm saying this, but I'm already sick of winter."

I look up to find Mom staring out the kitchen window at the snow coming down again. I can't remember the last time we've had this much snow so early in the season.

She's been a little subdued since I picked her and Paige up earlier today, and I suspect it's the holidays affecting her more than the actual weather.

I put a hand in the middle of her back and lean in to kiss her cheek.

"Are you missing Dad?" I ask carefully.

It's not really something we talk about often. Not anymore. Time just seems to move along, and what was at first a gaping hole, slowly fills in with everyday life.

I'm shocked when she turns to face me, the glisten of tears in her eyes.

"You know I loved your father to distraction, right?"

I drape my arm around her and give her a little squeeze.

"Of course I know."

"I met someone," she blurts out, and I see guilt written all over her face.

I ignore the small pang of hurt and smile at her encouragingly. Inside me a battle rages between the selfish need to hang on to that perfect memory of my parents' love, and my mother's happiness.

"That's wonderful," I force my lips to form.

"He is," she mumbles, returning her gaze to the softly falling snow. "He moved in two doors down, the week I stayed with Paige in New Jersey. He helped me with my suitcase when I got home. We bumped into each other a few times, and one day last month he gave me a hand with my groceries and stayed for dinner."

"Tell me about him," I encourage her.

She faces me again and I see a little blush high on her cheeks.

"His name is Ken. He recently retired from the police force and wants to travel. With me," she adds hesitantly.

I swallow down the knee-jerk 'mom' speech I want to give her, remembering just in time this is the woman who raised me and not the other way around. Still, it pays to be cautious.

"How did that come about?"

"We've spent a lot of time together and—"

"That's awesome, Gram." I hadn't heard my daughter walk in. "Glad you're getting some," she says, a big grin on her face.

I close my eyes. I don't care I'm in my forties; I still don't want to think about my parents *getting some*, especially with strangers.

"Paige!"

"Well, in case you haven't noticed, Gram's still got it goin' on. When we went out to dinner her last night in Newark, the waiter was totally hitting on her. Right, Gram? And I'm pretty sure he wasn't a day over fifty."

She's right, my mother looks phenomenal at sixty-eight. It's something I've never really thought much about because...well, she's my mom. She has great skin, her face is still youthful, and she rocks her full head of chestnut hair. Besides, Mom doesn't dress like an almost seventy-year old and always looks a bit artsy. Like now; in her faded boot-cut jeans, engine red finely knit tunic, and large chunky jewelry; she looks like she could've walked right out of a magazine.

Looking down at myself, I suddenly realize how much I've started mirroring her style.

"Now we just have to find someone for you, Mom," Paige says. "Gram's got Ken. I've got Josh." He's the new boyfriend we met in September. Nice kid and clearly smitten with my daughter. "It's gonna be harder for you, because Beaverton doesn't exactly have a large pool of single men, but I'm sure we can find you someone."

My daughter. I love her, but her mouth often runs unfiltered. I don't think she even realizes her words are a tad insensitive.

"But what happened to Gray?" Mom asks, and my daughter's eyes immediately widen.

"Gray? Who's Gray? You've got someone and didn't tell me?"

Shit. I've been able to push him from my mind since not hearing a thing from him, not even after I stopped by Olson's. The message now clearly received. For a while there, I imagined perhaps something was happening between us, but I guess that was wishful thinking on my part. Maybe he never looked at it the same way, or maybe he discovered he wasn't ready for where it was heading.

Either way, I'll get over it. I have what I need right here in this kitchen: my family.

"He's someone I saw a few times but it didn't pan out," I tell Paige with a shrug, as I head to the fridge to pull out the pie dough I had chilling. "Time to start on those apples." I indicate the large bowl on the counter.

We work in silence for a while, Mom and Paige peeling the apples, while I roll out dough for the three pie plates I buttered earlier. Don't ask me why three, other than there's three of us. A pie each may look like a lot, but spread it out over the four days of the long weekend and it's not so bad. Right?

To keep my mind off him, I start thinking about Mom and this Ken-guy.

"Does Ken have kids or grandkids?"

"A son in the military. No kids there yet, he's only twenty-five."

Yikes. That's just a few years older than Paige. I do some mental calculations.

"How old is Ken?"

I watch my mom closely and catch her glancing at me from the corner of her eyes.

"Fifty-five," she mumbles.

"Go, Gram!" Paige shouts. She raises a hand for a high five, which my mother, smiling nervously, slaps with hers.

Jesus. Thirteen years. I wince when I think how much closer he is to my age. Only nine years difference there.

"Yeah, good for you, Mom," I manage. "So what about this traveling? Where does he want to take you?"

"He has a time-share in Costa Rica."

"That sounds nice," Paige interjects. "Near a beach?"

Mom smiles at her. "On the beach, actually."

"Oh my God, you have to go."

Mom's eyes flit to me and back to Paige.

"Actually, he's leaving the middle of December. He'll be there until March. Wants to get away from the cold for a bit."

"And he's asked you to come?" Paige drops her peeler on the counter and grabs for Mom's hand. "Do it, Gram. You don't like the cold either."

I rip the crust I just rolled out when I try to lift it onto the pie plate. Swearing under my breath, I pound it back into a ball to start over again.

Three months. That would mean she's gone over Christmas. Selfishly I don't want to miss Christmas with her, but when I look at her face I can tell she's tempted. Who am I to hold her back? Sure there are safety concerns—after all, she hasn't known the man that long—but at least my mother is out there grabbing life by the balls.

"You should, Mom," I tell her gently, and I watch her face brighten with surprise. "Time to enjoy life again."

"But Christmas away from my girls…"

"It's just a day," I reassure her. "Paige and I will be fine."

"Actually," my daughter pipes up, a guilty look on her face. "Josh asked me to spend it with his parents in Florida."

Double whammy. A gnawing feeling settles in my stomach as I realize the world is moving except for me. Don't get me wrong, I want this for my two favorite people in the world, but it does make me realize how empty my life is. It also makes me wish things hadn't ended the way they did with Gray.

"Of course, Sweetie."

My smile is forced and everyone knows it, but still I roll a perfect piecrust this time. Better make the best of this Thanksgiving since it looks like I'll be spending the rest of the holidays alone.

———

Gray

"Not long now."

I look up to see Julie, one of Frank's nurses come into the room.

Frank was awake from time to time the first couple of days I was here, but that waned with the high doses of morphine they're giving him to keep him as comfortable as possible. I haven't seen his eyes open in the past twenty-four hours.

I rented a room in the motel across the street for a place to dump my stuff and occasionally grab a few hours of sleep or a shower, but the bulk of my time I've sat right here by his side, holding his dry, papery hand. Listening to his breath, which has become quite superficial.

The few times he was alert, he didn't speak much until the last time, yesterday morning.

"Good things come to those who wait is a load of shit," he said, his red-rimmed eyes clear, burning in mine. "Fucking go after what you want, son. Chase it. It'll be over in a blink." The hand in mine gave a squeeze. "Don't waste your life waiting."

I've been sitting here, thinking on those words since he drifted off. Already I've spent a lot of years waiting, at the mercy of others. I think I stopped thinking about what I wanted until I first saw Robin. I definitely wanted her.

Want, not wanted, it's not like I stopped.

Things aren't always as easy as that though, are they? Going after what you want, chasing dreams. It's not always about you. The fact I'm sitting here, by Frank's side, is testimony to that. He wanted to die alone; I needed to see him off. The outcome is the same but the path not that clear-cut.

I want Robin but I'm not sure I'm what she needs. Still, with Frank's last words on a loop in my head, I want to see if maybe there's a way. If she's still willing to try.

I watch as Julie takes a sponge swab from the glass on the nightstand and moistens Frank's dry lips.

"How can you tell?"

"Years of experience." She drops the swab back in its glass and checks his IV.

"Why do you do it? This work," I clarify.

She stills her hands and smiles at me.

"Because no one should leave this earth alone."

"He wanted to."

"No, he didn't," she disagrees, running a gentle hand over his sparse hair. "If he did, he wouldn't have come here."

She turns away from the bed and I expect her to walk out of the room. Instead she grabs a chair from against the wall and places it on the other side of the bed, sitting down and taking Frank's other hand in hers.

Less than an hour later, he breathes his last thin breath.

She doesn't jump into action, but sits there a while longer, still gently stroking her thumb over his pale, lifeless hand. As if giving the reality of his death time to settle in. With me, and maybe even with her.

I didn't know him as well as I did my sister and mother, but as I'm letting him go, I feel some of the guilt I've carried around their deaths let go as well. I'd like to believe, given the chance; I would have been there for them as well.

"I need to make some calls." I stand, my knees creaking, and let his hand slide from mine.

"You can use the small waiting room down the hall."

With a nod of acknowledgement, I leave Frank in her gentle hands.

"Olson's"

Jimmy's voice seems loud after hours spent in an almost silent room.

I take a seat in one of the club chairs in the room and drop my head back.

"It's me. He's gone," I tell my friend, fatigue lacing my voice.

"Made it past Thanksgiving after all."

"He did."

"You okay, brother?"

It takes me a moment before I can answer.

"Yeah, but I'm not sure what I'm supposed to do now," I confess.

After spending days by his bedside, it seems strange just to pick up where I'd left off. Sacrilegious somehow.

"Call his friends. Call Bunker. They'll feel better knowing you were there. You can do that."

"Okay. Do you have—"

My sentence is cut off with the ping of a message, and then another one.

"That's the contact information for Enzo Trotti and Bunk's cell phone."

"Thank you."

"No problem."

"I should be back tomorrow. Unless you want me to come back today?"

"No rush, brother. Take all the time you need."

The line goes dead and for a moment I rest my eyes and get my emotions under control. Then I dial Enzo.

"Who's this?" The bark on the other side startles me.

"Mr. Trotti, it's Gray. Gray Bennet. I'm here in Clare, with Frank Hanson. He...um...he just passed away."

"I know who you are, boy. Kicked you out of my restaurant enough times."

Despite the circumstances, I bite back a smile. As teenagers, Jimmy and I would hit the pizzeria with barely enough money for a slice each, but we'd wait for other diners to get up so we could nick their leftovers. Usually until the waitress spotted the extra plates and beer glasses on our table and would call Mr. Trotti, who would toss us out.

"So the old coot is gone, is he?" The words may seem harsh, but the man's feelings underneath are easy to detect.

"Yes. They kept him comfortable so he wasn't in any pain," I volunteer. "He woke up a few times and we talked some until yesterday. He never woke up again and maybe forty minutes ago he simply stopped breathing."

"You were there?"

"Yes, sir."

"That's a good thing you did, son," he mutters, and I can feel the approval down to my bones. "Things going down for you the way they did, it ate at Frank for years."

"That wasn't on him."

"Think I don't know that? The whole town carries some of that responsibility. People weren't blind, but no one stepped in."

"Was a long time ago, Mr. Trotti."

"You tell yourself that, boy?" That shuts me up. "Didn't think so. And fucking call me Enzo, that Mr. business makes me feel old."

"Sure thing."

"Gray?"

"Yes, Mr...Enzo?"

"Got a pie waiting with your name on it."

CHAPTER FOURTEEN

Robin

I don't know if it's the weather—which has been cold and gloomy —or the fact I don't have Christmas with my family to look forward to, but my ass has been dragging since Thanksgiving.

The days are long, the nights empty, and my own company leaves a lot to be desired. I don't know how to snap myself out of it. I've even started picking up shifts on my days off, just so I don't end up sitting at home feeling sorry for myself. It's pathetic.

"Your shift was over twenty minutes ago."

I look up from refilling the bottles of condiments to where Jason is sticking his head out of the kitchen.

"I know," I mumble. "I'm just finishing this up, then I'm out of here."

"You off tomorrow?"

"Yeah, unless you guys need me to come in?"

My voice is a little too hopeful and Jason picks up on it.

"Jesus, Robin. You've been here almost every day for the past few weeks. Take a break. I'm sure you've got Christmas shopping and stuff to do as well."

"I work Christmas, remember? I've got all I need."

He rolls his eyes and I can just hear his mumble before he ducks back into the kitchen.

"Except a life."

Isn't that the truth?

Donna slips behind the counter and puts in an order with the kitchen before turning to me.

"He's right you know."

Great. I guess she heard. I quickly look over to see if Becca heard as well, but she's talking to the family who just walked into the diner. I really don't want her to be privy to this conversation.

I brace an arm on the counter and plant my other fist on my hip.

"About?"

"Don't play coy. We've all see you mope around and that's not like you. Go out, do something fun, get a dog, join the book club. Anything to get you out of this funk."

Wow. I didn't realize I'd been that obvious.

"Don't hold back on my account," I snap defensively, even though I know she's right.

"I didn't," she says matter-of-factly. The straightforward mother of three boys shrugs. "Everybody's been pussyfooting around since whatever started with that public lip-lock outside weeks ago ended shortly thereafter."

She has to bring him up.

I heard from him, the Monday after Thanksgiving. A text message stating 'We need to talk,' and nothing since. Now I'd heard from Tank he'd been with Frank Hanson when he died, so I'd cut him some slack, but I promised myself I'd done all the chasing I would. So I waited until I saw him driving his old pickup truck past the diner last week, and it was clear that 'need to talk' was not that high on his list of priorities.

So I'm done. I'm consciously snuffing out that little spark of hope that after all these years there might be someone out there for me. My next step is to stop moping.

I pull my apron off and grab my purse from the drawer.

"I'm outta here."

"Grab the garbage on your way out?" Donna holds up the bag and I take it from her hands. "Enjoy your day off," she calls after me, and I lift a hand in response.

I'm in a foul mood.

Outside I duck into the dark alley beside the diner. The lid is heavy on the large bin, and I struggle to get it open. Swearing under my breath, I manage to lift it just enough to shove the bag inside.

A rustle sounds behind me and I swing around, letting the lid slam shut in the process. I squint and scan the alley. I don't see a thing, but when I turn toward the street I hear what sounds like a faint whimper behind me. My eyes do another scan of the deep shadows, and this time I see the glint of a pair of eyes peeking out from the far side of the dumpster.

Meeow.

A cat—or rather, a kitten no bigger than my hand—comes out of hiding and carefully walks closer.

Meeow.

I go down on one knee and hold out my hand for her to sniff, which she does tentatively. I don't really know if it's a *her*, but she strikes me as one; dainty and petite. Big eyes in a tiny face, she looks like a tabby, predominantly gray with some black-brown markings.

"Hey, little one," I coo, scratching behind her ear with a finger.

She leans her head into my touch but when I reach farther to pick her up, she suddenly darts past me. Straight for the curb.

I scramble to my feet and rush after her. Blind to the danger, she's already running into the middle of the street when I notice headlights shining on her and she promptly sits down on her butt. Oh hell no. Dropping my purse I dive for her, both hands out. The loud honk of a horn startles the kitten and she suddenly moves but it's too late; my fingers are already closing around her.

With her body pressed against me, and her little heart hammering out a staccato rhythm, I straighten up just as I hear a door slam.

"Do you have some kind of death wish or something?"

I don't have to look to see who the harsh voice belongs to. My whole body recognizes it. Bottled up anger bubbles to the surface, but rather than have it out in the middle of the street in front of the diner, I turn on my heel, snatch up my purse, and stalk toward my SUV.

Somewhere along the line, the kitten started purring and I feel the vibrations where I hold her against my chest. Luckily I locate my keys easily and unlock my door, relieved when I hear his truck door slam again before I get behind the wheel. Guess he's no more in the mood for a confrontation than I am.

The little fur ball curls on my lap when I try to fit the keys in the ignition, my hands trembling.

I half-expect the headlights of his truck to follow me home, and am surprised when I turn left but see him continuing north. I force down the disappointment that follows and focus on getting us home.

Us. It would appear I have a cat.

Not only have I become a grumpy reject, to add insult to injury, I'm officially a middle-aged cat lady. I'm also completely unprepared. I don't have food, I don't have a bowl; I don't have a goddamn litter box.

I almost turn around to hit up the grocery store, but remember I have a can of tuna in the pantry and an old box in the garage I can fill with newspaper. She'll be fine.

Ten minutes later, she's hungrily scarfed up half of the tuna, ignored her box, and peed on the kitchen mat. I see we have some

work to do. I picked her up and berated her—something she
seems to enjoy since the purring is back again—when someone
knocks on my door.

———

Gray

Fucking hell.

My heart almost stopped when I saw her diving into the damn
road, and the angry words were out of my mouth before I could
check them.

I know I waited too long getting back to her; things just kept
popping up.

I'd been full of good intentions after Frank's death, but then I
was contacted by a lawyer, stating he was the executor for Frank's
estate. That meant a trip back to Clare to his office, where I was
handed a copy of the will I already had and assigned with the task
of making Frank's funeral arrangements. Luckily only a small cere-
mony, he'd been very specific in his instructions and wanted no
fanfare.

Since then I've spent most nights at the bar, getting a feel for
the place, but also going through Frank's belongings in the apartment upstairs. Enzo had been willing to help when I asked him,
since a lot of the old man's belongings meant nothing to me, but
potentially a lot to someone else.

Frank had made it sound easy, just toss everything out you
don't want, but I didn't have the heart to do that. I'm just learning
how precious mementos are. All I have left of my life before are
memories I'm lucky I've retained, but I don't have anything tangi-
ble. It all disappeared when the bank sold my parents' place. All I
had was what had been in my possession when I was arrested, or
what Jimmy was able to salvage.

To my surprise, in going through shelves and cupboards and boxes in the old man's apartment, I discovered he'd retained a few mementos as well. A high school yearbook from the year my sister graduated, several pictures of her spread over the pages. A snapshot of the annual fair that showed my dad with me on his shoulders and my very pregnant mom tucked under his arm. Those were happier days, before Dad was laid off from General Motors.

Little things, hidden away among the seventy-some years of life accumulated in creaky drawers and on dusty shelves.

I don't know why, but it seemed important to sort through the past and find a new beginning to start a future from. That meant sorting through the stuff, cleaning the apartment, painting it, and getting a handle on my new and unexpected reality.

Then I was going to sit down with Robin, when I had something real to offer her.

Looks like fate wasn't quite as patient.

I lift my free hand and knock on her door, the other holding the supplies I picked up in town.

"Can I come in?" I ask when she opens the door, the damn cat snuggled against her chest, and looking pissed as all get out. Still beautiful, though.

"Why?"

The question stumps me for a moment. I should've expected her to be direct.

"Because there are things I want to tell you." When she looks at me dubiously, I quickly add, "And I bought kitty litter and toys."

Something passes over her face I can't quite identify, but she steps aside and waves me in. I walk straight into the kitchen and start pulling out the shit I just loaded up my cart with at the grocery store.

"How'd you know I needed that?"

I pivot my head to find her peeking over my shoulder.

"The fact you almost threw yourself in front of my truck to

rescue that cat made it pretty clear you'd be taking it home. You crawling behind the wheel still holding the damn thing confirmed it."

The corner of her mouth twitches.

"Smartass," she mumbles.

"No, I'm not," I contradict her, turning so I'm facing her. "I'm a little slow on the uptake."

She peers at me, judging me, and coming to a conclusion when she hands me the ball of fur and heads for the fridge.

"Hang on to her for a minute."

I look down in the kitten's big green eyes boldly staring back at me. Then I lift it up, scan the area between its hind legs and bite off a grin.

"What are you gonna call it?" I ask when she resurfaces with a couple of bottles of water, handing one over.

"Haven't had a chance to think about it yet. Maybe Ally? Since that's where I found her."

"You might scar him for life with a name like that."

"Why? It's a perfectly good—" Her mouth snaps shut and her eyes narrow as she reaches for the cat, holding him up much like I did seconds ago. "Son of a bitch. I was so sure..."

"He's probably too young to remember you thought he looked like a girl."

With the cat in one hand and her water in the other, she saunters into the living room, sitting down in the lone club chair, leaving the couch for me.

Message received.

Instead of agonizing over where to start, I tell her about Frank: his generous legacy, his guilt, his illness, and his death. The words come easy when I don't think too hard or worry about how they'll be perceived.

She listens intently, especially when I talk about the last days with him and repeat some of the things he told me.

"He was right," I confess looking straight at her. "I was wasting my life, going through the motions, and keeping expectations as low as I could." I run a hand through my hair, because here is where it becomes tricky. Where one wrong word could make all the difference. "I did that inside and continued after my release. Then I met you and suddenly everything seemed possible. The world I'd so tightly controlled and limited, suddenly open wide. It felt like...like craving the water but discovering you can't swim when you jump in."

Her hand, which has been absently stroking the sleeping kitten in her lap, scoops him up and sets him down on the floor. Then she gets up and sits on the couch with me. On the far side, with her knees pulled up, and her arms wrapped around them, but still on the same couch. Progress.

"I got scared. When you talked about the holidays, and family, it scared me shitless." I take a long swig from my water, buying time to sort through my thoughts. "When you're inside, you learn fast that hope is weakness. Hope is disappointment. Hope is pain, even crippling sometimes."

"I think I understand that," she says in a soft voice and my heart swells a little. "I don't mean to compare myself to you, or your experience, but 9/11 was the day I was set free and yet for the eighteen years since then, I've been scared to hope. I'm scared still."

The day she was set free was the day her husband died.

I'm starting to get a better understanding of the woman I saw with her arms spread and face to the sun. Much like I did when I stepped out of the gates of Rockwood Penitentiary. Feeling the clear air in my lungs and freedom on my face.

Perhaps we're not so different, she and I.

I stretch my arm along the back of the couch, my fingers lightly brushing at her hair.

"I am too," I admit, dropping my hand to her knee. A sigh of relief escapes me when she covers it with hers. Still an arm's length away, but infinitely closer. "Do you think we could try this again? Maybe wading in instead of diving off the cliff?"

A smile stretches over her face and her gorgeous eyes, glinting silver with a sheen of tears, meet mine.

"I'd like that."

Fuck, now I can feel my own eyes burning as that hope blooms inside my chest once again.

I lean over and kiss the top of her hand before I get to my feet.

"Where are you going?" she asks, looking surprised as she stands up as well.

"Home, so I can plan our first date."

She smiles at that.

"I'm off tomorrow," she offers.

"I'll pick you up for dinner at six."

Instead of claiming her smiling lips with mine, I press a kiss to her forehead and walk out the door.

But that smile stays with me all night.

CHAPTER FIFTEEN

Robin

This is ridiculous.

I discard yet another outfit onto the pile forming on the floor of my closet. The man has seen me naked, had his hands and mouth on my not so glorious curves. Those same curves are currently giving me a headache. Somewhere in the past few years I guess I've packed on a few pounds, because none of my dressy clothes fit anymore.

They date back to when I was casually dating Andrew, and I haven't really had reason to wear them since. God, I can't believe that was eight years ago. Time flies, and after the painful misunderstanding around the state of my so-called relationship with Andrew, it seemed safer to not date at all.

Until now.

I blow the hair out of my face and contemplate what's left in my closet. I snag a lonely pair of black jeans off the hanger and shoot up a little prayer they zip. They do, but now I have a little muffin top where my belly bulges. *Oh, for fuck's sakes. Get a grip.* I resolutely turn my back to the mirror and reach for a black V-neck T-shirt and a colorful duster cardigan that has seen better days.

My sudden nerves about dinner with Gray have nothing to do with how I look or what I wear, but those make for an easy distraction. Now that I'm dressed, with fifteen minutes to kill before he gets here, the real issue resurfaces.

He's shared a lot, both about his history and his thoughts. I've dropped hints about my past—he knows my marriage wasn't great, which is more than most—but there's a whole lot I left out.

Dinner out implies conversation and I know the idea is to get to know each other better, but there are some things I keep close to my chest for a reason. Heck, I've known Kim almost as long as I've lived here in Beaverton—she's a good friend—but she doesn't even know what little I told him. My mother knows some, but my daughter doesn't; at least not from me. Yet I get the sense someone as intense as Gray won't rest until he has answers.

My phone rings, and for a second before I check my call display, I wonder if perhaps Gray is cancelling, but it's Shirley's new number.

"Hey, lady. How are things?"

"Have you seen or heard from Mike?"

She sounds rushed and I'm instantly on full alert.

"No. Why?"

"The boys called. Their father contacted both of them yesterday. Apparently he stayed with his brother in Midland for a while, but was talking about coming back to Beaverton. They said he sounded desperate and claimed he wanted to make things right with me. He was trying to milk the boys for information. Almost two months he's been silent, but I knew it wouldn't last forever."

"Oh, shit, Shirley. Look, I was off today but maybe call Kim? At least to give her a heads-up."

"Yeah, I will. I'm just worried he's going to bother you guys at the diner."

"You worry about yourself, we can take care of things here." There's a knock at the door and I start moving in that direction. "Does he know where your aunt lives?" I glance through the peep-hole and see Gray on my doorstep.

"Last time he saw her, she was still living in Ann Arbor. I can't remember if I told him she moved to Grand Rapids. I don't think so."

I open the door and wave Gray in. Fuck me; he looks good in dark washed jeans and an untucked dress shirt over a white tee. I hold up my finger and mouth, *"One minute."*

"Still, be careful," I tell Shirley, as I watch Gray bend over the back of the couch, picking up the kitten. He's not even trying and I'm drooling. How sad is that? "Keep your eyes open, Shirl, okay? He's not gonna get far with us. We've got your back."

Gray's eyes come to mine and he raises an eyebrow. I shake my head as Shirley starts talking.

"Thanks, that means a lot. I figure with the trial date coming up, he's panicking."

"Trial coming up?" I ask, my attention suddenly snapping back to the phone call.

"February third. Gladwin District Courthouse."

"Shit, that's right too. I'll remind Kim. I'm sure she'll want to be there for you as well. I will for sure."

"Thank you, Robin. I appreciate you so much." She sniffles before she adds softly, "Ironic, isn't it? Working with someone for years and it takes something like this to form a friendship."

"I know, but we have that now. No use looking back, honey." I hear her cry softly and my heart goes out to her.

"I'll let you go. I should give the diner a call."

I barely have a chance to say goodbye before she hangs up.

"Hi," I tell Gray, who is still watching me closely.

"Let me try to do this right," he says almost grunting. "You look very nice tonight."

"Thank you. As do you."

"Right." He flares his nostrils as he sucks in air. "Now what the fuck is going on? That sounded like trouble."

"Not my trouble, Gray," I assure him, plucking my kitten from his arms and giving him a little cuddle before dropping him on the couch.

"Why did you say he wouldn't get far with you? Who are you talking about?" I can feel the tension coming off him.

"Can I tell you over dinner? I'm starving."

I tilt my head to the side and throw him a small smile. I watch as he seems to gather himself before taking a step toward me, grabbing my hand in his and leading me toward the door. There he helps me into my coat, and I can just snag my purse before he takes my hand in his again and walks me outside to his truck. I noticed he's cleaned it as he helps me in my seat and leans into the cab.

"Hi," he whispers, brushing a kiss over my lips.

It's tentative and sweet, and feels like the very first time.

————

Gray

It takes everything out of me not to interrogate her about the phone conversation I just overheard.

When I heard her plead with whomever she was talking to for caution and then mentioned something about a trial, the hair on my neck stood on end.

I grind my teeth and rein it in.

"Where are we going?" Robin asks, as I drive out of town.

There's no snow in the forecast until next week and the road's clear and quiet. Perfect night for a little drive.

"How do you feel about Chinese food?"

In my peripheral vision I catch her shift in her seat to face me.

"Love it. It's been ages, though. You have to go to Bay City for any restaurants."

"Not anymore. New place opened up in Pinconning a couple of months ago."

"Really? I didn't know that."

She sounds pleased, a smile on her lips. So far so good. Finding out about the restaurant had been a stroke of luck. I overheard one of Olson's customers recommending it to Jimmy last week and made a mental note. It's been a long time since I've had Chinese and I'm fucking elated Robin likes it too.

"That was Shirley by the way, the phone call?" she clarifies. "Waitress at the diner?" I draw a blank and I guess it shows on my face. "I guess you probably missed her at Over Easy. She left a couple of months ago. Anyway, she got away from an abusive marriage."

I feel the stirrings of my temper flaring at the mention of abuse.

"He beat her?" I grind out through clenched jaws.

"Yes," she answers before pensively adding, "although abuse has many faces."

My head swings around to look at her. I wonder if she is referring to herself.

"She charged him?"

"She did. He hurt her badly last time. The cops arrested him and she finally told them everything. Of course he walked out on bail just days later, then disappeared, until last week apparently."

"Is she safe?"

"Should be."

She proceeds to tell me about the two grown sons, the phone calls, and Shirley's concern he might approach someone at the diner. I can see her concern, but I'm only worried about one person.

By the time I pull into the parking lot behind the new restaurant, I'm resolved to make sure Robin stays safe.

We're led to a table by the window I had reserved. The woman on the phone assured me it wouldn't be necessary, but I didn't want to leave anything to chance. Even in my much younger years, I hadn't ever put thought or energy into wooing a woman, I'd been much too eager to get them into bed. It had been easy, much too easy. It's all I knew and when I first connected with Robin, it was a natural pattern to fall into.

But this is different. She is different. I was always focused on my own needs and wants. I'm not that secure or selfish anymore, so with Robin it seems important her needs match mine. I want her to *choose* me and therefore I have to win her.

"This is really lovely," she says, smiling at me from across the table. "I'm so excited about the food. Too bad I can't order everything." She glances over the menu offering way too many choices.

The waitress returns with Robin's glass of wine and my water.

"Excuse me." I raise my hand stop her when she starts to leave. "Is it possible to order a variety off the menu in smaller portions? Something we could share?"

"If you look at the back page, we have several sampler options for two or more people."

I see Robin's face light up when she scans the choices.

"What would you like?" she asks.

"I'm good with anything. You pick."

It takes her two seconds to choose and the waitress leaves with our order in hand.

"Thank you for this. I haven't been out in forever. I was actually really nervous, but you make it easy."

The fact she apparently suffered the same jitters I had immediately settles any remaining nerves.

"I could say the same," I admit. A sudden urge to haul her over the table has me grabbing my glass of water for a sip.

"You really must like water," she notes. "Other than coffee, it's all I've seen you drink."

"I don't have a problem with drinking, I just prefer keeping a clear head." She looks at me expectantly, waiting for me to elaborate, so I lean over the table and grab her hand. "It's about control," I admit. "I'm afraid to lose it."

"Because of what happened to you?"

It's a different way of looking at things, almost absolving me for my actions. I give her hand a squeeze; touched she chooses to see me as a victim of circumstance. It's tempting, but I can't allow myself to deny the responsibility I carry. Besides, I want her to know who I really am. What I'm capable of.

"Because of what I did," I say firmly, and she nods her understanding.

I'm amazed at this woman, so readily accepting my need to hold myself accountable. So willing to accept me where I'm at.

I open my mouth to tell her as much when the waitress appears with a stack of warmers, setting them down in the center of our table. A few minutes later, we are separated by a smorgasbord of fragrant dishes and when I look across the table at Robin, her gray eyes are bright and her lips smile wide.

"This looks delicious," she comments.

"It does," I agree, my eyes firmly fixed on her face.

Over dinner she asks about the bar and my plans, and I tell her I'm moving into the apartment over the Dirty Dog over the weekend, but plan to keep working at Olson's. At least for now.

She talks about her daughter, Paige, with great pride. She mentions her mother and the new man she's seeing. She confesses that despite wanting her mom happy after her father's death a few years ago, she struggles with the concept of a 'new man.'

When she asks, I find myself sharing a little about my sister, something that still isn't easy to do but she seems to understand that as well.

The night has cooled off significantly when we step outside, and I drape my arm around her shoulders, tucking her close as we walk to my truck.

"You're going the wrong way," she says when I purposely turn towards the lake instead of back home.

"I'm not."

"Oh, it's so pretty." She looks at me with a big smile when we head in the direction of the lakefront park.

When I checked into the restaurant yesterday, I saw mention of the annual Festival of Lights held here. Everywhere you look are Christmas light displays and at the center is a Christmas market.

This is my attempt to apologize for freezing her out after mentioning Thanksgiving.

"Are you sure?" she asks, putting a hand on my arm when I turn off the engine.

"Positive."

The chaste kiss she leans over the center console to give me is all the forgiveness I need.

When she slips her hand in mine as we walk along the displays, my chest swells.

For everything I've done wrong in my life, at least I got this right.

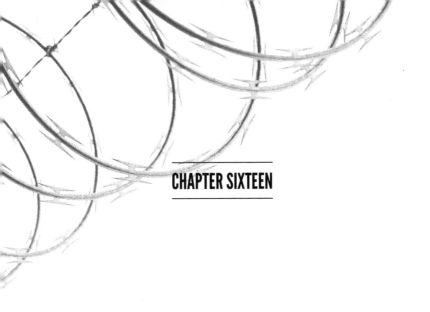

CHAPTER SIXTEEN

Robin

"I thought you were flying?"

I'm parked outside the Dirty Dog, talking to Paige.

Gray said I should drop in on the weekend, since he planned to get a lay of the land and work in the bar.

He stayed in touch via text, but I haven't seen him since our night out on Thursday. He messaged me this afternoon to tell me he was all moved in and if I wasn't too tired after my shift, to meet him for a drink.

I was definitely not too tired, but went home first for a quick shower and change before heading back to town.

Paige caught me as I was parking the SUV.

"We talked about it, but thought the road trip might be fun. We'll be careful, Mom. Josh found us an Airbnb not too far from Charleston to break up the trip. I've never been that far south."

I can hear the excitement in her voice and try hard not to let my motherly instincts spoil her mood. There are so many cautions on my lips, but I don't allow myself to give voice to any but one.

"Promise you'll call every day? At least while you're driving?"

"I promise, Mom," she says patiently. God, I raised a great kid. "Have you talked to Gram?"

"I did. They arrived safely yesterday and she says the place is even better than she imagined. She was going to take some pictures this weekend and send them."

"Does she even know how?" Paige asks, snickering.

"Apparently Ken does."

I lean my head back against the rest and stare at the ceiling of my car. I'm still having a hard time imagining Mom with any other man than my dad, let alone one who is so much younger, but she seems smitten.

"I talked to him for a few minutes before they left, you know?" I add.

"How is he?"

"Well, from what I could hear over the phone, he sounds nice enough. He gave me emergency contact information and the address, just in case. That helped."

I have to admit, when he told me he was sure I had concerns and wanted to do his best to alleviate them, it took me by surprise. He seemed quite taken with my mother as well.

"Gram may be a bit of an innocent, but she's not stupid, Mom," my daughter informs me. "In fact, when she met Josh while she was here, she gave him the third degree." She giggles. "He was duly intimidated."

I grin at the idea my mother would intimidate anyone. She's generally easygoing and sweet.

"Good for her."

"Are you going to be okay, Mom?"

My nose stings as I try hard to answer in a straight voice.

"You bet I am, sweetie. I'll be fine. You guys have fun and I call dibs on having you guys for Christmas next year."

"Deal, Momma. Love you."

"Love you too. So much."

I'm still sitting there, my head back and my eyes closed, well after ending the call, when a knock on my window startles me.

"Hey."

Gray smiles down at me when I open the door and get out.

"Hi."

"I thought maybe you couldn't decide whether to come in or not, so I thought I'd help you out with that."

"Oh?"

He wraps an arm around the small of my back and lowers his mouth to mine. This kiss, although still sweet and reserved, has his tongue sliding along the seam of my lips, politely asking entry. When I open for him I get a hint of hunger, but nothing like the voracious appetite of our earlier kisses. Not even my nails digging into his biceps or my pleading moan can shake his careful control.

I almost growl when he lifts his head, leaving me frustrated. His eyes are dancing and a smile pulls at the corner of his mouth, as he grabs my hand and starts walking to the bar. He knows exactly what he does to me. Bastard.

The long bar is on the left when you walk in, on the right a handful of tables and chairs, and toward the back I see two pool tables. There are maybe ten or so people inside, some of them I recognize, including Bunker behind the bar.

"Hey, Robin. What can I get ya, darlin'?"

"White wine, please. Thanks, Bunk."

Gray pulls out a stool for me and when I sit down I hear him whisper by my ear.

"Bunk? You know him?"

I bite off a smile as I turn to face him.

"I do." I point at the pair of seniors racking balls on the pool table. "I also know Enzo and John, as well as a few of the others." I put a hand on the arm he has braced on the bar and scan the deep creases of his face, softening my voice. "I know I'm new to you, but I've lived here almost as long as you've been away, Gray. I work at the town diner, and everyone's been in there at some point in time these past years."

The anger drains from his eyes and he hangs his head. I give his arm a squeeze.

"Fucked up already, didn't I?"

I shake my head and am about to say no when Bunker is back with my wine.

"Thanks."

At the sound of my voice, Gray straightens up and drapes his arm around my shoulder. Bunker looks from me to Gray, a smirk on his face.

"Ease up. Brought the woman wine, boss. Not like I propositioned her." With a wink for me, he turns to a patron waiting to place an order at the other end of the bar. I look up at Gray.

"To answer your question: no, you haven't fucked up. Yet," I tease him. "I actually think I'm flattered you're a little territorial, *but* if every time another man even comes in my vicinity you feel compelled to mark me like a vigilant dog does a fire hydrant, I'm afraid the shine will come off real fast."

The corner of his mouth twitches and I see humor bleeding into his eyes.

"Did you just call yourself a fire hydrant?"

I take a sip of my wine and shrug.

"Only if you consider yourself a vigilant dog."

———

Gray

I chuckle and pull out a stool before I make an even bigger idiot of myself.

"Fair enough."

Leaning over the bar, I grab the bottle of water I left there.

"So what had you sitting outside in the parking lot? Were you having second thoughts?"

She shakes her head before glancing at me, a little smile playing on her lips.

"Paige called just as I pulled up. She's leaving for Florida tomorrow. I thought they were flying, but she says they're driving."

"They? She going with friends?"

"Boyfriend. They're spending Christmas with his parents."

It's not hard to recognize Robin at the very least has mixed feelings around that. It's also becoming clear why she was happy to roam around the Christmas market with me, but didn't want to buy anything.

"What are you going to do? For Christmas? Celebrating with your mother?"

She throws me a pained smile and shrugs her shoulders.

"Actually, Mom left yesterday for Costa Rica with her... boyfriend." Sounds like it cost her to say that, but she quickly plasters a bright smile on her face. "Which is actually quite perfect since Kim always ends up working Christmas, and now she can spend it with her family for a change."

"The diner's open on Christmas?"

"Yeah. She started doing that five years ago for some of our regulars who'd otherwise be alone for the holidays. Jason comes in to cook with his wife, and Kim usually serves with a part-timer. We don't open until noon, though, and close the kitchen at eight."

"I'm sorry if I rubbed it in, taking you to that market the other day. I didn't know."

"Of course not, and you didn't. I enjoyed it. A lot," she adds putting her hand back on my arm.

I like it when she touches me. Maybe a little too much, given the current state of my jeans, which once again feel a little too tight. As much as I've told myself and promised her we'd go slow, my body is still not quite on board with that idea.

"Also," she says, tucking her hair behind her ear. "I'm sure you already have plans, but if not, feel free to pop in."

"I don't have plans," I find myself admitting.

She looks at me like she expects me to run off again, but I don't plan to. Don't get me wrong, I hate she clearly misses her family being around for the holidays, but it does simplify things for me. Meeting her at the diner for a Christmas dinner is easier than sitting down at the table as the odd one out at a family gathering.

"Perfect."

Her smile is just that. Fuck, the entire woman is conjured from my dreams.

I had planned to show her my new apartment, but I can't guarantee I won't maul her the moment we're out of the public eye. Instead, I nudge my head toward the one vacant pool table.

"How's your game?"

She tilts her head back and laughs heartily.

"Pool? The closest I ever came to a cue and balls was in college when I played field hockey. I sucked at that too." She grins and her eyes sparkle. "But I'm game to learn."

Well, hell.

It seemed the safer option just a minute ago, but now I'm thinking pool may have been an error in judgment.

Thirty minutes later, I know how big a mistake it was, when I lean over Robin to help her with a difficult shot and her ass presses into my groin. Bunker, the asshole, seems to recognize my pain as he encourages Robin to lean back a little more.

The shot goes wild and the ball ends up bouncing over the bumper and hits the floor to my bartender's great hilarity. Asshole. He has Robin chuckling along with him, while I covertly adjust myself. Apparently I'm not successful, since the two old coots at the next table over stop what they're doing and watch me with wide grins.

Liz, the lone waitress tonight, comes by to pick up empties and asks who wants refills.

"Round's on me," Bunker calls out to the bar, then he turns to us and says, "Haven't laughed this hard since Frank told Eddie Bank's cousin he was cut off because he couldn't see straight anymore, except the guy was legit cross-eyed."

Robin bursts into renewed laughter and this time I'm chuckling too.

We never finish the game, but spend the rest of the night sitting around a table with Enzo and John, who regale us with funny anecdotes. Robin has had a bit too much to drink and is still giggling when she gets up to announce she should get home. There's no way I'll let her drive home like this, but before I have a chance to say anything, Enzo gets to his feet.

"I can drive you."

The old bastard turns a shit-eating grin on me.

"You don't need to do that," Robin says, swaying a little on her feet as she waves a limp hand in the old man's direction.

I'm on my feet in a flash and put a stabilizing arm around her.

"No he doesn't, 'cause I am."

She twists her head and smiles up at me.

"You are?"

"Bunker," I call out. "Taking Robin home."

With a nod for John and a glare at a grinning Enzo, I wrap her coat around her and guide her to the door.

"What about my car?"

"We'll take care of it tomorrow morning."

"Mkay," she mutters, shivering under my arm.

It's freezing. I mentally cross my fingers my truck will start; it's been a little unpredictable these last few days with temperatures dropping.

"Oops." I have to grab onto her with both hands when she stumbles and almost falls in the parking lot.

"Easy, Sunshine."

I manage to lift her up in the truck and am buckling her in when she starts running her fingers through my hair.

"You've got nice hair."

I'm struggling to get the damn belt buckled, with her thick coat getting in the way, and all the while she plays with my hair.

"So thick. Don't you have any bald spots?" I can feel her fingers digging through my hair, looking for one.

Finally the buckle clicks in place and I immediately remove her hands from my head.

"No bald spots," I assure her, but when I look at her face she's gone pale. "You gonna toss your cookies?"

She shakes her head sharply.

"No. I just realized I have to work the early shift tomorrow. That's not good."

"You'll be a sore puppy. Let's get you home and to bed."

I close her door, round the hood, and get behind the wheel.

"I drank too much," she mutters, mostly to herself, when I pull away from the bar.

"Three glasses of wine," I remind her.

"Should'a stopped at one. I'm a lightweight, but I was having so much fun."

"That's good. I had fun too."

"I'm gonna hate myself in the morning."

It's on my tongue to agree with her, but she doesn't need me rubbing it in. Instead I focus on the road. She's asleep and snoring lightly when I pull up outside her house. When I open the passenger door, she blinks her eyes open.

"Give me your keys. Let's get you inside."

She fishes a keychain from her coat pocket and hands it over before I help her down from the cab.

Inside the kitten is waiting, and Robin almost goes down trying to pick the thing up.

"I need to check his food."

"You need to go to bed," I tell her firmly, taking the cat from her hands and giving her a nudge in the direction of her bedroom. "Go on. I'll look after the cat."

I watch as she cautiously moves down the hallway to her bedroom door. Then I take the cat to the kitchen, fill its bowls with water and some dry food, before setting him down on the floor. Like a growing boy, he immediately makes a beeline for his food bowl.

I dig through her cupboards, find some ibuprofen and fill a glass with water before heading to her bedroom.

She doesn't respond to my knock so I open the door, finding her half-dressed on her back on the bed.

"Too tired," she mumbles.

"Sit up for a minute, Sunshine." I hand her the pills and the glass of water. "Down both now. It'll help you feel better in the morning."

She does as I ask, and forcing my brain elsewhere, I quickly help her strip out of the rest of her clothes and tuck her in bed. The cat jumps up and curls up beside her, darting a suspicious look my way. I snatch the second pillow off the bed, press a kiss to her forehead, and head to her couch, where I make myself comfortable.

Tucking my arm behind my head, I close my eyes and feel a smile on my face.

I had a great fucking night and am starting to believe a decent life may be possible.

CHAPTER SEVENTEEN

Robin

Sweet Jesus.

The sound of my alarm carves like a blunt serrated knife into my skull, and I can barely peel my eyes open. Desperate to stop the torture, I slap my hand in the general direction of my nightstand, knocking shit off in the process, but the incessant beeping won't stop.

The door flies open and a disheveled Gray come barreling in, a wild look in his eyes.

"What the hell?"

"Make it stop," I groan pathetically.

He takes in the scene and immediately dives for my alarm clock, punching buttons until he finally rips it clear out of the socket. Then he sets everything back on the nightstand and sits down on the edge of the bed.

"I take it you still feel like shit?" he asks, brushing hair off my forehead. I nod gingerly. "Maybe you should take a day off."

"I can't. I have to do payroll today, so everyone gets their money before the holidays."

I fling back the covers and realize I'm only wearing panties. The rest of what I was wearing yesterday is piled on my dresser. Gray's eyes quickly avert and he's on his feet like a shot. Funny, since I'm pretty sure I recall him undressing me.

"Okay, then hop in the shower," he suggests, already reaching for the door. "And I'll bring you more water and drugs, and will get coffee going.

It's with a great deal of willpower I manage to get myself in the shower. The stream of warm water does make me feel a little better as I make quick work of washing my hair. When I pull back the curtain, I see Gray left me another glass of water and a couple of ibuprofen on the vanity which I down immediately.

In the kitchen, Gray is standing over the stove, the smell of coffee and frying eggs filling the air. I'm surprised to find myself hungry. No nausea, and the deep throbbing in my head seems to be waning.

"You stayed the night?"

His head swings around and I notice his eyes are clear, as opposed to mine looking bloodshot and bleary in the mirror just now. That'll teach me to drink more than one.

"Didn't seem safe to leave you," he says with a shrug before turning back to the stove.

It's a new experience having someone be protective of me. That's usually my job, to shield and protect. Rick was possessive; there was little caring involved in that and all about ownership. Dad had always looked out for Mom, so I automatically took on that role when he died. Although now with the new man, I wonder if he'll step in. That remains to be seen. Of course Paige has always been my responsibility, and I don't know if that will ever go away.

"Thank you."

He glances over and gives me the slightest of nods.

"Over easy?"

"Sounds good." I sit down and take a grateful sip of the hot coffee he slides in front of me, alongside a plate with eggs and a piece of toast.

It's still dark out when we head into town.

"Want to pick up your wheels now, or after your shift?"

"Now, please. I'm feeling better, but I'm sure I'll be crashing at some point. I'd rather not have to worry about picking it up then."

I look over at him and cover his hand on the gearshift with mine.

"And, Gray? Thank you for looking after me last night."

He glances at me sideways and a smile tugs at his mouth.

"Any time, Sunshine."

"Why do you call me that?" I ask, genuinely curious. It's not the first time he's used the nickname.

He doesn't answer immediately, and I'm about to ask again when he pulls up next to my Honda in the Dirty Dog's parking lot and twists in his seat.

"That's what you are to me. I spent most of my life living under dark clouds, and the first time I saw you I was able to feel the sun on my skin. Doesn't matter how gloomy the day, I catch sight of you and everything lights up."

I can't find adequate words, so instead I lift his hand and press a kiss in his palm to convey how deeply moved I am.

"I'm glad," I finally manage.

"Me too," he simply says, before leaning over and brushing his lips over mine lightly.

"I should go," I mumble.

"I know."

"I don't want to."

"I know that too."

I reach out and stroke a hand over his face before forcing myself to get out of the truck. When I'm behind the wheel of my

SUV, I look over and see him lowering his passenger side window. I roll down mine as well.

"Give me a shout when you're done," he calls out.

I smile, give him a thumbs-up, and drive over to the diner with a smile on my face and a warm glow in my heart.

———

I almost drop the tray with dirty dishes when I hear a loud scream followed by a crash. Quickly setting it down by the dishwasher, I dart out of the kitchen to find Kim and a few patrons crowding around Jess, one of our part-timers.

"Robin, we need a clean towel and water!" Kim calls over her shoulder.

I dart back in the kitchen where Jason hands me a mixing bowl to fill with cool water. I grab a couple of clean linen towels and soak them in the bowl of water.

This isn't our first rodeo; working in the food industry, burns are an almost daily occurrence, but mostly minor. It doesn't sound so minor this time and I can see why when I walk up to the group and see Jess sitting on a chair, tears running down her face.

Her right arm is stretched out over the table with Kim keeping a firm hold. Her skin on her forearm is already forming blisters. That's not good.

Someone must've dumped water on her already, judging from the puddle on the table, and I quickly fish the first towel out of the bowl and drape it over her arm. I follow it with the second one when I feel Jason at my back, handing me a roll of gauze he must've grabbed from the first aid kit.

"Hospital, sweetheart," Kim tells the girl. "That's a large burn. You need to have a doc look at it. I'll take you to Clare and we'll call your parents on the way."

"I'll stay," I offer, knowing it'll likely be at least a couple of hours.

When Jess is loaded in Kim's car, I head back inside where Donna is making sure the patrons are looked after. Luckily it's not that busy. Yet.

I clean up the area by the coffee station, where she apparently dropped a pot of hot water, and am just inspecting the floor for stray shards of glass when Becca walks in.

"What happened here?"

"Jess dropped the hot water," I tell her as I get to my feet. "She's pretty badly scalded. Kim took her to the ER in Clare."

"Well, shit. So we'll be short-handed?"

I take in the sour look on her face and am instantly annoyed.

"No, we're not. Donna can help until six and I'm staying until closing. We'll be fine."

I'm not looking forward to working with her. Not because she doesn't work hard—she does—but her attitude with me sucks. I've avoided her because I know myself; sooner or later I'm calling her out on it, and I'd rather not do that with a restaurant full of diners.

She huffs and rolls her eyes as she brushes by me to hang up her coat and grab her apron.

I take a deep breath in a prayer for patience.

———

Gray

"I'll go."

It started snowing around five, not long after Robin called to tell me one of the girls got hurt and she'd be working until closing.

We were just notified by the Sheriff's Office of an accident on the county road north of town. One car is off in the ditch and the other is blocking one of the lanes and is not drivable. Luckily, it's a Sunday night and not many folks are out on the road, especially in this weather.

I shrug on my coat and pull a beanie over my ears before grabbing the tow truck's keys off the pegboard.

"Be careful," Jimmy yells after me when I walk outside.

"Yes, Mom," I call back, mocking him.

I slow down when I drive by the diner, trying to catch a glimpse of Robin but catching one of Becca serving a couple sitting by window instead. She came by Olson's asking for me when I was out on a run last week. It would seem she's interested in rekindling something that's been dead for decades and wasn't much to start with, even back then.

I'd lived in Clare at the time, working at Brookwood Auto Repair, and Becca was a waitress at the local watering hole. I knew at the time she was looking to get hitched, something I had no interest in, but I was riding it out while it lasted.

I was a cocky bastard back then, high on myself and high on life. I sometimes wonder if things had been different if I would have turned into my father: a drunk, a womanizer, and an abuser.

Aside from the fact Becca bailed the moment trouble hit, there's a bigger reason I don't like her anywhere near my life; she reminds me of a time, and a version of myself, I'd rather forget. The fact she works side by side at the diner with Robin feels wrong.

I see the brake lights of a handful of cars stuck behind the accident and maneuver around them to get to the scene. The front of the pickup truck blocking both lanes is badly damaged, indicating a head-on collision. The car in the ditch is almost unrecognizable, a crumpled mass of steel. I can't see how anyone would've survived that kind of impact. The Beaverton fire department is already there. Behind me I hear the sound of sirens as the first ambulance pulls up.

A deputy points me to the side of the road and instructs me to wait until first responders have cleared the accident victims. In the back of his cruiser, I see an older gentleman I presume is the driver of the truck. He looks to be in shock.

The next twenty minutes, I wait and watch as a second ambulance arrives, while the fire department extricates someone from the wreck in the ditch. My heart sinks as I watch EMTs cover the body on the stretcher with a sheet. Somewhere someone is waiting for this person to come home and instead will find law enforcement at their door.

While the snow keeps falling, my heart grows heavy as my own grief blooms fresh and raw. Memories of the last conversation I had with my sister, the last hug my mother gave me, float to the surface like treasures I desperately cling onto.

When both ambulances leave, one with the distressed old man and the second with the other victim, I'm told to haul the pickup to the police yard in Gladwin. The other vehicle will go on a flatbed they called in. I'm relieved to finally be doing something instead of sitting in the truck surrounded by ghosts.

By the time I finally get back to Beaverton, I notice the lights at the diner are off. The roads are treacherous and I'm suddenly struck with a vision of Robin's SUV crumpled in a ditch somewhere. I've barely pulled in behind the dark shop when I have my phone out, already dialing.

"Hey."

I let out a deep breath at the sound of her voice.

"You're home," I confirm.

"Just got in, it's bad out there."

"I know, I just got back from a tow. Bad accident north of town." I get out of the tow truck and start walking to my pickup while I'm talking.

"Oh no. People hurt?"

"Yeah. One casualty," I find myself sharing.

"I'm sorry," she whispers, and I can feel her compassion like a comforting touch. "Are you okay?"

"I am now. Knowing you're home safe." The declaration is

followed by a drawn out silence as I climb behind the wheel. "Robin?"

"I'm here. I just...I should probably tell you not to worry about me, but...is it awful I really like that you do?"

I chuckle before I answer. "No. Besides, it would be useless. It's not like I could stop if I wanted to, and I don't want to."

"Good."

"How's the girl? The one who got burned?"

"Jess? She'll be okay, but out of commission for a bit, which means we're juggling the schedule again."

I'm sure it's a busy time of year too, like it is at Olson's. It'll only get worse if this snow persists. Jimmy does residential snow removal as well, which normally isn't that much. If what's fallen so far this season is any indication, we're in for a busy winter overall. We may soon need to put out a second plow.

Between both our work schedules, it may not be easy to find time to see each other.

"What time are you working tomorrow?" I ask.

"I start at lunch but will probably work 'til closing again."

"I'll try to pop in."

"Okay," she answers softly, and I can hear the smile in her voice.

"Get some sleep."

Like a fucking teenager I don't want to hang up. I should, because I'm freezing my balls off with my ass on the subzero vinyl seat, but I don't have the heart to start the engine and rush her off the phone.

"I will, you should too." She sounds like she's about to end the call when she adds, "Oh, and Gray?"

"Still here," I rumble.

"Thanks for caring. It makes life less lonely."

CHAPTER EIGHTEEN

Robin

I was here at seven thirty this morning and have been chopping and peeling ever since. It's still an hour before the diner opens and already my feet are sore.

"Take a break," Jason says, noticing my wince. "Kay and I can handle the kitchen."

Two giant turkeys are cooking in the large oven and an industrial-sized pot is boiling on the large burner with potatoes. Jason puts on a traditional Christmas with all the trimmings. He baked a bunch of pies yesterday already. It's going to be an elaborate spread.

I wasn't supposed to come in until ten or so, but after I got out of the shower this morning, the house felt too empty so I came in early. It's been a crazy week leading up to today, with Jess still off. I'd taken the bulk of her shifts since I was the only one without family around for Christmas. The day before yesterday, Becca had gone to spend time with her family for the holidays. That was a relief.

Working alongside her proved to be stressful. She wasn't overtly hostile toward me—not in public anyway—but she was far from friendly and refrained from talking to me at all when no one else was around. Of course it didn't help that the two times Gray could get away from work for a few minutes, it was during her shifts. I don't think it went over well he blatantly ignored her and even leaned over the counter to kiss me the day before yesterday.

Those are the only times we've seen each other. We've had snow almost every day this week, and it's kept him busy. Ironic, because I can't remember a single white Christmas since I moved here, and the one year I'm working it snows. Figures.

I'm just finished putting on a fresh pot of coffee when Debra, our other part-time girl walks in.

"Merry Christmas."

"Same to you, honey." I fold her in a quick hug.

Debra is a high school friend of Paige. She went to community college in Midland and chose to live at home. She's worked weekend shifts at the diner since she was eighteen.

"What do you want me to do?" she asks, hanging up her coat and tying her apron.

I duck into the small office and pull out a few bags of decorations I brought from home. We'd put up Christmas lights in the diner the weekend after Thanksgiving, but it still looks a little sparse.

"I thought we could spruce up the place a little."

"Awesome!" With a big grin on her face, she starts digging through the bags right away.

When we open the door at noon, the diner looks festive and the smells emanating from the kitchen are divine.

Most of the early customers stop in on their way home from church and are just looking for a coffee and a piece of pie. Then around three Mrs. Chapman shows up, a little branch of holly pinned to the lapel of her coat and a jaunty knit Christmas hat covering her hair.

Debra greets her and takes her coat, revealing the sweet lady is dressed up to the nines. A shimmering red blouse, matching the color of her painted lips, over a flared black skirt.

"You look lovely, Mrs. Chapman. Merry Christmas."

I swear the woman blushes with my compliment. I seat her in her favorite booth and offer to get her something to drink, but before I can get her the tea she ordered, the door opens again to let Eddie and Enzo in. Their buddy, John, and his wife, Marie, are probably visiting with their daughter's family for the holidays. Enzo is a widower, and from what I understand Eddie has been single his whole life.

The men kiss my cheek and wish me Merry Christmas before walking over to Mrs. Chapman, who seems to be blushing under their attention. It's like she was the Pied Piper leading everyone here, because over the next twenty minutes more people filter in. Some group together, and a couple choose to sit by themselves.

The last to walk in is Gray, and my heart does a little hop when I see he's dressed up. Well, the most 'dressed up' I'm likely to see him. He seems no different than I am with respect to clothes, but those dark jeans and white dress shirt he wore on our date last week look fantastic on him.

He walks right up to me behind the counter, hooks an arm around my waist, and plants a solid kiss on my mouth.

"Merry Christmas, Sunshine," he mumbles, rubbing his nose along mine.

"Merry Christmas, honey."

The endearment slips from my lips like it's the most natural thing in the world—and it is. It doesn't go unnoticed as Gray's light-blue eyes flare before they crinkle with a smile.

"Barring any emergencies, I'm hanging around until you're done and then I'm taking you home."

Now I'm smiling too, forgetting where I am as I lift up on my toes and press my lips to his. The promise in his words making my skin tingle.

"You'll get bored," I warn him, but he shakes his head.

"Not a chance. I'll be watching you."

"First order coming up!" Jason calls out, and slides a plate on the pass-through from the kitchen.

"You better take a seat," I tell Gray. "I've got dinner to put on the table."

I grab the plate Jason left and walk to Mrs. Chapman's table, watching from the corner of my eye as Enzo calls Gray over to their table.

"Here you go, Mrs. Chapman. *Bon appétit.*"

"Thank you, dear." She smiles up at me and covers her lap with the paper napkin like it's the finest linen.

The service bell rings and another couple of plates appear on the ledge.

"Add one more full order, Jason. Gray just walked in."

"Sure thing."

I grab the plates and turn to serve Eddie and Enzo when I notice Gray is not sitting with them, like I expected, but is sliding into the booth across from Mrs. Chapman. The glow on her face is unmistakable.

As if I needed another reason to fall for the man.

———

Gray

"About time you come to see me, Gray Bennet."

She says it in the stern voice I remember so well.

Mrs. Chapman, my high school English teacher. It was well over thirty years ago, yet I still remember the first time I walked into class. The short, middle-aged woman had looked like a sure pushover for the cocky, rebellious little shit I was back then. Boy, did I get it wrong. She ruled that classroom with an iron fist and actually got me reading my first book.

1984 by George Orwell.

I'll never forget my surprise when I finished the novel in one weekend. I devoured it. When I brought it back to her on that Monday, she just smiled knowingly and told me I shouldn't hide my light under a bushel. I had no fucking idea what she meant until much later.

I started reading everything I could get my hands on in high school. Thrived, got great marks, made it on the honor roll in my final year and was accepted to the University of Michigan in Ann Arbor. It was supposed to be my way out, but my father soon put a stop to that.

Things had been shit at home for years. Mom tried, but there was little she could do to please my father, especially when he'd been drinking. She'd been so happy for me when I got my acceptance letter, but my father thought it was a waste of time. It was the first of many on that subject. Mom wasn't one to provoke his anger but she went to bat for me on that. Until one day I came home to him beating her, and I had to drag him off her.

She wouldn't think of leaving, though, so needless to say I didn't go to college.

"Lost your tongue?"

Her voice snaps me out of my head and into the present.

"Sorry, Mrs. Chapman."

"As you should be," she says, but she does it smiling. "How have you been? Since coming back to town, I mean."

"Adjusting."

"I noticed," she says with a meaningful look at Robin.

"Your dinner's getting cold."

My attempt to distract her is futile. The woman may look meek, but she's sharp as a knife.

"It's not polite to eat until everyone's been served," she reminds me, just as Robin walks over.

She slides a steaming plate it in front of me and gives my shoulder a little squeeze before she moves to the next table.

"Now we can eat. Merry Christmas, young Mr. Bennet."

"Merry Christmas, Mrs. Chapman," I rumble, returning her smile.

We eat in silence, aside from a few comments about the amazing meal. I'm done first and let my gaze drift over the diner. Someone made an effort to make it look homey, with a candle in a small centerpiece on each of the tables, garland with clusters of balls along the edge of the counter, and soft Christmas music playing in the background.

I catch the eye of Enzo, sitting two tables over, who nods when he sees me. When I came in he invited me to sit with them, but then I saw Mrs. Chapman sitting alone and decided to sit with her. Robin crosses my line of vision, and I can't help but watch her make her way from table to table, the soft sway of her hips like a magnet.

"She was watching you earlier."

I snap my head back to my old teacher, who places her cutlery neatly side by side across her empty plate.

"That so?"

"You're both smitten," she concludes.

"So it would seem."

She tilts her head to the side and scrutinizes me.

"You sure you're ready for this?"

"For?"

"That woman deserves it all, Gray, are you ready to give her that? Because I know that's what she'll give you." When I open my mouth to answer she lifts a hand to stop me. "You don't owe me an answer. I just wanted to you to think about it."

"I don't have to," I grumble, but that only makes her smile. She's still not impressed by my attitude.

"Now," she suddenly changes the subject. "Read anything good lately?"

We spend a few minutes discussing books when the younger waitress comes by to clear our plates.

"Would you care for some pie? Coffee?"

"Just coffee for me," my dinner companion orders.

"What kind'a pie?"

The girl smiles at me. "Apple, banana cream, pecan, and pumpkin."

"Pumpkin with whipped cream if you have it."

"Sure thing. Coffee with that?"

"Please."

"Be right back."

I watch her move to the coffee station when the front door swings open and a man comes stumbling in.

I can't hear what he's saying to the girl, but I can see her taking a step back.

"That's trouble," Mrs. Chapman mutters under her breath, and immediately my hackles go up.

I'm already pushing out of my seat when I see Robin come flying out of the hallway leading to the washrooms and pull the young waitress behind her.

"...come in here and cause a disturbance..." I catch only snippets of what she's saying, but it's enough to have me double-time it to her side. "You need to leave right now, Mike," Robin says, reaching for his arm but he swats at her hand.

"Touch her and we've got issues," I growl, stepping in front of her.

"Where's my wife?" he yells, spittle flying.

"She's not here, Mike." Robin tries to nudge me out of the way and finally resorts to peeking her head around my elbow. "You need to leave or I have no choice but to call the police."

"Already done," I hear from behind me.

Jason, the diner's cook, steps around me and faces off with the irate man in the doorway.

"Enough, Mike. Go home."

"Do you know what she did?"

"Mike...come on, let's go."

Jason firmly grabs him by the arm and tries to spin him around, but the guy struggles against his hold. Ready for this scene to be over, I grab his other arm, twist it up behind his back and shove him unceremoniously out the door, Jason on his other side.

A police cruiser is just pulling up and an officer steps out.

"What've we got here?" the cop asks, over the loud protests of the idiot we're holding on to.

"He's drunk and making a nuisance of himself," Jason answers calmly. He doesn't seem fazed by the struggling man's swearing and cursing.

The cop's eyes come to me and his scrutiny makes me itchy.

"You're Bennet."

"I am." I lift my chin in a silent challenge.

It shouldn't surprise me local law enforcement is aware of my presence here and I've seen a couple around, but this is the first time someone's calling me out. It makes me uneasy.

The cop finally slides his eyes to the man still pulling against our hold.

"You causing trouble again, Mike? Told you two nights ago, when you were causing a ruckus outside your neighbor's place, I didn't want to get another call about you, didn't I?" He fishes a pair of handcuffs clipped to his belt. "Park him up against the cruiser, boys. He's gonna be sleeping this one off at the police station."

"This is a public place, you can't arrest me!"

"Be quiet already, Mike," the officer says, as he steps up and makes quick work of cuffing him.

He pats the man down for anything that can be used as a weapon and coming up empty, shoves him in the back of the cruiser, and slams the door.

"Derek Francisi," he says, reaching out his hand.

It takes me a moment to react but I eventually take his hand. "Gray Bennet."

"I hear you own the Dirty Dog now?"

"I do."

"Mind if I pop in at some point to talk about sponsoring the law enforcement baseball team this upcoming season? The Dirty Dog has for the past seven years, but we don't wanna assume you plan to continue."

"Fair enough," I mumble, taken aback. This was the last thing I expected.

Banging draws our attention to the man in the back of the cruiser, who is slamming his head against the window.

"Oh fuck, I better get going before he smashes his head open. I just had my cruiser detailed. Want him trespassed?"

"Probably best," Jason agrees.

"Consider it done." The officer tips his hat and slides behind the wheel. When he rolls past us he lowers his window. "Bennet!"

Instantly my spine straightens.

"Yeah?"

"See you at the Dog."

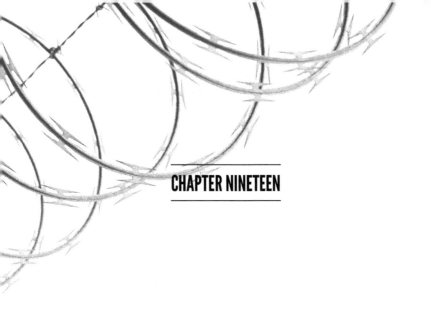

CHAPTER NINETEEN

Robin

I watch through the window as Jason and Gray stalk back to the diner, when the cruiser takes off with Mike inside.

"Coffee and pie on the house," Jason calls out when he enters.

Most of the guests who had been on their feet, checking out the goings-on in the parking lot, promptly take their seats.

To me he says, "Put on an extra pot."

"I'll help," Gray announces.

It's eight o'clock when I lock the door behind Debra, carrying half an apple pie to take to her family. Gray is wiping off tables and Jason is packing up the remainders in the kitchen. His wife, Kay, went home much earlier. We haven't had a quiet moment since the disturbance Mike caused. I suspect word must've traveled something was up at the diner, because people kept 'dropping in' for coffee and asking questions.

It's hard to keep anything here in Beaverton under wraps, and I think most people are aware of what happened between Shirley and Mike, but apparently that only made folks more curious about this latest incident. Most of the time I enjoy the close community, but in this case I find it a bit oppressive.

"You guys wanna take some of this home?" Jason calls from the kitchen.

I stick my head around the door.

"I wouldn't mind. Are you sure?"

"Plenty left." He indicates the overflowing containers.

"In that case, yes please." Saves me cooking tomorrow when I have the day off.

A few minutes later, we're saying goodbye in the parking lot when Gray throws an arm around my shoulders and guides me to my SUV. I'll admit I'm a little disappointed, I'd hoped he'd be taking me home, but then he grabs the keys I have in my hands.

"I'll drive."

"What about your truck?" I look around the parking lot but don't see it.

"I walked over."

He opens the passenger door and rounds the front of the SUV, getting in beside me.

"How will you get—" I start asking when the words dry up in my mouth at the look he shoots me.

He's not planning on going anywhere tonight.

A warm, electric sensation spreads out from deep in my belly down between my legs. My breathing is instantly shallow and his eyes are drawn to the base of my neck, where my rapid heartbeat is visible. A muscle in his jaw ticks, as he swallows hard before he turns the key in the ignition and forces his eyes front and forward.

Much like the last time he drove me home, the air charged with sexual tension, he opens the front door with my keys and pulls me inside. His mouth is on mine even as he's backing me up against the door. I drop the bag with the containers of leftovers on the floor and my hands find purchase in his hair.

Holy fuck, the man can kiss.

He pulls back when we run out of air, his eyes white-hot on mine as we both pant open-mouthed, catching our breath. But when I lift up to resume the kiss, he places two firm hands on my shoulders and takes a step back.

"Slow down."

"Why?" My voice comes out breathlessly.

He bends down, picks the plastic bag off the floor and carries it through to the kitchen. I follow behind and watch as he shrugs out of his coat before taking a couple of plates down from the cupboard.

"You haven't eaten yet."

"I'm not that hungry," I protest, hanging my coat on a kitchen chair. That's not entirely true, but I have more pressing matters on my mind right this minute. Distractedly I stroke the cat, who is curled up on the seat.

"Robin, I don't want to rush," he says, bracing his hands on the counter, eyeing me from under his eyebrows. "We don't *need* to rush, we have all the time, and I don't want to risk missing a single treasured moment. We've missed enough already."

"Okay," I respond immediately, moved by his words.

He's right. Time has moved along for both of us, but we had our eyes closed. I want to have them wide open from here on out.

A corner of his mouth pulls up and his eyes crinkle with his lopsided smile.

"Let's get you fed, and then in the shower."

He has already turned away when he adds the last, and a shiver of anticipation runs down my back. Visions of wet skin and droplets caught in the coarse hair on his chest. Soap-slicked hands exploring freely and bodies sliding together.

"Drink?"

I have to blink a few times to clear my vision and feel my face heating. Gray is watching me over his shoulder with heat in his eyes.

"Ice water," I blurt out and he laughs.

A hearty, genuine laugh that seems to come from his toes. It's a beautiful sound, and I file it away like one of those treasured moments Gray was talking about.

Determined to live in the moment, I pull a few candles and matches out of a drawer of the armoire and set them on the table. While Gray slides the plates on the table, I light them.

"Nice."

"It's Christmas, we should have candles."

"Yeah," he grins, sitting down at the table. "Nice."

I pick up the kitten and drop him on the couch before taking the seat across from Gray.

We eat in silence but manage to hold an entire conversation with our eyes, and the moment I put my fork down, Gray is already on his feet.

Leaving the dirty dishes on the table, I follow him to the bedroom. He's already taking off his dress shirt and the T-shirt underneath. I follow suit, stripping down and tossing everything in the direction of my hamper. I'll worry about laundry tomorrow.

His erection springs free when he pushes down his jeans and boxer briefs and I can't help staring. He slowly straightens, his eyes taking me in as well. I'm not sure who moves first but the next moment our bodies are plastered together, his mouth devouring mine.

"Shower," he mumbles against my lips, before grabbing my hand and pulling me behind him to the bathroom, where he bends down to turn on the shower.

"Lean your head back," he instructs when we step under the stream, and I do as he says.

His hands are heaven on my scalp as he washes my hair with more care than it usually receives from me. My eyes are closed as I take in the fresh scent of my shampoo and the sensation of his massaging fingers. He rinses it and I almost whimper when he pulls his hands away. Then it's my turn to do his hair and he groans with his eyes closed.

"Feels so good, Sunshine."

———

Gray

"Merry Christmas to me."

A little smile forms on her lips at my words as she lies back on the bed, her body and hair still damp from the most sensual shower I've ever taken. My hands have run over every inch of her, slicked with soap, discovering her body with my touch.

My own skin still tingles from her strokes, my dick is painfully hard, but what takes my breath away is the trust in Robin's eyes. Fucking makes me feel like a whole man instead of a shadow of one.

"Come here," she says, her hand reaching for me.

I put a knee in the mattress and crawl up between her legs. I kiss the tight nest of curls at the apex of her thighs, the scar running across her lower abdomen, the soft skin of her belly, the swells of her generous breasts, the heartbeat at her throat, and finally her luscious lips. Her arms and legs wrap me tightly and with our mouths fused, I slide into her.

Time doesn't exist, only the feel of her welcoming body enveloping me.

———

"Mom?"

The house is silent when I push open the door.

"Mom?"

From the hallway I get a glimpse of the kitchen where the cordless phone is in pieces on the floor, in front of the stove.

I can feel it, I can even smell it, and my feet seem frozen to the floor. I force myself to move, my eyes locked on the black plastic shards of the hand-set, unwilling to scan any further.

My last connection with her. She was talking to me, whispering to me that my father was home and angry. She was packing and I was getting ready to pick her up when she called. I can imagine the scene, he'd have been drunk, would've found her with her suitcase, and gone ballistic.

She's rolled on her side and for a moment I think maybe...but then I see the blood. So much blood.

"Mom..."

I drop down on my knees beside her, sliding in the cooling puddle. If not for the earring my sister gave her last Christmas, shimmering in her earlobe, I might have been able to convince myself this is not her.

"Gray, honey..."

Looking away from what is left of her head, my eyes catch on the cast-iron pan Mom always has sitting on the stove. The one she uses to cook eggs in, except now it's sticky with her blood.

Something snaps inside me at the sight of that pan and I scramble to my feet, only to find my father standing behind me, a dripping baseball bat in his hand and his own head misshapen and bloody.

"Please, honey, wake up."

I shoot up, sucking in lungfuls of air as I blink the lingering visions from my eyes. It takes me a second to recognize my surroundings and glance at the woman beside me in bed. Her hand is stroking my back firmly, anchoring me in the moment, as I rub my face with my hands.

Jesus.

"Come here." She softly echoes her words from last night and I lower myself in her arms.

We lie like that for a while, my heart slowly returning to its normal rate, and the last strands of the dream evaporating under her gentle touch.

"Sorry," I mumble.

"Don't be. Want to talk about it?"

I don't—not really—but somehow the words start flowing and I find myself telling her about my dream.

I can feel tension in her body as I describe the scene I walked in on so many years ago. Her body tenses up and I immediately feel guilty, but she encourages me to get it out, so I do. I tell her everything, about the earring, the cast-iron pan, my blind rage as I tracked down my father stumbling out of the Dirty Dog, and how I took it upon myself to mete out justice with the baseball bat I grabbed from the sports bag in the back of my truck.

As she lightly runs her fingers through my hair, I tell her how Frank pulled me away from my father and had to pin me against the wall until the cops came. How I waived my rights and told them everything.

"Is this a recurring dream?" she asks softly, her breath brushing against my forehead.

"No. I don't dream, ever."

"What do you think triggered it?"

I push up and brace myself on an elbow, looking down in her sleep-swollen eyes.

"Christmas, maybe. You," I offer, registering shock on her face. "Learning to feel again can be painful. Like a muscle you haven't used in forever suddenly called into action. The last time I let myself feel anything was on that kitchen floor."

"I'm sorry." Her eyes are shiny in the shadows of the room.

I pick up her hand and flatten it against my chest.

"I'm not. If it hurts, it's healing."

I roll on my back and take her with me, settling her head on my shoulder and pressing her body close. Her lips brush my chest and I sigh with contentment.

"You okay?"

I press a kiss to her forehead.

"Yeah. I really am."

My head shoots up when I feel something climbing up my legs. The kitten walks casually up my body, his eyes bright.

"Hey, Zeus, can't sleep either?" Robin gives the cat a scratch behind his ears, as he curls up in the middle of my chest.

"Zeus? For that little thing?"

She tilts her head back and I can see the white of her teeth when she smiles up at me.

"I'm sure he'll grow into his oversized attitude."

Seconds later, I hear her breath even out as the cat's purring vibrates against my chest. Moments later I feel myself drift off into a dreamless sleep.

CHAPTER TWENTY

Robin

It's been mild these past few days. Whatever accumulation remained on the ground after the early snowfalls has since disappeared.

The diner has been busy, not uncommon for the week bridging Christmas and New Year's, with people returning to the small town to spend time with family. Over Easy has always been a gathering place to catch up with friends and neighbors.

Our staffing issues have been resolved since Jess is back on the schedule, and I've happily slid back in my regular day shift. That means that out of the past five nights, I was able to spend four with Gray.

Last night he finally took me back to the Dirty Dog, where I had a single glass of wine before reverting to water, and watched the three musketeers—John, Eddie, and Enzo—play pool. I passed on the offer to try the game again, mostly instigated by Bunker, and instead chatted with him while Gray swept the floor with a very grumpy Enzo.

"No pie for you," had been his comment after, sending both Bunker and me into fits of laughter.

It had been a fun night ending with a very brief tour of Gray's apartment that never got farther than his bedroom. For two people who have hit their midlife, our sexual appetite only seems to grow. I always thought by this age I would be slowing down in that department, but the opposite is true. Maybe we're catching up for years lost, or perhaps we've simply found the right partner, because I've never experienced this kind of insatiable hunger.

This morning I was touched to find, sometime in the past few days, he picked up a bottle of my favorite shampoo—which was sitting on the little shelf in his shower—a spare toothbrush, and a package of disposable razors.

"It's going to be another nice day," I comment, as he pulls his truck up to the diner to drop me off. My SUV is still parked in the same spot I left it yesterday.

It's still mostly dark, but the moon and stars are clearly visible against the cloudless sky.

I lean over the console and slide my hand along his neck, pulling him down for a kiss.

"Thank you."

"No problem," he mumbles against my mouth before I reluctantly let him go. "I'll drop your key off after I've fed Zeus."

Since I was running a little late, after he joined me in the shower for the kind of exercise I'm going to feel for days to come, he offered to go feed Zeus. Poor cat has been home alone since yesterday morning and I feel a little guilty, despite the extra dry food I always put out.

"Appreciate it."

"Small price to pay for that kind of wake-up call."

He grins lasciviously and I roll my eyes but can't help grin as well, as I get out of the truck.

I've noticed him smiling more these past few days. More easily. I've been wondering if perhaps that dreadful nightmare and subsequent talk Christmas night has somehow provided some release. He seems more relaxed and less guarded.

I open the door to the diner, closing it behind me right away as I flip on a few of the lights. We don't open for another half hour, but I'm always early to help Jason with prep. He usually parks in the back and comes in through the back entrance, but the kitchen lights are still off.

My phone rings in my pocket as I'm hanging up my coat. It's Jason.

"Morning."

"Hey, Robin, I'm running a bit late. My car isn't starting and Kay just jumped in the shower. She'll drive me when she's done. Can you crank up the griddle? That way it's ready to go when I get in. Pull the eggs from the cooler as well?"

"Not to worry, I've got this. I bet you, between Donna and I, we can even manage to fry a couple of eggs," I tease him. Donna should be here at six.

"Just don't poison the customers," he fires back, chuckling before hanging up.

I shake my head and grab my apron, tying it around my waist. I slide my phone in my pocket and head for the kitchen first, flipping on the lights in there.

I fire up the griddle so we won't have to wait for it to heat once the orders come in, and head for the cooler to pull out the eggs and bacon. Then I dive into the pantry to grab the vegetables and potatoes.

I'm just rinsing the peppers under the tap when I hear something. Shutting off the faucet, I listen carefully.

There it is again, a slight shuffle. It sounds like it's coming from the hallway to the bathrooms.

Maybe Donna is early.

I wipe my hands on my apron and head out of the kitchen to say good morning, but the hallway is dark and empty.

Except for a faint strip of light coming out from under the office door.

"Donna?" I call out, simultaneously opening the door.

I barely step a foot inside when a hand clamps around my wrist, yanking me into the dim room, the door slamming shut behind me. I can just stay standing and swing around.

"Mike?" I'm stunned finding Shirley's husband, who immediately shines a penlight in my eyes. Anger hits me immediately as I pull my arm free from his hold. "What the hell are you doing here? How did you get in here?"

"I need to find her. I need to talk to her."

His hands are waving with frantic urgency. The light is no longer blinding me, but his behavior is concerning and fear starts to penetrate my initial burst of anger.

"Whatever you're looking for you won't find it here. You should leave, Mike. Jason will be here any minute."

His wild eyes come to rest on me, and I know I have to get out of here.

"Where is she, Robin? Where is my wife? Did you know she's out to ruin me? I'm facing jail time because of her!" His voice grows more irate with every word, and I fish around my apron pocket for my phone.

"You need to leave," I repeat, but I already know he won't listen. He can't hear anything.

I curse my iPhone and wish I had my old Nokia so it would be easy to blindly punch in numbers. I try to free my phone from my pocket inconspicuously but he notices right away. Even as he takes a threatening step toward me I try to unlock my screen, but to no avail.

He slaps the phone out of my hand before backhanding me in the face.

I barely hang onto the edge of the desk and gasp as the pain vibrates through my skull. Eyes blurred by the sting of tears and fueled a surge of rage, I grab on to the first thing I can find and throw my arm back as I swing around. He curses loudly as I catch him in the face. When he grabs for his cheek I aim for his crotch, my fist still clutching the stapler. When he howls, bending over, I don't hesitate and dart past him into the hallway.

I aim for the door, but don't get farther than the coffee station when a fist closes in my hair. I'm jerked back hard and can't keep my footing. I hit my head on the edge of the counter before I land hard, ears ringing and seeing stars.

A sharp kick lands in my ribs and I instinctively curl into a fetal position as a heavy body lands on mine. Blows land on my head and my back, when I hear a loud crash followed by an inhuman roar.

The next moment the heavy weight is lifted off me.

———

Gray

All I hear is the roaring of my blood and the thuds of my fists.

I just got out of my truck when I spotted Robin inside the diner, rushing toward the door. I was already running when her head jerked back and she disappeared from view. When I got to the door, all I could see was someone sitting on her, fists flying.

I never slowed down and dove right through the window in the door.

"Gray! Stop..."

I barely register the voice, lost in the heavy rhythm of my punches until hands start tugging at my coat.

"Gray! Stop! You're killing him!"

Robin.

My fists freeze in midair and the blurred face of the man on the ground slowly comes into focus.

Not my father.

I jerk back and land on my ass, caught in arms banding tightly around me, a soft body cushioning my back.

"It's okay. I'm okay. It's okay..." She chants the words over and over again with her lips pressed against the shell of my ear. "I'm all right, Gray. I'll be okay."

I pull from her hold and turn, taking in the swelling of her face, the trickle of blood escaping her hairline.

"Robin," I breathe out, my fingers wiping at the hair hanging in her face. "Oh, God, Sunshine."

I manage to switch places with her, pulling her onto my lap and resting my back against the base of the counter. My arms encircle her as she grabs fistfuls of my jacket.

"What the fuck?" Jason walks in from the kitchen, confused at the scene in front of him. Then his eyes get caught on the man's prone body on the floor and he drops to his knees, pulling a phone from his pocket.

I listen with half an ear as he talks to the 911 dispatcher, concentrating on the chest of the man on the floor. It's moving, barely, but moving. My eyes don't waver until I hear the sound of sirens outside.

———

"He's coming with me," Robin says firmly, when the EMT tries to block me from the ambulance. "He comes or I'm not going."

"Let him go."

The unexpected support comes from Officer Derek Francisi; first cop on the scene. Robin started talking to him the moment he showed up. She told him what happened, how she tried to get away but that motherfucker caught her. She explained how I crashed through the glass of the door and fought the guy off her. She swore high and low I was protecting her and that's how he got hurt.

She didn't leave me a chance to speak.

Derek's large hand lands on my shoulder.

"Looks like a pretty clear case of self-defense to me. I can catch you later for your statement. Go on."

I climb in the back and sit on the narrow bench beside the EMT, with Robin on the stretcher in front of us. Immediately she reaches her hand and I grab onto it.

Unlike the other ambulance, which already left with lights and sirens on, our trip is silent.

The entire time I'm trying to come to terms with the fact I almost killed another man—at least I fucking hope I didn't succeed—if it hadn't been for Robin pulling me off. Robin, who also jumped to my defense, conveniently leaving off she'd had to hold me back or things might've ended differently.

At the hospital, right before they wheel her inside, she calls me close. Her hands come up to cup my face and her heart shows in her eyes.

"Thank you. You saved me."

CHAPTER TWENTY-ONE

Robin

"I'm fine."

"You don't look fine," he counters stubbornly.

Gray has been hovering over me like an angry bear since we got home late last night. They closed the cut on my scalp, where I'd hit the counter going down, and made sure no bones were broken. The only other issue was the minor concussion, which is what has him sitting like a sentry by the side of my bed.

I agree, I may not be at my prettiest with my face swollen and bruised, but he's taking the doctor's suggestion to keep an eye on me for twenty-four hours a little too seriously.

I wasn't surprised to find out, when Jason and Donna showed up at the hospital, Kim had closed the diner for the day. They came to deliver my purse and coat, as well as my phone the cops had found in the office. One of them had also driven my SUV so we'd have wheels.

During the entire time we were in the hospital, Gray had said maybe five words. Even when the cops came, snapped some pictures of my injuries, and took my statement as well.

The eventual ride home had been mostly silent as well, which was welcome because my head hurt. He put me to bed and left the bedroom only to walk in seconds later, carrying one of my kitchen chairs. I didn't question him then, I was too exhausted and fell asleep, but seeing him still sitting there, now hours later, I wonder if his eyes ever left me. It's a bit too much.

"Have you even slept?"

He doesn't need to answer; I can see it in the pallor of his skin and the red-rimmed eyes glaring at me.

I fling back the covers and swing my legs out of bed, hissing when my body aches in response.

"What are you doing?"

"I need to pee," I announce snippily. "Pretty sure I remember how to do that."

When I return from the bathroom after brushing my teeth and washing up at the sink, both he and the kitchen chair are gone. I slip into a pair of old yoga pants and a sweatshirt and head for the kitchen. He's standing at the sink, staring out into the trees bordering my backyard.

I'm already regretting my sharp words. Giving myself a few minutes to think about it, I recognize all he's trying to do is keep me safe to the best of his abilities, even if it means spending the night sitting on a kitchen chair, staring at me.

I place a hand in the middle of his back.

"I should be thanking you, not bitching at you. I'm sorry."

He slowly turns around and folds his arms around me, holding me loosely. I'm struck by the conflicting emotions passing over his face.

"What is it?" I fist my hands in his shirt and give him a little shake. "Gray?"

"I lost control yesterday," he whispers in a raw voice. "I almost killed that man. Would've, if you hadn't stopped me."

My heart hurts hearing the desolation in his tone.

"You were protecting me," I'm quick to defend. "He was hurting me and you stopped him." Even as I'm saying it, I realize that's not the problem. It's losing control at all that has him spooked.

"What if you hadn't been able to? Or even worse, what if I got mad at you? Who's to say—"

"That's enough," I cut him off. "You would never do that."

He removes his arms from around me and grabs my wrists. The only thing I can read from his face now is agony.

"You don't know that," he mumbles, turning away and creating a distance between us I don't like.

"I *do* know that," I counter firmly. "Everything I know about you tells me you are a good man to the core. For God's sake, Gray, you jumped through the glass pane of a door to protect me." He'd had a cut on his face and a few on his hands they'd cleaned up in the hospital. "I don't believe you could ever touch me in anger."

Despite his rigid posture, I walk right up to him and plaster myself against his body, not allowing for any space. It takes a few moments, but eventually I feel his arms close around me as he buries his face in my hair.

"How do you do that?"

"Do what?"

"Have such blind faith in me?"

I lean back so I can look in his face.

"Easy," I tell him. "I know what evil looks like."

———

Gray

"I was told at Olson's I could probably find you here."

Officer Derek Francisi is standing on the front steps when I open the door. I'd been half-expecting the cops to come knocking at some point.

"Come in. Robin is just getting out of the shower."

She walks in as I'm handing the officer a cup of coffee.

"Ms. Bishop, how are you feeling?"

"Robin, please, and I'm fine. A bit banged up is all."

"Coffee?" I ask her.

"Please."

She turns to me with a kind smile and her eyes hold a promise.

We never finished our earlier conversation, when I asked her what she meant by knowing what evil looked like. Kim called, interrupting. Then I remembered I should probably get in touch with Jimmy, during which Robin headed for the shower. So that comment of hers still burns in my mind, but it'll have to wait.

She sits down at the table facing Francisi.

"What can I do for you this morning?"

"Just following up. Anything more you've remembered from yesterday morning's events?"

"Not really, except maybe wondering how the hell he got in? I didn't notice any signs of a break-in, and I know I locked the front door behind when I got there."

Derek shoots a glance in my direction before responding.

"That's because he had a key to the back door."

She sloshes coffee on the table when she sets her cup down too hard.

"How would he have a key?"

"That's the question we haven't been able to ask him yet."

"How is he?" I can't stop myself from interjecting, an uncomfortable feeling creeping under my skin.

"Rough," he says, giving me a hard look. "But he'll live. You messed him up good, though: he'll need surgery to fix his face." He turns back to Robin. "As to how he'd have a key, that's part of the reason I'm here."

"Not from me," she blurts out indignantly.

"I figured as much, but thanks for confirming. Who else has a key to that door?"

"As far as I know Jason, Donna, me, and of course, Kim, the owner. She's the one to ask if you want to make sure."

"I plan to. Right after I leave here."

"So..." Robin puts a hand on my knee under the table before she continues. "What will happen now?"

Francisi moves his chair back and gets up.

"Once he's back on his feet, he'll be heading for jail and new charges will be added. No judge is gonna let him go before his trial, so you don't have to worry about that."

"And that'll be the end of that?"

I cover her hand with mine. I know what she's digging for and apparently so does Francisi.

"Robin, the only charges coming out of this incident will be felony charges against Mike Hancock. We'll keep you updated."

I push a hand on her shoulder when she tries to get up, "I've got it," before following the officer to the door, stepping outside with him.

"You sure?" I ask him, partially pulling the door closed behind me. "Prosecutor may remember my name."

"Got nothin' to worry about, Bennet. I understand your concern, but I suspect your reputation isn't half as bad as you may think it is. Your father's reputation was another thing altogether. Not a lot in this town goes unnoticed."

Feeling a weight lifted, I watch as he ambles to his patrol car and gets behind the wheel. I'm still standing there when he passes another vehicle coming up the drive. A silver compact driven by a woman I don't recognize. Not at first anyway.

"Excuse me, who are you?" she snaps, getting out of the car.

She's young, in her twenties if I had to venture a guess, and something about the challenging look she shoots me is familiar.

"Paige, right?"

"Where is my mother?"

She looks over my shoulder at the partially closed door and shoves her hand in her purse, and I lift my hands up defensively. As I suspected, her hand comes out holding a small can I assume is mace.

"She's inside."

The young woman gives me a hard look and I step out of the way when she barges past me and shoves open the door, yelling for her mother. I follow in a little slower to find the two women facing off in the living room.

"What the hell?"

"Calm down, Paige, I'm fine," Robin soothes. "Let me—"

"Your face is a mess! My God, Mom!"

She must've heard me walk in because she swings around, aiming her mace at my face.

"Whoa. Easy."

"Paige, put that thing down and let me—"

"What is going on?" The girl's eyes dart from me to her mother, and I use that moment of distraction to close the distance and grab the canister from her hand.

"If you'd give your mother half a second to explain, you'd know," I grumble.

Robin jumps right in.

"Gray didn't do this, baby. There was a little incident at the diner yesterday."

Understatement of the year, but I'm not going to correct her when she's trying to calm her clearly upset daughter down.

"What incident?"

Robin pulls the younger woman down on the couch, their heads close together.

"Why don't I put on another pot?" I mutter at no one in particular, since the two of them are too engrossed in each other to pay me any attention.

It's just noon and already I've had more social interaction than I'm accustomed to or even comfortable with. Instead of escaping out the back door—or 'running away' as Robin likes to refer to it —I busy myself making coffee.

I'm at the sink, looking out the window, when I feel a tugging on my jeans. I drop my gaze to Zeus, sitting by my feet, his big eyes blinking up at me.

"What do you want?" I ask the little terror.

He complains urgently in response.

"Demanding little thing, aren't you?"

Meowww.

"You have a cat?" I hear Paige exclaim inside when I open the cupboard for the cat food. "Oh my God, she's so cute."

"It's a he."

Robin's daughter looks up from where she's crouched on the ground, plying Zeus with attention the cat seems to lap up. Then she scoops up the cat and straightens, holding out her free hand.

"Sorry about earlier," she mumbles when I shake it.

"No worries. Name's Gray."

"Paige. So Mom says you rescued her when that old piece of shit car of hers broke down?"

She tilts her head to the side and the move reminds me of her mother. In fact, now that I'm looking at her a little closer, the family resemblance is quite obvious.

"Technically we first met in New York at the 9/11 Memorial," I correct her.

I watch her eyes grow big before she swings her head around. Robin is walking in from the living room, a concerned look on her face as she bulges her eyes at me.

I'm not sure what, but I'm positive I did something wrong. The air in here has just gone electric in a significant way I don't quite understand.

Robin is blushing, looking guilty, and her daughter is staring daggers at her mom.

"Mom? When were you at the 9/11 Memorial?"

———

Robin

Well, *fuck*.

I guess there was always a chance she'd catch on at some point. Especially now she's an adult. For years, I was able to get away with my annual trip around the beginning of September by telling her I was meeting up with my old sorority sisters.

It had been an excuse both Paige and my parents accepted easily. My parents thought it was a nice distraction for me around the anniversary of Rick's death, assuming any 9/11 memorials would be too painful for me. I never bothered to disavow them of that notion. Over the years it had become an easy tradition for everyone to get used to.

Paige had been the first to suggest we see the Tribute in Light when she first went to school in New Jersey. I would still go during the day, supposedly to meet up with friends, and would return with Paige at night.

As far as Paige is concerned, her father was one of many to die an unfortunate death when she was only five. She holds no real memories of him—thank God for that—and I wasn't about to refresh her limited recollection.

I remember clearly how he held a gun to her head the last time I tried to leave with her, stating how he'd kill us both. I'd believed him. How could I not? He'd never hit me but I was painfully familiar with that gun. He knew all too well I would sacrifice everything for my child.

I remember how terrified Paige had been, her eyes big and not understanding what was happening. I remember trying to smile at her reassuringly, all the while screaming inside. After he saw his message had the desired result, he left me to lie down with Paige.

I coaxed her back to sleep and stayed with her the night. The next morning I explained to her she'd had a bad nightmare.

When Rick died so unexpectedly, I felt safe for the first time in years. Free. I never saw the point of burdening Paige with the truth about her father, or my parents with knowledge they could do nothing about. That's why I moved back to Michigan the first opportunity I had.

Looking into my daughter's face, I realize she's become too savvy for me to try and lie my way out of this one, but before I have a chance to respond, Gray speaks up.

"I should probably check in at the shop," he announces, his gaze sliding from Paige—who is still glaring—to me. "And maybe leave you two to talk. I'll check in with you in a bit."

Despite my daughter's sharp attention, he closes in on me, brushes his lips against mine, and heads for the door.

I'm not sure whether to be upset or relieved he's leaving.

CHAPTER TWENTY-TWO

Robin

"So when? When you were staying with me?"

I reluctantly look at my angry daughter as the door closes behind Gray.

"Yes," I admit.

Moved to find out she'd caught a flight home so I wouldn't be alone for New Year's as well, I hate ruining her sweet gesture.

"I don't understand," she says agitated. "For years you told me you would never set foot in Manhattan. That being there would be too overwhelming. Why?"

I don't immediately answer, wondering how much or how little I should tell her. Is it time for the truth? A truth I had hoped never to have to share if I could help it? A truth I'd prayed had gone down when those towers fell?

Even Mom assumed I'd sit in Liberty State Park by the dock, staring at the Manhattan skyline while grieving the loss of my husband. She had no idea I was heading to the Memorial Pools.

Tired of waiting, Paige rages on as tears well in her eyes and the betrayal she feels is visible on her face.

"For years I asked if perhaps we could visit the memorial, until I finally went to see it by myself when I moved there. I wanted desperately to see his name on the memorial, but you wouldn't come any closer than Liberty State Park and watch the Tribute in Light from there. Why would you go without me? Why lie about it?"

"Honey, it's...it's something I needed to do on my own." I take her hand and pull her with me to the living room where I sit down, waiting for her to do the same. "People deal with loss differently," I say carefully when she finally sits. "I have my way to cope but never wanted that to influence the way you grieved his loss. The way you remember him."

She yanks her hand from mine and abruptly gets to her feet.

"You have no idea how I remember him, Mom. Or maybe I should say how I've tried hard to forget him."

My mouth drops open.

"Why would you want to—"

"Oh, come on, Mom," she interrupts me, cutting her hand through the air. "You can't be that blind. The man held a gun to my head. He threatened to kill me—it left me with nightmares for years—it's the most vivid memory of him I have."

"But..." I sputter, but nothing more comes out. I'm too stunned.

I remember right after he died she would sometimes come in my room at night to ask me if I was sure her daddy wasn't coming back. Those were the only times she talked about him. I always thought she missed him and wanted to sleep with me for comfort. Turns out I was wrong.

"Why didn't you say anything?"

"Because I was afraid to upset *you*. Mom, I was five—not stupid. Dad always scared the crap out of me. Did you know my nightmares stopped when I saw his name chiseled in stone? I needed to see it for myself."

She turns on her heel and disappears in the direction of the bedrooms. When I hear a door slam, I drop my head in my hands.

How stupid of me to think I could make her forget what he put us through. She's right, even at five she had been sharp as a tack. Never said a word out of place when her father was around. Hell, other than occasionally asking me to take her to the 9/11 Memorial since it opened when she was fifteen, she never mentioned his name.

I should've known.

I rub my face in my hands and force myself to my feet, following her down the hall. My daughter is an adult and she deserves to know.

She's lying on her old bed, facing the wall when I walk in.

"Oh, honey..." I lie down in bed beside her, staring up at the ceiling. "I'd hoped you'd never have to find out your father wasn't a good man," I start. "I was still so young and wide-eyed, living in the big city. I didn't have a lot of experience and was swept off my feet when this older, handsome, and successful man paid me attention. I got pregnant, he wanted to get married, and you know? Life was pretty good for a while."

I keep my eyes on the ceiling but can feel her turning in the bed.

"Until?" she asks softly.

"Until after I had you. I'm not sure exactly when it started, but I blamed myself at first. I was a brand-new mom and my support system lived halfway across the country. I didn't recognize it as postpartum depression at the time. Your father was a busy man, he didn't adjust well to sharing my attention and forced me to see a doctor, a friend of his, who put me on anti-depressants."

I roll on my side and find myself looking into my daughter's identical eyes.

"I saw less and less of him and days would go by where I

wouldn't see or hear from him at all. Whenever I had a chance to question him, he blamed it on me. It took a while, but I eventually started getting angry. I stopped taking the pills without telling him and booked a flight for you and I to go see Gram and Pap. I needed some space to get my head clear."

She has a pained look on her face and I take one of her hands in mine.

"He wasn't happy with me when he discovered. Told me, given my fragile mental state, he wouldn't hesitate taking you from me. Claimed his doctor friend would attest to the fact I wasn't of sound mind. He threatened if I tried as much as to leave the house with you without his permission, he'd have me committed. I was cut off from Gram and Pap, any friends I'd made. He canceled our landline and took my cell phone. If I wanted or needed to call, he..."

"Oh, Mom," she sighs.

"I tried to get away, honey. Several times, but I couldn't risk losing you. Your father worked for some shady characters. Dangerous and powerful people."

"What do you mean? What kind of people?"

An image of a meeting in Rick's home office I walked in on, after putting Paige down for a nap, surfaces. The door I'd just pushed open ripped from my hand, and a gun pressed to my forehead was my first real indication my husband's business dealings weren't aboveboard. I could read the ruthlessness from the eyes of the goon on the other end of the gun, and I promptly let go of my bladder.

Rick yelled at me. I can't even remember what he said, but I do remember leaving the room and shutting the door behind me before I ran straight for Paige's room. He found me there hours later, sitting on the floor in shock, with my daughter in my arms.

"The kind of people you don't ever want to be associated with, sweetheart. That incident scared the crap out of me, and I was desperately thinking up ways I could get us safely away, but he always seemed to be a step ahead of me."

"Is that what happened when he had a gun to my head?"

I nod. "I still don't know how he discovered, but he walked in that night with a bag of necessities I'd been hiding under the back deck."

"Jesus, Mom."

I stroke the back of my hand over her cheek.

"That was September fourth."

———

Gray

"I thought you said you weren't going to be in?" Jimmy's head pops up from under the hood of the Cherokee he's working on when I walk in. "Robin okay?"

"She's fine. Her girl showed up. Giving them some space."

"Her girl?"

"Paige. Her daughter." I take a look around the shop and notice two other vehicles. "What's with those?"

"Oil change and tire rotation. Kyle was supposed to get to those, but he's out with the tow truck. Accident at the on-ramp to Highway 10."

I grab my coveralls off the peg on the wall and pull them on. May as well make myself useful. Jimmy lifts his chin before ducking under the hood again in silent acknowledgement.

We work in silence with Jimmy's favorite rock radio station blaring classics, when someone taps me on the shoulder. I jump and swing around, not having heard anyone approach.

I bristle at the sight of a smiling Becca in front of me.

"What do you want?"

She blanches, her face instantly falling at my gruff tone, and behind me Jimmy coughs in warning. Right. Customer service.

"What can I do for you?" I mellow my tone.

"Well..." she drawls, tucking her hair behind her ear. "I'm having some problems with my car."

I try to wait her out, but when it appears there's not more forthcoming and she bats her eyes at me, my impatience finally wins.

"What problems, Becca?"

"Oh, well...it makes an odd noise."

To stop myself from rolling my eyes I close them, take a deep breath in, and wipe my hands on a rag.

"Let's hear it."

Her aging Toyota is parked in the drive outside the bay doors and I walk past her out of the shop. Her footsteps sound behind me as she follows.

"Keys?"

She hands them over and I climb behind the wheel, putting the key in the ignition when the passenger door opens and Becca slides in.

"What are you doing?"

She turns to me with surprise on her face at my snapped question.

"I...uh...assumed we were going for a test drive?"

"Not planning on it," I grumble, cranking the engine.

"You know, I was thinking—"

I hold up my hand to cut her off, while I try to listen for whatever odd sounds she thinks she hears. There it is, a faint rustling. Leaving the engine running, I pop the hood and get out.

A firm brush of my hand to clear leftover fall leaves from under the vents solves the problem immediately. I slam the hood closed, reach in the driver's side, and turn off the engine.

"There. Fixed," I mutter, dropping the keys on the seat before backing out.

I turn to head back to the car I was working on when she calls out behind me.

"Wait!"

Reluctantly I stop in my tracks and wait for her to catch up.

"I was just thinking...do you have something going on New Year's Eve? We could—"

Aside from the fact Becca clearly still hasn't gotten the message, she knows damn well I'm seeing Robin, which rattles my chain even more.

"No."

"But I haven't even—"

"Doesn't matter what you have to say, the answer is no. I thought I'd been clear I have no intention of going there. I'm with Robin and you know it, so why you would think I'd be even remotely interested in doing anything with you fucking boggles my mind. Go home, Becca, I'm not interested."

Jimmy is standing in the open bay door when I approach, and I realize I may have been loud enough for him to hear. I don't bother looking back when I hear her car door slam and the engine start up.

"Ouch," Jimmy comments when I reach him. "Harsh."

"Not a word of a lie."

"True, but still..."

"Why don't you take her out then?" I snap.

"Fuck no," he says immediately, sharply shaking his head.

"Right, that's what I thought."

Indicating this discussion over, I dive back under the car I was working on.

It's late afternoon when the last vehicle is picked up and I head back to my apartment for a quick shower and a change. I strip out of my clothes and dump them on the floor beside the hamper, since it's already full. I should probably head over to the coin laundry downtown; I'm running out of clean clothes.

A muffled ringing sounds from the pile of laundry on the floor and I scramble to fish my phone from my dirty jeans.

"Hey."

"Am I disturbing you?" Robin asks, and at the sound of her voice my flaccid cock immediately stirs to life.

I chuckle. "Not in the way you're thinking. Just about to have a shower. How are things there?"

"Good. Thanks for giving us some time to clear the air."

"Since I'm the one who overshared, it was the least I could do. Other than to say I'm sorry."

"Turns out it was a talk that was long overdue, so don't apologize, I should probably be thanking you."

"Oh?"

There's a moment's silence on the other side before she responds in a soft voice.

"I'll share, just not right now, please? I'm still processing."

"Sure thing, Sunshine," I consent easily. "Thought about what you guys want to eat? I'm heading out to get a load in at the Laundromat so I'll be downtown anyway. I'll pick something up."

"Paige is actually cooking dinner."

Shit. The food had been a good excuse to see her.

"All right, no problem. I'll...uh...be in touch."

"Bring it here," she says, and it takes me a minute to realize she's talking about the laundry. "Paige is counting on you, and I'm doing laundry anyway."

"You sure?" I ask, realizing I sound a tad eager, evidenced by her deep chuckle.

"Positive. Your boxer briefs can party with my granny panties."

"Mom!" I hear Paige's voice in the background and bite my lip not to break out laughing.

"Oh, keep your shorts on," Robin mutters at her before addressing me, "Not you."

I lose the battle with hilarity when I hear her daughter's outraged cry on the other end.

Fuck, I like everything about this woman. Even the teasing way she interacts with her girl.

"Give me half an hour. Do you need anything from town?"

"I think we're good here. Paige? Need Gray to bring anything?"

"Gray! Bring me a gag for Mom!"

CHAPTER TWENTY-THREE

Gray

It's been a couple of days since Paige showed up.

I started keeping a bit of a low profile at Robin's place when it became clear concern for her mother was only part of the reason the girl cut her visit to Florida short. Apparently the boyfriend—or now ex-boyfriend—turned out to be a spoiled little son of a bitch. His wealthy parents had looked down their noses at Paige after discovering her mother worked at a diner in nowhere Michigan. She hung in there for almost a week, being made to feel inferior, before she packed her bags and told them they could keep their precious boy.

Paige was still a bit reserved around me and I'd slept in my own bed every night, giving them some much-needed time alone. I've kept busy at the shop; joining them for dinner a few nights when weather didn't have us work overtime at Olson's.

I miss Robin. I never thought I'd be that guy pining over a woman, but I seem to be doing a fair bit of it.

For almost two decades I've worn my solitude like a protective cloak and within a few months it's become an uncomfortable weight I can't wait to be rid of.

Because of her.

Robin hasn't yet enlightened me on exactly what the drama was about when her girl first arrived, but with Paige leaving to get back to New Jersey tomorrow, I plan to remind her.

Despite the early hour on a weekend, the diner already looks quite busy when I walk in. My eyes are immediately drawn to Robin, who appears to be dropping an order with the kitchen. When she sees me, I'm greeted with a big smirk and a slight nudge of her head in the direction of Mrs. Chapman's table. Enzo Trotti is sitting across from her.

I shake my head at Robin, a grin on my face. Then she raises her eyebrows and points at a booth in the back where Paige is sitting by herself staring out the window. Understanding her message, I walk over.

"This seat taken?"

Paige ducks her head and swipes at her eyes. Shit. Not sure how equipped I am to deal with tears.

"Go ahead," she says in a soft voice.

I slide in the bench opposite her.

"Have you ordered yet?"

She shakes her head. "Not yet."

I don't have to look at the menu; I know what I want. Instead I carefully touch the back of her hands, clenched on the table in front of her.

"Not known for talking, but I'm a decent listener."

She looks at me with the same hesitation I've seen on her face the past week.

"I don't even know you."

"You haven't tried," I counter her snippy comment. It seems to startle her and I use her momentary shock to soften my accusation with, "Please."

"Men are pigs." She lifts her chin in challenge.

"Not gonna argue that."

I struggle not to chuckle, especially when she narrows her eyes on me. Glad to know at least some of her reservation with me is because I'm one of *them*.

Finally she drops her eyes to her still-wringing hands.

"I called him last night," she whispers and I lean forward to catch her words. "I'm heading back tomorrow and hoped maybe we could clear the air beforehand."

"I take it that didn't go as planned?"

She shakes her head and I notice her swallowing hard before she speaks.

"No. He wasn't very nice. Said he'd made a mistake. That I'd upset his mother." She suddenly snorts derisively and continues with a hiss, her eyes shooting fire. "His mother? You should've heard what that stuck-up cow said about Mom."

Fierce little thing is protective of her mother, and I understand her reluctance toward me better. Still, I get the sense she may have held hope he'd come after her.

I reach out again and take her hand in mine, giving it a squeeze.

"He's a little sniveling weasel, hiding behind his momma's apron. Clearly he's no match for you. He's not man enough."

She shows surprise, a small, pleased smile tugging at her mouth.

"Sorry to keep you waiting."

Becca's voice is like a pitcher of ice water down my back as I straighten to look up at her. I didn't see her car in the parking lot and assumed she was on a later shift. Guess not.

To avoid my anger rising to the surface, I turn to Paige.

"What do you want, sweetheart?" I ask her, the endearment slipping from my mouth, but before she can answer I feel Becca leaning over the table.

"Oh? Is this a new one already, Gray? Bit young, don't you

think? I guess after all those years in the slammer, you've got plenty of pent-up energy to burn off."

I hear Paige's sharp intake of breath as she backs away from the table as far as the booth will allow. I thought Robin might've mentioned my past to her, but clearly it's news to the girl. That'll teach me to assume so much.

"Awww," Becca drawls, a calculating glint in her eyes. "You didn't know he's an ex-con? Murder too."

I push out of my seat, ready drag her out of the fucking diner but Robin already has her by the arm.

"You're fired," she snarls at Becca.

"You can't fire me," the bitch sputters.

"The way you're treating the customers? Absolutely I can."

"Here, I can help," Enzo comes walking up, taking Becca's other arm.

"You're not very nice," Mrs. Chapman contributes, leaning out of her booth.

"Let go of me!"

Becca shrugs free and tears her apron off, flinging it in the direction of the counter where Kim stands, glaring at her.

"Key," Kim says, holding up her hand as Becca stomps past her to grab her stuff. "I'll need the key."

I notice the quick glance the bitch throws at Robin before she straightens her shoulders and turns to Kim.

"I lost it."

With that, she turns on her heel and marches out the door.

The diner is dead silent for a second before people turn back to their meals, and I sit down across from a wide-eyed Paige. She's not looking at the door Becca just disappeared through, but straight at me.

"Sorry about that," Robin says approaching our table, and looks from her daughter to me and back. "Everything all right here? Can I put in your order?"

"I lost my appetite," Paige mumbles, scrambling out of the booth and darting past her mother.

Robin throws me a pained look and takes off after her.

I get up too. Not feeling much like breakfast now.

"Don't let it get to you," Enzo says when I pass him and Mrs. Chapman.

I grunt in response but keep walking.

———

Robin

"Hold up!"

Paige ducks into the bathroom, but I'm right behind her, finding her leaning on the sink with her head down.

"Are you insane? Murder, Mom? Do you have a death wish or something? God! You have the worst taste in men."

Ouch.

That hurt.

I want to lash out, put her in her place, but yelling at each other is not going to improve this situation. I should've told her, but she was already so leery of Gray, I really didn't want to feed into it by telling her his history. Hindsight being twenty/twenty, I should've told her right away.

"Don't jump to conclusions, Paige. Don't make judgments until you have all the information."

She pushes off the sink and swings around.

"Was he in jail for murder?"

"Second-degree, but—"

"Oh my God, Mom!" Both her hands come up and grab at her hair, a grimace on her face. "I can't even talk to you right now." She ducks into one of the stalls and slams the door shut.

I close my eyes and tilt my head back when the door hits me

in the back.

"Oops, sorry, dear." Mrs. Chapman slips inside and turns to face me. "Kim is looking for you. The orders are piling up."

I groan, looking at the stall door where my daughter is hiding out.

"You go ahead. I've got this," she says placing a hand on my shoulder.

"Mrs. Chapman, I—"

"Go. I'll look after your girl."

With one last look at the firmly closed door, I nod at Mrs. Chapman. I'm not sure I'll be able to get through to Paige in this state, but maybe she'll have better luck.

Kim's head turns my way when I come down the hallway. A few people are waiting to pay at the counter and the pass-through is loaded with plates. Yikes.

I mumble a quick, "Sorry," to Kim and grab the first order.

My eyes go straight to the table where Gray had been sitting just minutes before, but is now empty. Damn. He took off. I briefly consider if he might be running again, but I have a diner full of hungry people and quickly file it away to worry about later.

In no time I have food in front of waiting patrons and am taking orders for new ones. I'm handing those in with the kitchen when Mrs. Chapman appears, a subdued Paige following her as they make their way to the booth where Enzo waits. They were in the bathroom for a good fifteen minutes, and I'm struggling to keep my curiosity in check as I go about my work.

"You okay?" Kim asks, when I stop to make a fresh pot of coffee.

"Yes. I'm so sorry about all that."

"Not sure why you think any of that had anything to do with you. It wasn't the first time she was rude with customers. Good riddance if you ask me."

"But it leaves us shorthanded," I protest.

Kim shrugs.

"Not for long. Holidays are over. This is the last weekend before everyone's back to work and it'll slow down. Besides, I talked to Shirley last night; with Mike safely locked away, she plans to return to Beaverton some time next week. She wanted to know if she still had a job to come back to."

"That's good news."

I feel a little guilty I haven't been in touch with Shirley as much since Paige got here, but I'm glad to hear she'll be back home soon.

"Orders up!" Jason calls from the kitchen.

I collect the plates and bring them to Mrs. Chapman and Enzo, who seem deep in conversation with my daughter.

"What can I get you, Paige?" I try again.

Paige looks at me from under her eyebrows.

"Can I have a coffee and a muffin or something?"

She doesn't have to say anything; I can see the apology in her eyes. I stroke my hand over her hair while sending my own silent message to Mrs. Chapman, thanking her for whatever it was she conveyed to my daughter.

"Coming right up."

"Oh, and Mom?"

"Yeah?"

"Can you put in an order for whatever Gray likes for breakfast for takeout?"

God, I have such a great kid.

My heart swells in my chest and I smile down at her.

"You bet, sweetheart."

Fifteen minutes later, I hand her a container with a Western omelet for Gray and a carryout cup of coffee.

"Can we talk when you get home?" she asks.

"Of course. I'll be home midafternoon. Want me to bring home something for dinner?"

"No, I'll take care of it."

She leans in to kiss my cheek before she walks out. I see her get in the rental car and watch as she drives off, turning right toward Olson's.

When she's out of sight, I head straight for Mrs. Chapman's table.

"Should I be worried?" I ask her.

"Good Lord, no. You raised a sensible young lady. It didn't take her long to realize she may have overreacted. Something she's determined to set straight herself. It's commendable."

"Whatever it is you said to her; thank you. Maybe I should give Gray—"

"Let them figure it out," Enzo interrupts. "They're both adults, they can handle it."

"He's right," Mrs. Chapman agrees. "And while I have you here, could I have the bill, please?"

"Actually," her breakfast companion offers. "I'll take the bill."

"You'll do no such thing," Mrs. Chapman protests, her spine suddenly ramrod straight as she visibly bristles.

"Watch me. You're not paying for me, Madeline. End of story," Enzo declares firmly, putting his words into action when he produces a billfold and pulls out a few bills, handing them to me. "Keep the change."

"Well, I never..." she continues to sputter, but I notice it's not quite as convincing.

Enzo grins wide and reaches across the table the moment I clear their dishes, covering her hand with his.

"Tell you what; next time you can buy me breakfast. But only if you let me buy you dinner the night before."

"Enzo!"

Chuckling and slightly mortified at the surplus of information, I rush to settle their bill.

———

Gray

. . .

I've barely started on the transmission flush when I hear Kyle call
me over the sounds of the Eagles coming from the radio.

"Yeah?"

As soon as I straighten I see Paige, shuffling a little nervously
in the open bay door, a Styrofoam box in her hands. I'm surprised
to see her here, given her reaction earlier. Kyle is lingering close
by, his eyes honed in on Robin's pretty daughter.

"Yo, Kyle!" I call out, getting his attention as I wipe my hands
on a rag. "Don't you have work to do?"

Even at this distance, I can see a blush color his cheeks as he
quickly returns to the car he was working on. Smart kid.

"Hey."

"Hi," she mutters when I approach. "I brought you breakfast.
As an apology. I'm...I wasn't...I overreacted. It's just Mom hasn't
had—"

I hold up my hand to stop her.

"I get it, girl. It's all good."

Surprisingly I find I mean it. That easy.

"But I was rude, then I yelled at Mom until Mrs. Chapman
explained a few things..." I'm starting to realize there's no way I'm
going to stop the flow, so I'll just wait her out. "...And then I saw
you'd left. I felt so bad for making a scene, and being rude to you
the whole time, and I'm so sorry."

"You done?" I finally ask.

"Yup," she says, nodding. "Totally done."

"Good." I grab the container from her hands and start walking
to the office.

Halfway there I check over my shoulder to find her still
standing in the same spot.

"Well, come on," I call out. "You can get to know me over
breakfast. I'm fucking starving."

A smile tugs at her mouth as she hustles to catch up with me.

CHAPTER TWENTY-FOUR

Robin

I want to cry but I don't.

I'll save it for later, when I don't have my daughter sitting beside me as I drive her to Lansing to catch her flight back to Newark.

She's struggling, she told me as much last night, no longer sure what she's doing in New Jersey. Josh—that little prick—turns out to have had a lot to do with her wanting to settle there after she graduated last year. Had I known it was over a boy I'd have cautioned her, which I'm sure she knew when she decided to keep his existence a secret until I visited in September.

I hate she's hurting, but in hindsight I'm glad she went with him to see his family over Christmas. Being around them had brought out Josh's true colors, and luckily, my girl had enough self-worth to remove herself from that situation. Doesn't mean it's not painful, that much is clear from the drawn and pale girl sitting beside me.

Last night she announced she didn't want to go back to her

apartment or her job. As tempting as it was to tell her to stay home, I don't want this to be another decision made because of that guy. I wanted to be her friend but knew I had to be her mother. So I reminded her she had a responsibility to her employer, an apartment she couldn't simply abandon, and friends she couldn't just drop.

In the end, she'd agreed and would give herself a month or two to really consider what *she* wanted.

The parent in me is happy with that decision, but my mother's heart is heavy.

"When is Gram coming home again?" she asks, when we see the first traffic sign for the airport.

"Not sure of the exact date, but I believe she said the third week of March." I glance over and catch her chewing on her bottom lip, something she tends to do when she's thinking hard. "Why?" I prompt her.

Her eyes flash to me.

"I just wonder if I decide to come back before she's supposed to return, whether I could maybe use her place until I find something of my own."

"I'm sure she won't mind, but why don't you just come home?"

There's a bit of a pause before she answers.

"No offense, Mom, but you have a boyfriend. I don't want to cramp your style any more than I need to."

"You're not cramping my style and besides, my 'boyfriend' has a place too."

She snorts. "I can't see you frequenting the Dirty Dog, Mom."

"Did he say something to you?"

I immediately have my bristles up. Nobody's shared with me any details of what they talked about when Paige dropped off her peace offering with him yesterday, but I assumed they'd worked things out. Maybe I was wrong.

"No. Geeze, Mom. You should know him better than that."

Put in my place by my child. She's right, I should realize

there's no way the man I've gotten to know over the past months would say anything that could hurt my girl or me.

"You're right. I should."

Fifteen minutes later, I pull up in the drop-off zone at departures.

"Are you sure you don't want me to come in with you?"

"I'll be fine, Mom. This is easier."

She doesn't add she doesn't want to prolong goodbye any longer than is absolutely necessary, but she doesn't need to; I feel the same. Funny how neither of us have been particularly emotional at previous goodbyes over the last few years, but seem to be this time around. Not all that surprising though, given the deep heart-to-hearts we've shared this past week. Both of us are pretty raw, but probably more in tune than ever before.

Honesty has scraped some wounds raw, but hopefully now they can heal without ugly scars.

"Love you, Mom" Paige says, once her bags are waiting on the curb.

I open my arms to her and hold her securely to me, taking in a deep breath of her scent. I wish I could hold her safe like this forever, but I know the best thing I can do for her is let her go. Let her make her own mistakes and find her own solutions. Parenting never gets easier.

"Love you too, sweetheart. So much." Reluctantly I let go and force my tears back. "Call me when you get there."

"I will."

She smiles through tears, grabs her bags, and heads for the entrance. I stand there until she disappears inside when I'm startled by a car horn. I quickly slide behind the wheel, making room for the waiting car behind me.

I manage to hold it together until I pull up outside Mom's house. I know she's made arrangements for her mail to be picked up, and a friend has her plants to look after, but I want to make sure everything is in order. Especially since it's entirely possible Paige will be staying here for a while.

It's appropriately raining when I get out of my vehicle, cold sleet hitting me in the face, mingling with my tears.

The house smells like Mom when I step in the door and I have a sudden urge to hear her voice. Hanging up my coat and kicking off my shoes, so I don't track dirt onto her pristine carpet, I head for the kitchen, grabbing the towel hanging on the stove handle to wipe my face. Then I sit down at the island and pull out my phone.

"Is she gone?"

My mom, so intuitive when it comes to her *girls*.

"Yes." My voice sounds wobbly even to my own ears.

"Oh, honey. Where are you now? You're not driving are you?"

"I'm at your place. Just wanted to check on things here."

"Why? Is everything all right?"

"It's fine, Mom."

For the next few minutes I recount the conversation with Paige about her staying here for a bit. Mom is instantly on board, which makes me feel a little better. Whatever Paige ends up deciding to do, she's covered with all her options.

As always, talking with my mom is like a warm blanket around my shoulders, and by the time we end the call, I feel better equipped to face the drive back. I do a quick check of the house —everything appears in order—and lock back up.

During my drive home I start thinking about Gray. I missed him last night. He messaged me at some point, letting me know he wouldn't be coming by so Paige and I had the night to ourselves—which was sweet—but I missed him anyway.

We hadn't made any plans and part of me was nervous about facing him alone. I'm not sure what—if anything—Paige shared with him about her father, but I know I at least owe him some explanation. I had tightly guarded the truth about my marriage to protect my family. However, discovering my daughter already knew more than I thought, there's no real point in keeping it a secret. At least not from Gray.

My mother is another matter. I'm not sure how much to tell her, but I have a couple of months to figure that out.

Gray is my first concern, and when I hit town limits—instead of taking the turn home—I keep driving and pull into the Dirty Dog parking lot.

———

Gray

Un-fucking-believable.

With the garage closed and Robin out of town, I spent the day in my apartment reading. Sounds from the Dirty Dog downstairs started filtering through and I could smell the grill up here. Getting hungry and more than a little claustrophobic, I made my way down the outside stairs, thinking maybe I could grab a burger and play a game of pool if any of the old guys are around.

I was about to round my truck parked at the bottom of the stairs, when I noticed it was sitting lower than it should be. All four of my goddamn tires sliced.

"Who'd you piss off?"

I lift my head to see Derek Francisi walking up. I called the police right away. No way this was an accident, as the clean slices in each of my tires attest to and Francisi clearly agrees with.

"I didn't see and it's possible there are some people out there still holding a grudge, but if I had to venture a guess..."

He bends down to examine my rear tire and whistles between his teeth.

"By all means, do."

I share my suspicions and the reasons behind it. He does little more than raise his eyebrows when I mention Becca's name.

"Interesting. That's a name that has come up in recent days."

Now it's my turn to look surprised.

"How so?"

"Mike Hancock was the first one to mention her when I finally had a chance to question him a few days ago. Claims the woman asked him to pick something up she'd left in the office at the diner. Of course, he also claimed he'd just been defending himself when, according to him, he was attacked by your lady friend." He chuckles when I mutter a heartfelt profanity and a promise of substantial physical harm. "Anyway, things came up and I haven't had a chance to speak to Ms. Simms to get her side of things. I did happen to talk to Kim Hudson at the diner yesterday, who mentioned Ms. Simms no longer worked there."

I flip up my collar when the slight drizzle turns into sleet coming down in earnest. Francisi tucks away his notepad and motions me to follow him to his cruiser. I barely flinch when I open his passenger side door and slide in.

"What is the woman's hang-up with you?" he asks, turning sideways in his seat.

"Fuck if I know. When 9/11 happened, I never saw or heard from her again. Not even an attempt. Then I'm released and suddenly she shows up here in Beaverton, wanting to reconnect and not taking no for an answer."

"And you don't know why?"

"Not a damn clue."

"Okay, guess I'll have to pay Ms. Simms a visit, but first let me see if anyone at the Dirty Dog has seen anything."

The sleet has let up again so we make our way inside. The smell of hot grease has my stomach grumbling as we sidle up to the bar. Bunker is chatting with a few regulars at the far end but comes over when he sees us.

"What can I get you guys?"

"Actually," Francisi answers. "I'm working, I just have a few questions."

Bunker glances questioningly at me but I shrug.

"I'll wait 'til he's done."

"Fire away, Francisi."

"Have you by any chance noticed anything unusual out in the parking lot today? Anyone hanging around who didn't have reason to be there?"

"Here? Why?"

"We'll get to that," Francisi answers firmly.

Bunker takes his time thinking before he responds.

"Not really. I opened up at noon and it was pretty quiet for the first hour before people started dropping in. Probably no more than three or four vehicles in the parking lot until maybe an hour ago."

"Anyone come in or out of the side door?"

The door Francisi is referring to is right underneath the stairway to the apartment. The dumpster is on the other side and I heard the door open and close a few times this afternoon, but that's not unusual. Staff is tossing out garbage all the time. The kitchen is right there.

"No. Not that I know of."

"I heard the door at least twice," I contribute, turning to the cop to clarify. "My apartment is right upstairs."

"Could've been Sammie," he suggests.

Sammie is one of the kitchen employees. An old guy, probably in his seventies, who's apparently been a staple at the Dirty Dog for twenty or so years.

"That the only one?" Francisi asks.

"As far as I know." Bunker shrugs. "Well, except for my cousin. She popped in when I was still cleaning up from last night. She offered to take the garbage on her way out the door."

"Your cousin?"

"Yeah. She lives in Clare but has crashed at my place from time to time, since she started working at the diner."

I don't realize I've gotten to my feet, my knuckles white

holding onto the bar, until I feel Francisi's restraining hand on my shoulder.

"Fucking Becca? She's your cousin?" I bite off, faintly registering the stunned look on Bunker's face.

"You know her?"

His surprise seems genuine enough, but I'm still unable to let the tension go from my hands.

"Any idea where I can find her?" Derek asks.

"At the diner."

"She got canned yesterday," I volunteer.

"What? She never said anything." He shakes his head in confusion. "Wait, how do you know Becca?"

I take in a deep breath to try and get my temper under control before I repeat to Bunker what I told the cop earlier, noting the look of disbelief on his face when I fill him in.

"Look," he says when I'm done. "I'm sorry, man, I had no idea. She never let on she knew you, not even when I mentioned..." he lets his words trail off and clenches his jaw.

"Mentioned what?" Francisi asks.

I catch a mix of anger and regret when Bunker throws a glance my way.

"*Fuck,*" he hisses. "My aunt's birthday in October; I took my mother to Clare to see her. Becca was there. I may have mentioned Frank leaving you the Dirty Dog."

My blood roars in my ears and white-hot anger is beating its way to the surface. *That miserable bitch.* I grab the first thing I can find—the inverted glass covering one of the beer taps—and haul out, flinging the glass to the far wall.

"Jesus fucking Christ, man!" I hear Bunker call out, as I'm spun around and pinned to the edge of the bar, Francisi's bulk holding me in place. Now panic is creeping in. Snaps of being pressed face forward into whitewashed concrete and held there by too many hands start flashing in front of my eyes. I struggle against the hold, hearing a man's voice muttering something by my ear but the words all blend together.

"Let him go."

That I hear loud and clear through the roaring in my ears and I grab on to the sound of her voice, rising like a beacon from the ruins of my life.

"You're okay," she whispers, and I feel her cool hand on my face. "Just breathe. You're fine."

CHAPTER TWENTY-FIVE

Robin

"Eat a little more."

I watch his silver head shake. He's barely eaten half of what I've seen him put away before, but I'm not going to push him.

He hasn't spoken a word since I coaxed him away from the bar and into the passenger side of my SUV. Not on the drive here, not while I heated up some of yesterday's leftovers for us, and not during dinner.

I take his half-finished plate and my empty one and set them on the counter in the kitchen.

I'm not sure what to do at this point. He's in a weird place where I don't feel I can reach him. Something happened back in that bar and Officer Francisi's explanations only go so far.

I'm beyond furious at that bitch, Becca. Not only does it appear her pursuit of Gray had little to do with him and everything to do with what she thought he could provide for her, but it turns she also doesn't take rejection well, judging by the four slashed tires on Gray's truck.

Francisi mentioned he had reason to believe she also may have had a hand in last week's break-in at the diner. The logic behind that eludes me at this time, but I'm sure he has his reasons for saying that.

"Let's watch something mindless on TV," I suggest, finally pushing away from the counter. When I notice he's not moving, I walk over and take his hand. I sit down on the couch and he sits beside me. "Unless you want to talk," I try.

His unreadable eyes meet mine, a spark of heat burning through when I put my hand on his thigh.

"Nothing to say." His voice is raspy, the way it can be when he first wakes up.

"Okay," I decide to concede instead of forcing him to speak.

Hopefully giving him some space he'll eventually feel comfortable opening up. His reaction is not just about anger; I get the sense it's about pain. Maybe if I open up first.

I grab the remote, find an old episode of *Criminal Minds*, and pull my legs up under me. Then I coax him to put his head on my lap so I can massage his scalp, something I've discovered helps him relax.

"My husband was an accountant," I start softly.

He tries to lift his head but I push it back down, never changing my soothing touch as I explain the history behind his first glimpse of me last September. The hand he has resting on his thigh occasionally clenches into a fist, but he doesn't make another attempt to lift his head.

Not even when I'm done talking and my eyes drift back, mindlessly watching whatever is on TV.

"Paige didn't know?" he finally asks.

"I didn't want her to, but it turns out she remembered enough to know he wasn't a good man. Killed me to fill in some of the details." Then I snort at the irony. "Seems we were each trying to protect the other."

"Probably shouldn't say this." Gray suddenly sits up and places his hands on either side of my face. "But I'm glad the fucker is dead."

"Me too," I admit a second before his mouth slams down on mine.

I groan at the loss of his lips when he ends the kiss too soon. I've missed getting lost in him.

"Can we go for a walk?"

I'm a little surprised at the request.

"Now?"

It's dark outside and it's probably cooled off quite a bit, but there's a plea in the way he looks at me, so I don't argue and get to my feet. Zeus lifts his head briefly when I pass the chair he adopted as his bed. We shrug into our coats and shoes and make our way outside.

It's gorgeous. The cold temperature comes with a beautifully crisp, clear sky filled with stars.

One of the perks of living in a small community, a fair distance from any large cities, is the amazing night skies.

"Zip up," Gray grumbles, turning me so he can close the zipper on my coat, tugging my hood over my head. Then his large warm hand closes over mine and tucks both in his coat pocket.

We head down the driveway to the road. There are trails behind the house but it would be too dark under the tree cover. There are hardly any cars on this road and this way we can see the stars.

"It's easier to talk out here," he finally says when we've been walking for a bit. "Not enclosed. It still bothers me sometimes. Gets my heart rate up. Makes me anxious."

My hand warmly in his spasms at his confession.

"I like walking," I say clumsily, but he seems to understand what I'm trying to express and gives my hand a squeeze.

"I lost it today."

Sensing he needs to share at his own pace, and afraid I'll blurt out some other inane comment, I keep my silence and wait him out.

"I didn't hear them coming," he says, so low it's hard for me to hear. "Three of them. I hadn't been inside for forty-eight hours yet. Fucking cell block C."

My hand is getting sweaty in his big paw, not liking where this is going.

"They got me from behind and I was shoved face-first into the shower wall. One of them was ready with a balled up shirt he stuffed in my mouth when I opened it to yell. Pinned against that wall...*fuck*...I knew what was coming. I'd heard the taunts. *Fresh meat*."

I hear a whimper I realize is coming from me and his hands squeezes mine again.

"They didn't. Didn't get the chance. A guard walking by must've had a feeling something was off and came in to check."

I can feel a shudder run through his body.

"Never turned my back on anyone after that. Never."

"My God, Gray..."

"Lost my temper earlier, flung a glass at the wall and Francisi was pinning me."

"From behind," I fill in, and turn my head to find his eyes on me.

"Yeah."

"You went back there," I conclude.

"Sure did."

"That's understandable."

He stops us and pulls our hands from his pocket, bringing them up to his chest. He curves his other hand around the back of my neck and drops his head until the tip of his nose almost touches mine.

"Is it? I've been so repressed all these years, so controlled, but lately it's like all my emotions have been unleashed. I can't rein them in; anger, fear, even love... *shit*... What if I hurt you?"

"You wouldn't." I grab his wrist firmly and pull myself up on my toes so our noses touch. His eyes hold mine with an intensity that makes me want to cry.

"I couldn't," he finally admits. "You're the light at the end of the tunnel. You're sunshine and fresh air. *Jesus*, I'm fucked up beyond imagination, but you look at me like that and make me feel whole."

Instead of tears, I feel a smile spread over my face.

"Good."

I lift my face and kiss him sweetly. Then I turn and start walking back to the house, his hand still in mine.

"Robin?" he says.

"Yeah?"

"I love you."

I turn my head and find the truth of his words in his gorgeous eyes.

"I know."

————

Gray

I can't get her clothes off fast enough.

She backs into the bedroom, already kicking off her jeans as I'm pulling her sweater over her head.

"You too," she urges me, yanking at my belt while walking backward to the bed. The mattress catches her behind the knees and she tumbles, landing on her back, her hair fanning out on the comforter.

Christ, she's beautiful; her eyes shining with passion, a deep flush high on her cheeks, and those lush, wet lips slightly parted in anticipation.

I'm out of my jeans in seconds, ripping my boxer briefs down with them and toeing off my socks. When I straighten up and pull my shirt over my head, Robin's eyes drop down to my cock, jutting out eagerly.

Her skin contrasts pale against the black bra.

"Take it off."

My voice is hoarse with barely contained lust as she arches her back to reach behind her. I have no idea where the garment lands when she flings it off the bed, since my eyes are glued to her creamy soft breasts. My gaze slides down over the swell of her belly to the edge of her black panties. Immediately her hands move down to her hips hooking thumbs underneath the elastic.

"Let me."

I brush her hands away and slide the panties down her legs, the scent of her arousal tempting my senses. Sinking down on my knees, I drag her body close to the edge of the mattress and pull her legs over my shoulders. Her fingers restlessly dig into the comforter; I don't hesitate lashing the flat of my tongue along her crease.

My eyes close and a satisfied groan works its way up from deep in my chest when her flavor hits my sensory receptors. I'm not in a hurry, savoring every moan from her lips and tremble of her body. Time, once all-important, becomes meaningless when her thighs clamp tightly on my head and Robin cries out her release.

My scruff still slick with her essence, I kiss my way up her body, nipping and tasting her soft, pliant skin. She doesn't flinch when I reach her mouth. Her hands pull my face close, kissing me back hungrily. Without losing our connection I slide my arm underneath her, moving us farther onto the mattress. She wraps her legs around my hips, as I align my straining cock to her center and sink myself deep inside her.

"Gray..." she sighs, ending our kiss.

Her hands slide down to my ass, fingers digging into my flexing muscles as I pump into her body. Already I can feel tightness building at the base of my spine and my movements grow erratic.

"Honey…" she whispers, her eyes holding mine captive. "Love you back."

My thin thread of control snaps hearing those words.

"*Fuuuck* yesss," I grind out as I buck, spurting hot streams of my cum inside her. A full-body shiver makes me weak and I collapse on top of her, my face buried in her neck.

I may have dozed when I hear her soft strangled voice at my ear.

"I can't breathe."

"Sorry," I mumble, rolling over and taking her with me so she's on top. "Better?"

"Much." She nuzzles the hair on my chest. "But I'm leaking all over you."

I chuckle at that. She's not lying; we're virtually glued together.

"Fine. Shower."

I hold onto her firmly and swing us both out of bed. She giggles in my arms, grabbing onto my shoulders, as I walk us to the bathroom. I take great pleasure in washing her clean under the warm stream, and I gladly let her return the favor.

Zeus is curled in the middle of the mattress when we get back to the bedroom. He protests loudly when Robin picks him up, plants a kiss on his head, and sets him on the floor before crawling in bed. I flick off the lights and get in to spoon her, tugging her body close.

I stroke the pads of my fingers lazily along her skin and breathe in the freshly washed scent of her hair.

"You love me."

It's more a statement than a question, but she answers anyway, twisting her head to look at me.

"I do."

"Why?"

She snorts and rolls toward me. "Why? Well, because..." She hesitates and then shakes her head. "It's really not that simple." She pushes me to my back, and props her chin on my chest.

"There's darkness inside me."

"And there's light," she counters.

"I get angry."

"And you can be exquisitely sweet."

"I'm violent."

That earns me a narrowing of her eyes.

"Bullshit. You're one of the most gentle men I've known."

I shake my head and don't bother hiding the small smile tugging at my lips.

"Do you have an answer for everything?"

"Try me," she challenges, and I wrap my arms around her while my body shakes with laughter.

CHAPTER TWENTY-SIX

Robin

Shirley slips past me with the order for table seven, tossing me a little smile over her shoulder.

She arrived back in town last week and after getting herself sorted, started at the diner yesterday. She seems like a different person from the woman I'd worked alongside for years before.

That woman had been distant, reserved, and rarely cracked a smile. The woman who showed up yesterday looked like the weight of the world was lifted from her shoulders. She hugged everyone, cried happy tears, and has treated customers to wide smiles and kind words all day yesterday and today.

"Do you have a second?"

"Sure." I barely get the chance to answer when Shirley grabs my arm and pulls me toward the ladies' room. "What is it?" I ask when she shuts the door behind us.

"I owe you an apology."

"For what?"

Her eyes flit to a point beyond my shoulder and she visibly steels herself.

"It may have been my fault Mike came after you."

"That wasn't your responsibility," I assure her, but she shakes her head sharply.

"It was. I told my boys you'd dropped me off here. I didn't know my youngest shared your name with his father. He knows Mike attacked someone, but didn't put two and two together until he called me last night to see how my first day back had been and I happened to mention you. He feels awful."

The poor woman has tears in her eyes, and I quickly put my hands on her shoulders and give her a little shake.

"None of that. The only responsible person is locked up," I state firmly. "Besides, I'm totally fine. I think you've wasted enough energy on that man. Let it go. Fuck, let *him* go. Trust me on this."

She blinks her eyes a few times, takes a deep breath in, and manufactures a wobbly smile.

"You're right."

"You bet I am, and tell your boy to put it out of his head." I give her another little shake before letting her go. "One of these days, when we have a moment of quiet, I'll tell you my story, but for now let's get some food on those tables."

Kim is at the cash register and eyes us closely when we approach.

"Everything all right?"

"Yup," Shirley answers, making a beeline for the pass-through lined with orders.

I just give Kim a wink and grab the next order. It's for the threesome of regulars at their customary table.

"Two eggs over easy, bacon, sausage, biscuits and gravy?"

"That's mine." Eddie Banks lifts a hand and I slide the plate in front of him.

"You know that's gonna kill ya, right?" John tells him before turning to me. "Egg white, spinach omelet is mine, darlin'."

"You bet."

I serve him his breakfast and the final plate, a tall stack of pancakes, has to be Enzo's. He smiles his gratitude and doesn't hesitate digging in.

"Up for a game tonight?" he asks with his mouth full.

"Game?"

"Pool, girl. I hear you've been practicing quite a bit."

I grin. Sneaky old geezer. I bet he's seen my CRV parked outside the Dirty Dog a few nights a week. Not that I was practicing my pool, or even in the bar for that matter. I probably had my hands full with—or should I say of—the man living upstairs.

It had been Gray's idea to stay over at his place when I have an early shift. Mostly because it saves me fifteen minutes in the morning, which he apparently likes to spend in other ways. The other nights he's spent with me. There have only been a couple of nights we haven't been together when our schedules didn't align, and it was just easier to sleep in our respective beds.

Zeus is becoming a well-traveled cat, and has taken a liking to car rides. I may have melted a little when I discovered Gray had bought food and a matching bed for the cat to keep at his place.

"You just want an easy win," John accuses his friend.

"So? You guys are a bunch of sharks," Enzo fires back.

"Come on, guys, no fighting," I admonish them with a smile. "Eat your breakfast."

Eddie pulls his wallet from his pocket, takes out a twenty-dollar bill and slaps it on the table in front of John.

"Twenty on Robin."

John glances at me before he turns to Enzo, who is busy glaring at Eddie.

"Now, guys..." I try, but already John is fishing money from his pocket.

"Enzo's got this." He slaps a matching bill beside the other on the table before he turns to me. "No offense, Robin, but you suck."

"None taken, John. You guys want a top up?"

The collective mumbles are approving and I borrow the carafe from Shirley as she walks by.

"Enjoy your breakfast," I tell them when I've filled their cups.

"Thanks, girl."

"Bring your A game tonight, Robin," Eddie says.

As I walk away, I can just hear John's response.

"You are so going down, my friend."

I pick up the next order with a grin on my face.

————

"Hey, sweetheart. How are you?"

I toss my purse on the couch and sit down, kicking off my shoes.

"I'm okay."

Her listless voice sends off alarm bells. Paige has been home for a few weeks now and I've talked to her a few times, but haven't heard her this dejected.

"Talk to me," I invite.

"He showed up after work today. Let himself in while I was in the shower and was sitting on my bed when I came out. I almost had a heart attack."

"Hope you took back his key."

"Technically he threw it at me, but yeah, I got it back."

"Little shit needs to—"

"Mom, it's fine. It may have been after I pelted him with my hairbrush."

"Tell me your aim was accurate," I blurt out, pissed on my girl's account, but I soften when I hear her snicker.

"Bloodthirsty much, Mom?" She falls silent after that, and I can feel the tension through the phone. "It was ugly," she finally says in a subdued voice. "He came to collect the Kate Spade purse he got me for Christmas. Can you believe that?" I make a sympathetic sound, but I'm guessing she doesn't really want me to answer. That is confirmed when she continues with a great deal more piss and vinegar. "I told him he could have the damn thing, but I wanted back the wireless Powerbeats Pro earbuds I got him. He got me a pink purse, Mom. Pink. You know I don't like pink. It should've been a sign, but I guess I wasn't ready to see it yet. He's totally clueless. Guess what he said?" Again, I know better than to say anything, so I do no more than make an encouraging sound. "He said he'd be willing to forget everything and take me back if I apologized to his mother."

"I hope you told him where to get off."

"Well...sort of. That's when I chucked the brush at him."

"I don't blame you, sweetheart," I soothe, hearing the tears in her voice.

"He was right, you know?"

"Josh?"

"God," she wails dramatically. "To think I used to like that name. No, not him, Gray."

"You talked to Gray?" Guess I missed something.

"Yeah, at the diner. Remember? Before that woman—"

"Right. I remember," I quickly interrupt, holding up my hand. Don't want to revisit that scene.

"He said Josh was no match for me. That he wasn't man enough."

A smile spreads on my lips as I put a hand on my heart. I love he said that to her. Love he found the exact right thing to say to my baby girl. It's the truth; that momma's boy was not a good match for my daughter. I'm not sure anyone is.

"Gray is right, sweetheart. He wasn't. You deserve someone who knows your favorite color is blue and your favorite ice cream is plain vanilla. Someone who always puts you first and will do anything to see you happy."

"Is that Gray for you, Mom?"

For a moment I wonder if it's too soon to share my feelings with my daughter, but she's an adult and I want her to know there are good men out there.

Men like Gray.

"He is."

"Tell him 'thank you' for me."

"I will. Love you, baby."

"Love you more," she says, like she has since she was three years old.

————

Gray

"It looks a little rough."

A snort escapes me.

"Ya think?"

It's a little slow at Olson's, so Jimmy suggested we pick up the old bike from his parents' garage and get to work on it. He's determined to have it ready so I can join him and his buddies when the weather gets better.

Back in September, when I'd gone on a ride with them to a swap meet, I managed to pick up a few new parts, but I never got around to working on the bike.

The Knucklehead had been protected with a tarp, but it hadn't been in great shape when I dragged it from the dump all those years ago. I just forgot how much work it needed.

We load it on the back of my truck—no mean feat, the fucker is heavy—I thank Jimmy's dad, who came out to see what we were up to, and drive back to the shop.

"Sweet," Kyle calls out when we back the truck into one of the bays.

He's already climbing into the cargo bed to get a closer look by the time we round the truck.

"Fuck. I don't even know where to start," I admit when we get the bike down and set up against the back wall, where it's out of the way.

"Take it apart and clean it up."

"That's a fuckload of parts to try and fit back together," I tell Jimmy.

"Might as well do it right."

We spend the next couple of hours taking apart as much as we can—with a fair bit of cursing at the numerous bolts and nuts almost fused with rust—until we have a bunch of bins filled with parts and only the frame is left standing.

"Look what I found." Kyle holds up his phone, the picture of a buddy seat up on the screen. "They've got all kinds of original parts. You're gonna need one of those." He taps the picture and grins.

A mental image of Robin snug behind me on the back of the bike, her arms around me, stirs my blood.

"How much?"

Kyle stifles a chuckle, but Jimmy doesn't hold back, he starts laughing out loud.

"You're predictable," he snickers.

"Yeah?" I pin him with a sharp look. "Last time I checked you had a bitch seat. Difference is, mine won't be empty." I turn to Kyle and repeat. "How much?"

Half an hour later I climb up the stairs to my apartment, a few hundred dollars lighter, but a grin on my face.

———

I walk into the bar, just catching Robin throwing her head back and laughing.

I'm not the only one paying attention, the three musketeers

sitting with her at the table watch her too. Fuck, who wouldn't, she radiates when she as much as smiles. It's no wonder the old geezers flock to her; they're as hungry as I am for her light.

"There he is," Enzo announces when he sees me approach.

Robin twists her head around and greets me with a brilliant smile. It's all I need. Seeing happiness on her face at the sight of me makes every struggle I've faced in my life well worth it. Heck, if I'd known this was at the end of it all, I would have greeted each day of my past with a smile of my own.

"Hey, honey," she says softly, when I walk up to her. Ignoring everyone else I bend down, cup the back of her head, and kiss her soundly.

"Sunshine," I mumble against her lips, before releasing her and finally looking around the table. "Guys."

The three wear similar grins as they mumble their greetings.

"Need refills?"

"Not gonna say no," John says, holding up his half empty beer. The other two follow suit and I turn my eyes back to Robin.

"You? Another wine?"

"Sure, I brought Zeus and left him upstairs."

Her way of telling me she was spending the night. I'm good with that.

"Be right back."

Bunker is cleaning glasses behind the bar.

"Refills for them," I tell him, cocking my thumb at the table. "And I'll have a draft."

His mouth falls open.

"I thought you didn't drink?"

I shrug. "I used to. Before I went in. Only if I had something to celebrate, though."

His eyes knowingly flit in Robin's direction and he grins.

"I see."

I'm sure he does.

"I talked to Becca last night," he suddenly says as he fills my order.

Not sure why he would bring her up, and I don't know if I really want to hear what he has to say. Still, I raise my eyebrow in question.

"She's leaving for Florida with my aunt. Just so you know."

"Good."

I know from Francisi, who had shown up at Olson's last week, he caught up with Becca, who claimed she had no idea Mike had taken her key to the diner when he left her place. Said she didn't miss it until later and she was scared she'd get in trouble. Bullshit, of course, but Francisi had nothing but Mike Hancock's say-so, which isn't worth spit.

"So you know; I reamed her a new one. Apparently my aunt got wind of what she'd been up to, so I wasn't the first. She admitted she'd come here thinking she could get you back after discovering you'd inherited the bar. Fuck, I know it doesn't excuse anything, but she's been living hand-to-mouth her whole life, guess she was hoping to be looked after."

I grunt, keeping my thoughts to myself. Truth is, she's always been one of those people who expect a good life to drop in her lap. My eyes drift to the table. Not like Robin, who put in the effort and managed to carve out a new and decent existence not only for her, but also for her daughter.

"Look," Bunker says in a low voice, as he places the drinks on a tray. "She admitted she was out to make trouble for Robin. Maybe hoping that...fuck, I don't even know what she was thinking. She says she never meant for Robin to get hurt, but I'm not sure I even believe that. Anyway, she won't give you any more trouble."

"Appreciate it."

"We good?" he asks, handing me the tray.

"Course we are. You're not her keeper."

I take the drinks to the table and sit down beside Robin,

pulling her chair closer. She tosses a quick grin my way before turning back to Eddie, who is telling a funny story. I don't pay attention; I'm too focused on the feeling of utter contentment as Robin leans against me, her hand on my knee as she tilts her head to my shoulder.

Enzo draws my attention when he slaps both hands on the table.

"How about a game of pool?"

CHAPTER TWENTY-SEVEN

Robin

"I think Paige is coming home."

Gray props himself up on his elbow and looks down on me, his free hand brushing a strand of hair from my flushed face.

"I'm not sure how I feel about you bringing up your daughter when I'm still trying to catch my breath here."

I snicker at his dismayed expression.

"Only because it would seriously curb these amazing sexual adventures you take me on."

He cracks a shit-eating grin and wiggles his eyebrows.

"Amazing, huh?"

"Creative, that's for sure."

Who'd have thought at forty-six, I still had so much to learn about one of the most basic of human urges. Gray has certainly awoken a sexual beast in me, because I can't recall there ever being a time where I was constantly horny.

Gray has been an enthusiastic teacher and I've been a very willing student.

"It does lead one to wonder where you would've acquired all knowledge," I tease.

"I read a lot of books," he says on a shrug, making me laugh.

"I can't recall any Clive Cussler or John Grisham containing erotica," I point out, pulling myself up so I have my back against the headboard.

I'm not even worried about how my breasts instantly give in to gravity. In fact, I don't really worry about the way I look at all. I don't need to; Gray seems to love every part of me.

"That wasn't all I read," he admits with a wink, as he makes himself comfortable against the headboard as well. "Besides, with little else to do but fantasize, I've built up quite a bucket list of things to try."

"Mmm. I'm all for trying new things, which is why..." I circle back around to my earlier comment, "...we should talk about what we're gonna do when Paige comes back. I was thinking..." I glance over at him and see I have his full attention. "And you can shut me down if you don't like it," I quickly add. "But what if Paige took your apartment? She'd be close but still independent. Then you could move here? I mean, I know we haven't really talked about it, but we're either here or at your place most nights anyway, so—"

"Hey," he interrupts my ramble, turning toward me and cupping my jaw with his hand. "Makes sense to me."

"Yeah?"

I grin and scoot closer.

"Hell yeah."

He pulls me on top of his body so I'm straddling his hips. His face is at level with my breasts, something he immediately makes good use of. His nipping and tugging soon has me rock my hips on the hardening ridge of his cock as my body sparks back to life.

"Gray?"

"Mmmm," he mumbles around my nipple.

"So...what else is on that bucket list of yours?"

———

I walk out of the office to get a coffee refill. God knows I need it.

This past week I've been trying to catch up on the diner's bookkeeping. Taxes are due on the fifteenth of next month and I've barely looked at the books since before Christmas.

It's like this every year, I have the best of intentions and then stuff happens distracting me.

"How is it going?" Kim asks when I pass her.

"I may require wine instead of coffee to fuel me soon," I grumble.

"Take a break." She indicates a stool. "It's about lunchtime anyway, Jason can whip you up something."

I start telling her I can't, I need to get this done before Paige comes home this weekend, but I stop myself. I'll probably be more productive if I can clear my head and fill my stomach.

"I'd kill for a home burger," I announce, sliding onto a seat.

"Jason!" she hollers over her shoulder. "Robin needs feeding. Home burger."

"Coming up!"

"You could've just stuck your head in the pass-through," I suggest.

She grins. "Now what would be the fun in that?"

Donna throws me a wink in passing on her way to the kitchen with a tub of dirty dishes. There are only two straggling tables but most of the breakfast crowd is done. Lunch won't be quite as busy, at least during the workweek.

"You know Amanda Kerns?" Donna asks me when she reappears.

"Isn't she the redhead? Pregnant?" Kim says.

"That's the one. She's a nurse at the Great Lakes Medical Center in Gladwin."

I nod. "Yeah, I think I know who you're talking about."

"Well, she's about to go on maternity leave, and I hear they're having a hard time finding someone qualified. I was thinking maybe that's something for your girl? May be only until Amanda comes back—if she does—but it could be a start?"

It might actually be perfect. Paige isn't clear on what she wants, so something temporary while she figures it out wouldn't be a bad idea.

"Thanks, that might work for her. She's getting in this weekend, so I'll pass it on. Anyone in particular she should get in touch with?"

"Don't know, but I'll give Amanda a call tonight and find out."

That bit of potentially good news—and the fat juicy burger and fries I inhale ten minutes later—fuel me sufficiently to breeze through my afternoon. By the time I'm ready to head home, I have a number for Dr. Ashram at the Gladwin clinic, courtesy of Donna, and call Paige on my hands-free while I'm driving.

"Hey, Mom."

"Hi, sweetheart. Do you have a pen ready?"

"Yeah, I'm at my desk, why?"

"You're still at work?"

"Just tying up a few loose ends before I head home. Why do I need pen and paper?"

"I may have a lead for you." I tell her about the clinic in Gladwin and give her the contact information. "I don't know if they'd still be open, but you could give them a call now, see if you can set something up for next week when you're here."

"Thanks, Mom," she says with a bit of an edge. "Not sure if I would've thought of that myself."

Definitely sarcasm there.

"Just looking out for you, Paige."

I can hear the sigh through the phone.

"I know, but I've lived on my own for a few years now and I've managed to survive, so give me some credit here."

That shuts me up for a minute. She's right, she's not a child anymore and as happy as I am for her to be coming home, I have to recognize her need for independence. Otherwise I'm afraid she won't hesitate moving away again soon. I know my daughter.

Every so often the mother hen in me rears its head.

"So noted. I didn't mean to—"

"It's okay, Mom. I'm a little stressed, that's all."

"Understandable, sweetheart. Do you have a lot left to do?"

"The trailer is packed, I just need to throw my bedding, the air mattress, and a couple of odds and ends in the car before I hit the road. I plan to leave before traffic gets nuts tomorrow morning, so I'll make an early night of it tonight."

I turn into my driveway.

"All right, honey. I'll let you go then. Let me know where you end up tomorrow night. Not because don't I trust you," I quickly add. "But because I'm a mom and we worry."

Her soft chuckle is music to my ears.

"So noted, Mom."

———

Gray

"Go on. Take it for a spin."

Jimmy, Kyle, and I are standing side by side, looking at our handiwork.

It took a little over a month, but between the three of us we have the Knucklehead rebuilt. Kyle did an amazing job spraying the frame in a deep blue so dark; it looks almost black from a distance.

"It'll have to wait. I've gotta get over to the bar and load the last of my shit in the truck."

"Damn, I almost forgot," Jimmy says. "Paige is gonna be here this weekend, right?"

"She's supposed to start driving tomorrow."

She's pulling a U-Haul behind her small SUV, so Robin told her to take it slow and divide the drive over two days.

"She's driving?" Kyle does not sound pleased.

Jimmy and I look at each other, simultaneously raising an eyebrow before we glance at Kyle.

"What's it to you?"

His eyes shoot to me.

"It's hardly safe for a woman alone on the road. What if she hits bad weather?"

"Listen here, kid; if her mother trusts her enough to make the trip, why the hell would you worry?"

"Her mother doesn't see what I see," Kyle persists, not so wisely. "Paige could stop traffic, she's that hot."

"All right, Valentino," Jimmy jumps in, throwing an arm around his shoulders and steering him into the garage. "You're poking the bear," I hear him mumble at the kid.

I'm starting to rethink the favor I was going to ask of the guys to come and help empty Paige's trailer when she gets here. Maybe that's not such a good idea, given the way Kyle talks about her.

I pull out my phone and dial Robin as I head around the side of the shop to the apartment stairs.

"Change of plans," I tell her when she answers my call.

"What?"

"Kyle won't be helping this weekend."

"That's too bad. Is he busy?"

"No."

I open the door and let myself inside, flicking on the lights. I've left the furniture for Paige to pick through, but other than my clothes and books, there's not much left for me to load up.

"He said no? Well, that's a surprise; I actually thought he might be a little sweet on her. Guess I was wrong."

It would probably be easier to let her assume that.

"He didn't say no," I admit anyway.

"Okay, now I'm confused."

"He thinks she's hot," I clarify.

"So I *was* right. I knew it," she says triumphantly. "So why isn't he helping?"

Normally Robin is sharp as a tack, I can't believe she's not clueing in.

"Because he thinks she's *hot*," I repeat. "Sunshine, the kid almost bit my head off when he found out she's driving here by herself."

"Awww, that's sweet," is her chuckled reply. "Almost sounds familiar, Gray. You think maybe you're being a little overprotective here?"

Now I'm getting a little pissed. Doesn't she realize I'm just using common sense?

"You wouldn't say that if you knew what guys his age spend their time thinking about, Robin. They're horndogs."

Apparently I said something funny because she's suddenly laughing loudly. I'm about to hang up on her when she seems to gain control.

"Gray?"

"Yeah."

"Why don't you come home and explain it to me. Maybe we can scratch another item off your bucket list," she teases in a sultry voice.

Fuck. The blood that was trying to keep from boiling suddenly heads south, flooding my dick. Just like that, every argument on my lips evaporates.

"I'm just packing up," I tell her, as I empty the contents of my drawers straight into the laundry basket.

Her chuckle is sexy as shit.

"I'll be in the garage."

Holy crap. We exchanged fantasies last week and enacted hers, but she's clearly not forgotten about mine. I already moved my Mustang to her place and I know exactly where I'll find her.

My voice comes out sounding strangled when I respond.

"Be right there."

Fifteen minutes later, hornier than a teenager at a Playboy party, I slam my truck in park next to Robin's Honda. I don't even bother taking my shit out of the truck but head straight for the detached two-car garage, set back from the house.

Soft light flickers in the single window on the side of the building, but I aim for the left bay door behind, where the Mustang is parked under a dust tarp. I roll up the door, wincing when my jeans prove to be tighter than I anticipated.

The inside is lit with a single lantern sitting on the work-bench. My immediate focus is drawn to the Mustang, the dust-cover off, and the paint gleaming in the sparse light.

Leaning back against the hood is Robin; naked as the day she was born.

"Welcome home, honey."

CHAPTER TWENTY-EIGHT

Robin

"What's wrong with your arm?"

Of course the first thing Paige notices is the stress bandage wrapped around my wrist. I shoot a quick glance at Gray, who is suddenly very interested in his boots.

I'm not about to tell her it's the result of a very enthusiastic—but probably ill-advised—effort to scratch an item off Gray's bucket list. Luckily she can't see his swollen knee, or she might guess.

Our adventure in the garage was all very sexy, until I got a cramp in my calf in the middle of... Anyway, Gray attempted to lift me off the hood, had forgotten his jeans were around his ankles, and started going down. He sacrificed his knee and I tried to brace for impact by sticking out my hand.

The whole thing was a clusterfuck—quite literally.

I plaster a smile on my face for my daughter's sake.

"I tripped over the cat," I lie, silently apologizing to Zeus for throwing him under the bus. "It's just a sprain. Now, do I get a hug?"

Paige takes the few steps separating us and I can fold her in my arms.

"Hey, Mom," she mumbles in my neck.

"Hey, sweetheart. So glad you're here." I glance over her shoulder to Gray, who is observing us with a faint smile on his lips.

The next moment she lets me go and turns to him.

"Hey, Gray."

"Paige," he barely gets out, before Paige plants her face in his chest and wraps her arms around his waist. I almost laugh out loud when I see the brief look of panic on his face before he awkwardly pats her back. "Your drive okay?"

She lets him go and steps back, and he quickly tucks his hands in his pockets.

"Yeah. I lucked out with the weather. Not a snowflake in sight."

"That's good," he grumbles, still looking a little uneasy. "If you give me your keys, I'll drive it over to the apartment. I've got someone meeting me there to help. We can get started on unloading, while you catch up with your mom."

"If you're sure. I just wanna grab a quick bite of something and we'll be on our way."

"Positive."

She hands him her keys and he leans in, pressing a kiss on my hair. We watch as he gets behind the wheel of the small SUV, quickly adjusting the seat for more legroom. Paige quietly snickers beside me.

"You sure you don't wanna stay here tonight?" I offer, hooking my arm through hers as Gray drives off.

"I'd rather get this done today, so I can drop the trailer off in the morning." She starts pulling me toward the house. "But first you need to feed me."

It always amazes how natural it feels when my daughter is home. I grin when she heads straight for the kitchen.

"What've you got?" she asks, her head already in the fridge. "Oh, apple pie."

She pulls out the pie, grabs a fork from the drawer, and starts eating right from the pan.

"I have plates, you know," I scold her, only partially meaning it.

"No need to get any dirty," she says with an apple pie filled grin, as she sits down at the table.

Shaking my head I pour her a glass of milk, setting it beside the pie plate she's guarding with her arm curved around it.

Some things never change. She may be all grown-up, but to me she's still that little pigtailed girl.

"That was nice of Gray to offer, by the way." She glances up at me and I bite off a grin.

"It was," I agree, pulling out a chair and sitting across from her. "Although I have a suspicion there was a little more to it than just being nice."

Paige raises an eyebrow.

"What do you mean?"

"He may have had second thoughts about asking Kyle to help move your stuff."

"Kyle? Isn't that the guy at Olson's?"

I recognize the way she tucks her hair behind her ear and widens her eyes in mock-innocence. Oh, my girl knows exactly who I'm talking about.

"Mmmm," I mumble in confirmation.

Paige suddenly gets up and shoves the massacred apple pie back in the fridge, drops her fork in the sink, and moves toward the bathroom.

"I'm just gonna freshen up before we go," she mutters, as she disappears from sight.

This should be interesting.

———

I'm chuckling at the stormy expression on Gray's face as Kyle stubbornly hauls my daughter's coffee table up the stairs to the apartment by himself. Paige is waiting in the doorway.

"Down boy," I whisper in his ear.

"He's a punk," Gray grumbles.

"He is not. He's a nice kid, who works hard and obviously aims to impress my daughter."

He harrumphs, sounding so much like my dad used to it hits me with a pang of bittersweet nostalgia. I slide my hand in his and entwine our fingers.

"Go easy, honey," I caution him, my tone drawing his attention as he turns his head to look at me. "Paige hasn't exactly been exposed to protective men before. You may want to introduce her gently."

He tries to smile but the annoyance isn't quite gone from his eyes, so I hook a hand behind his neck and pull him down, lifting my mouth for a kiss.

"All right!" I hear my daughter's voice coming from above. "I did not need to see that. Are you guys gonna just stand there or are you helping?"

Gray ducks his head, but I catch the grin on his face as he pulls me along behind him and up the stairs.

An hour later, we've got the apartment the way Paige wants it, and tossed some of the furniture she no longer wants in the back of Kyle's truck so the guys can run it to the dump. She and I have sorted the kitchen, put clean sheets on the bed, and are putting away her clothes. There are only a few boxes left with odds and ends she says she'll go through tonight.

"Have you talked to Gram?" she asks, when I hand her a stack of folded T-shirts to put away.

"I was going to try and reach her tonight. Why? Did you talk to her?"

"She called me this morning when I was on the road. She said they might stay on another week or two."

Mom was originally supposed to get back next weekend. I've missed her, but her wanting to stay longer means she's having a good time and I'm happy for her. I can wait an extra few weeks to hug her.

"Good for her. It'll probably have warmed up by then, so maybe we can have a barbecue at my place. See if we can get her to bring Ken for us to finally meet."

My daughter's dancing eyes meet mine.

"Can we invite Kyle?"

I only hesitate for a second, grinning when I think about Gray's reaction to that.

"Sure. I'll ask him."

———

Gray

"I'll get it."

I watch Paige jump up from her seat on the steps and dart inside to answer the door.

She was keeping me company while I clean the grill. She and Robin have been cooking all morning. Enough damn food to feed all of Beaverton. Crazy if you ask me, since it's only Robin's mother and her boyfriend coming, but the two younger Bishop women seem intent on making an impression. I tried to steal a potato from the salad Paige was putting together earlier but almost got my fingers chopped off. I was banned after that.

Not a hardship, exactly. I enjoy sitting at the kitchen table with a book in front of me, listening to the two of them chatter in the kitchen. Something that's happened a few times since Paige moved back. Two women, both fiercely independent, but still so tightly connected. I imagine Robin's mom will be like that too. It seems to run in the family.

Family.

Hard to believe not that long ago, I didn't know what that meant, or maybe I'd just forgotten. Either way, I'm learning quickly what family can be: uninvited smiles, warm touches, easy disagreements, comfortable silences, and food—lots and lots of food.

"Look who's here?"

I turn away from the grill to find a smiling Paige coming through the sliding door, fucking Kyle right behind her.

"I don't recall inviting you," I snap, annoyed he'd have the gall to show up out of the blue.

"That's because you didn't. Robin did," he answers, the shit-eating grin on his face starting to piss me off.

I'm about to give the little punk a piece of my mind when Robin steps outside, and I catch a sharp glare from her before she turns a bright smile on the kid as she sidles up to me.

"So glad you could make it, Kyle. Would you like a drink?"

"Wouldn't mind a beer."

I may have made a sound, because the next thing I know I have an elbow in my ribs.

"Coming right up." She hooks her arm in mine. "Can I borrow you for a sec?"

I don't get a chance to answer; she's already dragging me to the door.

Inside she swings on me, fire in her eyes as she plants her hands on her hips.

"Do you think you could lose the attitude before my mom gets here?"

"What attitude?" I grumble.

"That one," she snaps, poking her finger in my chest. "I haven't seen Mom in months, it's my first time meeting Ken, and I'd really like us to try and make a good impression."

There's a lot more I can hear her saying between the lines, and I immediately regret adding to her stress. All she wants is for everyone to like each other and get along, and right now there are already plenty of question marks in play. Last thing she needs is me adding to the tension.

It's not that Kyle is a bad guy—he's not, from what I can see he's smart and a hard worker—but his cocky attitude gets to me sometimes. Maybe because he reminds me of me at that age, and God knows I was a punk.

I step toward her and slip my arms around her waist, tugging her close. I bend my head down and kiss the tip of her nose.

"I'm sorry. I'll behave."

"She could do worse, Gray," Robin says, a plea in her eyes. "She already has."

She's referring to that little weasel. That guy ever shows his face here, he and I will have words. Of sorts.

"I know, Robin."

"He's a good man," she insists, her lips a firm line.

I save myself from responding by kissing her. I tease her with my tongue, satisfied when I feel her mouth finally relax, letting me in. One of my hands tangles in her hair, tilting her head back. With her slim neck exposed, I slide my lips down until I find her heartbeat in the soft hollow at its base.

"Love you, Sunshine," I mumble against her skin, before lifting my head and looking in her eyes.

"Me too," she whispers.

"Hellooo!"

Robin's eyes go wide at the sound of a woman's voice from the front of the house, but before she can wrestle herself from my hold, a pretty woman, who could be Robin's older sister, and a tough-looking guy walk into the kitchen. The resemblance between all the Bishop women is undeniable; all brunettes, all beautiful.

Robin and her mother hug and the man, Ken, and I take measure of the other over the women's heads.

"You look so good!" Robin exclaims, holding her mother at arm's length. "Look at your tan."

"And you, honey, you look fantastic," her mother replies.

With those two chattering away, and remembering my promise to Robin to behave, I approach Ken offering my hand.

"Good to meet you. Gray Bennet."

"Ken Saunders."

His grip is firm and his gaze discerning. The guy can't be that much older than me, but there's something authoritarian about him. Must be the cop in him. Robin told me he was retired law enforcement.

"Beer?"

"Dying for one."

By the time I pull a couple from the fridge and hand one to Ken, the women have turned to us, both smiling big. Further introductions are made—which included a hug from Mrs. Bishop —something else they have in common.

"Gram!" Paige's squeal triggers more hugging and introductions.

I make my way to the door and slip outside, the kitchen becoming a little claustrophobic with all those bodies. I take in a few deep breaths to release the tension in my chest.

It still happens every so often—an enclosed space, an unexpected hand on my back, an occasional nightmare—but nothing Robin's soft touch or a little deep breathing can't erase.

"You don't drink?" Ken's voice sounds behind me.

He must've seen me hand the other beer to Kyle.

"I do, but not often." I turn around and face him, leaning my back against the railing. "You know," I challenge him, catching another scrutinizing glance.

"Didn't know it was a secret," he fires back.

"So? What's the verdict?"

I know I'm being an ass but it slips out anyway. I don't expect the grin stretching on his face.

"Thought you already served your time?" he deadpans.

I bark out a laugh, surprised as hell.

"Every last second," I tell him.

"Good," he says, turning so he's facing the sliding doors as well. "Now that we have that out of the way, what do you make of that cocky little bastard in there?"

Minutes later, Robin walks outside with a platter of meat, her eyes on me.

"What are you grinning about?" she wants to know.

I'm not about to tell her I may have backed off Kyle, but Ken is planning to put the thumbscrews on. I take the platter, slide it to the side of the grill, and take her in my arms.

"I'm happy."

She tilts her head, not sure if she should believe me.

"How come I get the feeling that's not all?"

I take her face in my hands and lean my forehead against hers.

"Sunshine, it's everything."

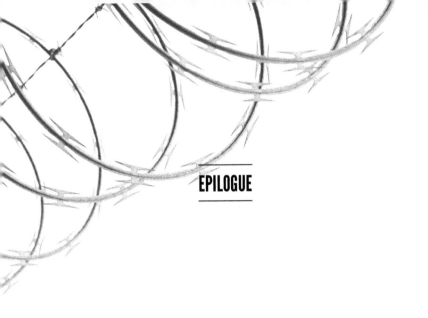

EPILOGUE

Gray

Fresh air.

I stop when I hear the door slam shut behind me and suck in a deep, liberating breath. I'll never take this free feeling for granted, my lungs fully expanding and the hit of oxygen instantly clearing my head.

I'm not sure why it was important for me to visit the museum again. Last time I'd come here to remind me of what I had lost, maybe even to acknowledge my own part in it.

Perhaps this time I needed to let go of the guilt, of the grief, both of which I'd been guarding so carefully for years. There's no place for either in my life now. Guilt has been replaced with gratitude, and the grief—although never completely gone—with happiness.

My life is nothing like I'd expected it to be, and that has everything to do with the woman I saw standing in a crowd last year. An unexpected source of brightness in a world that seemed perpetually overcast.

I still can't believe fate—who'd been nothing but a bitch until then—ended up being so kind to me.

We'd each been a victim of circumstance; invisibly connected for many years by this place. We'd come here from different directions but when we left, our paths were aligned.

Fate. Not something I've ever subscribed to, but this past year has made a believer of me. To everything there's a purpose, even when we can only see it looking back.

I flip up the collar on my leather jacket against the gloomy drizzle coming down, and start walking through the crowd.

I trust my feet to find her.

———

Robin

I'm not here for me. Not anymore.

I don't need to celebrate my freedom by thumbing my nose at my long-dead husband. If I've learned anything this past year, it's I was deluding myself before.

Where's the so-called freedom in visiting a place year after year, just to remind yourself you won? Where's the victory in denying yourself any chance at happiness just to hang onto that autonomy?

I've never felt more unencumbered than I am when I'm with Gray.

So no, I'm not here for me, I'm here for him.

Gray may have been released from prison a year ago, but he wasn't yet free of his restraints. That's why we came, and that's why I didn't join him down in the museum.

Tonight we're going to the Liberty State Park to watch the Tribute in Light. Paige and Kyle are meeting us at a nearby restaurant and will be joining us then.

I grin when I think of Gray's reaction when he heard Kyle would be joining us in New York. He and Paige have only been together since this summer. My girl hadn't been ready to jump into anything when she moved back home, and all credit to Kyle, he hadn't pushed. That didn't mean he stayed in the background. Oh no, he was up front and center at every opportunity, not about to let her forget she held his interest.

Gray had warmed up some; until he caught them kissing outside Olson's one day in the summer, and Jimmy had to intervene before it came to blows.

Luckily Paige finds it mostly endearing, although she may well have felt differently if she'd had to put up with his overprotectiveness her whole life. He loves her—Gray does—and I think Paige understands in part, he sees his sister in her. It makes sense, when he lost her she was the same age as her. So she indulges him, because the truth is, she loves him too.

I sense him before I see him, walking toward me with determination in his gait and love in his eyes. The crowds fade away until all I see is him, all I hear is the rain on my hood. His hands cup my face as he kisses my forehead, my eyes, and then my lips, rain dripping from our hair.

"I want a dog," he says, momentarily confusing me.

"Uh, sure."

"And I'll never expect anything of you that you're not willing to give."

I'm pretty sure my mouth falls open.

"Okay?"

"And I'll understand if you want to keep Bishop as your last name."

A light dawns and I grab onto his wrists.

"Gray?"

"But I need you to marry me, Sunshine."

"All right."

"I can't even imagine what it was like before I met you."

"Okay, Gray."

"I know I'm fucking this up, but—"

I press my hand over his mouth and manage to get his attention.

"When you ask a question, you need to listen to the answer, honey."

Since I'm still covering his mouth he has to resort to nodding.

"Good. Now listen..." I rise up on my toes until my lips are next to his ear. "Yes, Gray."

THE END

ALSO BY FREYA BARKER

Click here to see all my books!

Standalones:

WHEN HOPE ENDS

VICTIM OF CIRCUMSTANCE

Arrow's Edge MC Series:

EDGE OF REASON

EDGE OF DARKNESS

PASS Series:

HIT & RUN

LIFE & LIMB

On Call Series:

BURNING FOR AUTUMN

COVERING OLLIE

TRACKING TAHLULA

ABSOLVING BLUE

Rock Point Series:

KEEPING 6

CABIN 12

HWY 550

10-CODE

Northern Lights Collection:

A CHANGE OF TIDE

A CHANGE OF VIEW

A CHANGE OF PACE

SnapShot Series:

SHUTTER SPEED

FREEZE FRAME

IDEAL IMAGE

Portland, ME, Series:

FROM DUST

CRUEL WATER

THROUGH FIRE

STILL AIR

LuLLaY (a Christmas novella)

Cedar Tree Series:

SLIM TO NONE

HUNDRED TO ONE

AGAINST ME

CLEAN LINES

UPPER HAND

LIKE ARROWS

HEAD START

ACKNOWLEDGMENTS

I'm so fortunate. Over the years I've assembled an amazing crew of people who are always at my back. To promote me, to guide me, to support me and encourage me, and to correct me. This amazing group of people make it possible for me to write my stories and bring them to you;

My editor, Karen Hrdlicka, and alpha reader and proofreader, Joanne Thompson; from the first word to paper they keep me on track and make me look much better than I am!

My agent, Stephanie Phillips of SBR Media, I'll be forever grateful for her constant faith in me.

My publicists, Debra Presley and Drue Hoffman and my PA Krystal Weiss of Buoni Amici Press; these ladies are invaluable, they organize and manage me when many gave up on that long ago!

My awesome beta team—Deb Blake, Pam Buchanan, and Petra Gleason who are always up for scrutinizing my stories, making sure they are good enough for you to read.

To all the fabulous blogs and early reviewers who help get the word about my books to you.

And last, but far from least, you, my readers, you are who make me want to keep writing with your enthusiasm and appreciation. Where would I be without you?

Lots of love!

Freya

ABOUT THE AUTHOR

USA Today bestselling author Freya Barker loves writing about ordinary people with extraordinary stories.

Driven to make her books about 'real' people; she creates characters who are perhaps less than perfect, each struggling to find their own slice of happy, but just as deserving of romance, thrills and chills in their lives.

Recipient of the ReadFREE.ly 2019 Best Book We've Read All Year Award for "Covering Ollie, the 2015 RomCon "Reader's Choice" Award for Best First Book, "Slim To None", and Finalist for the 2017 Kindle Book Award with "From Dust", Freya continues to add to her rapidly growing collection of published novels as she spins story after story with an endless supply of bruised and dented characters, vying for attention!

https://www.freyabarker.com

If you'd like to stay up to date on the latest news and upcoming new releases, sign up for my newsletter:
https://www.subscribepage.com/Freya_Newsletter

Printed in the USA
CPSIA information can be obtained
at www.ICGtesting.com
LVHW011942191123
764357LV00013B/1160

9 781988 733470